PRAISE FOR *MAMA DOES TIME*

"Who knew that a who-dun-it would not only keep you guessing—but have you laughing! Deborah Sharp is the new Edna Buchanan."

—Hoda Kotb, *NBC's Today show* co-anchor

"With a strong, funny heroine, colorful characters, and a look at a part of Florida the tourists rarely see, Deborah Sharp has an engaging new series. Make sure *Mama Does Time* does time on your bookshelf."

—Elaine Viets, author of
Clubbed to Death: a Dead-End Job Mystery

"Deborah Sharp's witty way with words makes *Mama Does Time* as much fun as a down-home visit with your quirky Florida cousins."

—Nancy Martin, author of the *Blackbird Sisters Mysteries*

"Not since the late Anne George has there been such laugh-out-loud Southern fried fun. Deborah Sharp's *Mama Does Time* is a hilarious page turner with crisp and intelligent writing."

—Sue Ann Jaffarian, author of the *Odelia Grey Mystery* series

"Deborah Sharp is the freshest, funniest voice to come along since, well, since I can't remember when. She's wise, she's wily and, what matters most—she knows the hearts of people. *Mama Does Time* has it all—murder, mystery and a brand new take on Florida's particular version of mayhem. Mama, aka Rosalee Deveraux, is an absolute hoot. And Mace Bauer, her middle daughter and the savvy, surefooted heroine of this romp of a book, is a most welcome addition to the ranks of detective fiction."

—Bob Morris, fourth-generation Floridian and
Edgar-nominated author of the *Zack Chasteen Mystery* series

FORTHCOMING BY DEBORAH SHARP

Mama Rides Shotgun
coming July 2009

Deborah Sharp

FLORIDA 2008
MAMA
A MACE BAUER MYSTERY

DOES TIME

MIDNIGHT INK
WOODBURY, MINNESOTA

First Edition
Second Printing, 2008

Book design and format by Donna Burch
Cover design by Lisa Novak
Cover illustration © 2008 by Mark Gerber
Editing by Connie Hill

Midnight Ink, an imprint of Llewellyn Publications

Library of Congress Cataloging-in-Publication Data
Sharp, Deborah, 1954–
  Mama does time : a Mace Bauer mystery / Deborah Sharp. — 1st ed.
    p. cm.
  ISBN: 978-0-7387-1329-8
  1. Mothers and daughters—Fiction. 2. Florida—Fiction.   I. Title.
  PS3619.H35645M36 2008
  813'.6—dc22
                                                      2008018947

Midnight Ink
Llewellyn Publications
2143 Wooddale Drive, Dept. 978-0-7387-1329-8
Woodbury, MN 55125-2989 USA
www.midnightinkbooks.com

Printed in the United States of America

To the original Mama, Marion Sharp,
and to my husband, Kerry Sanders.
I love you both to pieces.

ACKNOWLEDGMENTS

The good folks of Okeechobee, Florida, and the state's cattle belt inspired fictional Himmarshee. You might recognize a few landmarks, but most everything else is made up.

Any mistakes in the book are mine, and not the fault of the experts I consulted. Henry Cabbage, spokesman for the Florida Fish and Wildlife Conservation Commission, and two of the agency's biologists, Lindsey Hord and Steve Stiegler, guided me on 'gators. Allen Register, owner of Palmdale's Gatorama, also helped.

Okeechobee County extension agent Pat Hogue answered my cattle questions, and the Clemons family welcomed me to the Okeechobee Livestock Market, in the same spot since 1937. Jack Knight showed me how a cattle buyer bids at auction.

The staff at the SPCA Wildlife Care Center in Fort Lauderdale allowed me to tag along on the care and feeding of critters.

My mom and real-life sisters encouraged me, and loaned their best traits to Mama, Mace, Maddie, and Marty. My husband gave his gorgeousness to Carlos Martinez. Any negative resemblance to these fictional counterparts is pure coincidence. (Y'all believe me, right?)

A long line of newspaper editors, including USA Today's, taught me to ask questions, listen carefully, and write tight. (Okay, so maybe this could be tighter, but I can't leave anyone out!)

Several writers' groups in Fort Lauderdale assisted my transition from journalism to fiction writing. Thanks to leaders Carol Lytle, Jon Frangipane and Wendell Abern, Shelley Lieber, and, especially, to my friends Joyce Sweeney and the super-talented members of the Thursday Night Group. A special nod to Kingsley Guy for the great title.

Former acquisitions editor Barbara Moore saved me from the slush pile, and the creative folks at Midnight Ink shepherded my book to publication.

Agent Whitney Lee held my hand (electronically, anyway), calmed my insecurities, and combed over my contract.

Thanks to those above, to those I've missed, and especially to YOU, for reading Mama Does Time.

ONE

MAMA JUST WANTED TO look pretty for high-stakes bingo night at the Seminole casino.

But her beautician left the peroxide on too long, and she's been shedding like an Angora sweater ever since. Now, it turns out a patchy dye job is the least of my mother's worries.

It all started with a phone call. I was just about to plop down with my left-over fried chicken in front of the TV, wanting to see if I could spot any of my ex-boyfriends on *Cops,* when the damned thing rang.

"Mace, honey, you've got to come down here and help me. I'm in a lot of trouble."

Mama's voice was shaking. She sounded scared, like the time the raccoon came crashing from the attic through the bathroom ceiling while my little sister, Marty, was in a bubble bath.

"Slow down, Mama," I told her. "Now, take a deep breath."

My mother is excitable. I'm used to such calls. Maybe she needed me to solve a romantic crisis, or come pluck a snake out of the engine of her vintage turquoise convertible. I work outdoors in Himmarshee, Florida, in the wild regions north of Lake Okeechobee. I'm accustomed to snakes.

"Start at the beginning and tell me what's wrong," I said.

I heard a shuddery sigh, and then silence. She cleared her throat. Finally she spoke.

"They've got me down here at the police station, Mace. They think I've killed a man."

If the kitchen counter hadn't been there for me to grab a hold of, I'd have fallen out flat on the checkerboard pattern of my linoleum floor. I leaned my back against the wall and slid down slowly until my butt hit the baseboard. There I sat, clutching the receiver and searching for the proper response when your mother announces she's got one foot behind bars for murder.

"Just sit tight and don't say another word. I'll be there as soon as I can."

I knew my advice would go untaken. The only time Mama's mouth is shut is when she's chewing on something.

"There was a man's body in my trunk, Mace."

A strangled sob came through the phone. Then the story started pouring out.

"There was an accident," she said, running the words together. "Everything started at the Dairy Queen. Or maybe at bingo. I'd ordered me a butterscotch dip. Then, two police cars came. I couldn't even get a second cone. A pretty young girl hit me. The man had a diamond pinky ring." She stopped for a breath. "You'd better call your sisters, Mace."

The ability to make sense deserts Mama under stress. That doesn't mean she stops trying. I needed to get to her before she conversated herself right into a correctional facility.

"Not another word. Do not say another word to anyone, you hear? You can fill me in when I get there. And Mama? Don't worry. Everything's going to be all right."

Even as I said it, I didn't believe it. But I hoped I sounded like I did. My two sisters and I spend a lot of time reassuring our mother that things will turn out fine. The amazing thing is, they usually do. But getting Mama from Point A to Point A-OK requires delicate maneuvering, truckloads of patience, and a fair amount of prayer.

I wasn't sure this time if all those things together would be enough.

TWO

I GRABBED MY KEYS from inside the toothy grin of a stuffed alligator head I keep on my coffee table. It's a trapping souvenir from a ten-foot nuisance gator my cousin and I wrestled from a swimming pool. The pool's owner, a newcomer, thought he wanted country living until the country came to call.

Within minutes, I was on my way to town to rescue Mama. I live twenty miles out, in a cottage made of native cypress cut from local swamps. But downtown Himmarshee itself isn't much more than a bug speck on the windshield of a cattle-hauling truck. It seems like every week developers plant a new subdivision sign on former pastureland. But so far, the big cattle trucks still rumble along these narrow old highways north of Lake Okeechobee.

I opened the Jeep's windows in addition to cranking the AC. We're fifty miles from the nearest ocean breeze. Even at night, the summer heat in middle Florida is like a prelude to hell.

As I sped south, a full moon spilled light on fields dotted with palmetto scrub. Cows herded together under Sabal palms, dark shadows in the distance. The Monday night traffic was light. I was at the police department in no time at all.

Inside, I rounded a corner into the lobby and spotted my mother—Rosalee Deveraux, sixty-two years old last Fourth of July. She was clad in an orange-sherbet-colored pantsuit and matching pumps, perched on a desk like she owned the place. Someone must have just said something funny, because Mama's head was reared back in a laugh.

The sound was reassuring. Strange, under the circumstances, but reassuring.

"Well, look who's here." She grabbed the receptionist's elbow and turned her in my direction. "Emma Jean, you remember my middle girl, Mace. You know, the one who works at the nature park and traps critters on the side?"

Mama was grinning at me like I was Santa Claus bringing that baby doll she'd always wanted. "Honey, c'mon over and say hello to my bingo buddy, Emma Jean Valentine."

I raised an eyebrow at my mother, who appeared to be in full hostess mode.

"Nice to see you again, Ms. Valentine." I extended my hand across the desk, over a decorative family of Troll dolls, to a plus-sized woman in her mid-fifties.

Emma Jean, whose short skirt was in reverse proportion to her big hair, gave me a girlish grin. It was a marked contrast to her bone-crushing handshake. I offered her the pleasantries that small town manners demand. Then I put my hands on my mother's shoulders and looked her in the eyes.

"What in the hell's going on, Mama? When you called, you sounded like you were strapped into Ol' Sparky, and the warden was ready to throw the switch. Where's your car? Where's the body? Are you being arrested?"

My mother licked a finger and reached over to smooth my bangs. I jerked away, like I've been doing since I was six.

"I'm sorry, Mace. I was awful upset, what with that poor dead man and all, God rest his soul. But Emma Jean says this brand-new detective is gonna get everything straightened out. Now, calm down, honey."

That was rich. *Her* telling *me* to calm down.

She swiveled on the desk back to Emma Jean. "Mace isn't usually so excitable. My youngest, Marty, is the one who falls to pieces over the littlest things. Mace is usually my rock."

Emma Jean had been watching us. For all I knew, she'd concealed a tiny tape recorder somewhere on her person. That might be hard to miss, though, since her pink denim outfit looked spray-painted on. A kitty-cat pin glittered on the jacket she'd tossed over her bustier. Could one of those rhinestone eyes hold a miniature microphone to capture Mama's confession?

I was staring at the sparkly cat, plotting how to get my mother alone, when Mama spun to Emma Jean. "Would you be a doll and fetch me a dash more of that heavenly coffee?" She flashed a smile so luminous it could melt snow. "Extra cream, lots of sugar."

Turning, my mother winked at me. She might be flighty and infuriating, but occasionally a sharp mind makes itself known from beneath that badly dyed 'do.

Emma Jean heaved herself from her leather chair. Looming over Mama, she waggled an index finger six inches from her face. The nail was bright red, with a tiny white heart. "You're not going

6

to run out on us, are you, Rosalee? The detective will be with you shortly. And, don't forget, we know where you live."

Her tone was playful. But it seemed there might be some menace in the message.

Emma Jean punched in a code and passed through a plain white door, her high heels *click-clicking* down the hall.

My mother sipped from the coffee dregs in her cup, then made a face. "Ice cold. And it never was nothing but lukewarm. Now I know why all my TV shows make a big deal out of bad coffee at the police station."

I looked around for eavesdroppers. Himmarshee isn't exactly a criminal hotbed. We were alone in the reception area. "Should I find you a lawyer, Mama?"

Her eyes widened. "You can't be serious, Mace. You don't really think I've murdered a man, do you? You, my own flesh and blood?" She shook her head. A few stray hairs floated to the surface of Emma Jean's desk. "Your daddy's rollin' in his grave, girl."

Mama always says that Daddy, who died young of a heart attack, was her one true love. Even so, she's seen no harm in hoping Cupid will aim true again. She's been married four times.

"Mama, tell me—quickly. What happened?"

"Well, first I got dressed to go to bingo. What do you think of this orange, Mace?" She ran a hand down the pantsuit's fabric. "Is it too much with the shoes? I was afraid with my white hair, I'd look like a Creamsicle. I did re-think an orange-and-white scarf I'd planned to wear. "

"The man you're accused of killing, Mama? Remember him?"

"Mercy, Mace. You're wound tighter than an eight-day clock. Of course I remember. I'm the one who found the man, dead in my trunk. I was just trying to tell you how I came to be at the Dairy Queen. I'd already started out of the parking lot, when I decided at the last minute to go back and buy me a second cone."

A photo on Emma Jean's desk caught my mother's eye. She traced the image with a finger, a far-away look on her face. It showed a young Emma Jean pushing a child on a swing.

"Mama?"

"Hmmm?" She looked up, her eyes unfocused. "Sorry, Mace. So, that was when I felt a tap on my bumper. The cutest young girl in a red sports car had tail-ended me. Do you think I'm too old for a little sports car like that, honey?"

"Mama," I warned.

"Anyway, the girl noticed my trunk wasn't shut right. I tried to slam it, but it wouldn't catch. You should have seen her face when I lifted up that heavy lid to see what was making it stick."

I was afraid to ask.

"It was a man's hand, catching that little metal doohickey that makes the trunk close. His sleeve was bloody. The back of his fingers were hairy. When I close my eyes, I can still see that diamond pinky ring."

"How'd you know he was dead?"

She looked at me like I was slow. "I grew up on a farm, Mace. Don't you think I've seen enough animals, dead and alive, to know when any one of God's creatures has taken its last breath? Besides, his wrist was right there. I put my fingers on it real careful, and felt for a pulse. He didn't have one. And his skin was colder than a car seat in January."

Mama stared out the window into the night. "There was a blanket tossed over his face." Her voice sounded soft, distant. "I wasn't about to go messing around. I watch *Law and Order*. You never contaminate a crime scene. And that's what my car was, Mace, a murder scene."

Mama walked over to the trash and dumped her coffee cup. Then, she tore yesterday's date—September 13—off a wall calendar. A gift from the Gotcha Bait & Tackle shop, the calendar pictured a large mouth bass leaping over the month. When she started rubbing at a scuff mark on the wall, I knew Mama was more upset than she let on.

Putting my arm around her shoulder, I led her back to the desk. At barely five feet in her sherbet pumps, the top of her head didn't reach my chin.

"C'mon, let's sit down." I lowered her gently to a chair beside the desk. "Everything will be fine."

"I know, Mace." She managed a shaky smile. "I'm just thinking of that poor dead soul. He must have had a family. I bet someone is wondering right now where he's at."

I steered her back to the Dairy Queen.

"When we found the body, the girl started screaming," Mama said. "I believe her name was Donna. Or maybe Lonna. Before I knew it, people were pouring outside. Everyone was staring, their ice creams melting all over the asphalt lot. Policemen in two different cars came, squealing tires."

"What'd you tell them?"

"That I had no idea how that man got into my trunk, of course. That I'm innocent."

I didn't want to picture that conversation.

"They made me wait inside until a detective came. He had a Spanish last name. Awfully good-looking. He seemed real impatient with my answers."

Imagine that, I thought.

9

"He finally got up, all red in the face, and ordered the officers to bring me here to wait some more. He has more questions, he said. He acted like he thinks I'm guilty."

"Is the detective someone we know, Mama?"

"He's brand new. Emma Jean says he used to be a policeman down in Miami, but something bad happened down there. No one talks about exactly what."

Just then, the door opened. My mother nudged me in the ribs and bent her head. "That's him. That's the detective," she whispered.

The man in the doorway was in his late thirties or early forties. His hair was black and wavy. His dark eyes looked like they hid plenty of secrets. He wore creased jeans and a white dress shirt. His tie, light blue with white stripes, was loosened at the neck. He wasn't exceedingly tall, maybe an inch more-so than me. But he filled the frame of the door, the way confident men do. And Mama was right: he was good-looking, if you're partial to dark and glowering. Which I definitely am not.

"Who's she?" the detective asked Mama, crooking a thumb in my direction.

I knew people were rude in Miami, but this was ridiculous. Good looks are no excuse for bad manners.

" 'She' is Mason Bauer, Detective." I used my given name and straightened to my full five-foot-ten inches. "I'm Ms. Deveraux's daughter."

"And I'm Detective Martinez." He gave his last name a little trill. Neither of us offered to shake hands. "You can't be here while I talk to your mother. She may be involved in a homicide."

"I'm aware that a man's body was discovered in the trunk of her car. I want to assure you my mother had nothing whatsoever to do with the man getting there."

"Assure away." He crossed his arms over his chest and scowled. "I'm still talking to your mother alone, Ms. Bauer."

"Excuse me, Detective?" Mama held up a finger like she was trying to raise a point on orchids at the Garden Club. "That's *Miss* Bauer. My daughter isn't married. And, please, call her Mace. Everybody does."

"Mama!"

"Well, they do, honey." She turned back to the detective. "I gave old family surnames to all three of my girls. The youngest is Marty, which comes from Martin. We call Madison, the oldest, Maddie for short. It's a Southern thing."

Mama didn't mention these fine old English names appear nowhere in our own family background, which is Scotch and German. She didn't think it sounded as classy to name us "McDougall," "Zumwald," and "Schultz."

She raised her finger again. "I just want to add that Mace is smart, too. She graduated top in her college class at Central Florida."

A vein started throbbing at Martinez's temple. I had the oddest impulse to trace it with my thumb.

I felt a flush spreading from my hairline south. "Mama, please. Nobody cares what kind of grade point average I carried ten years ago."

Just then, the door behind the counter swung open, rescuing me from Mama's compulsive matchmaking. Emma Jean pushed through backwards, balancing three coffees. She propped open the door with her ample rear end, sheathed in the same bubble-gum shade as her bustier. Setting the coffees down, she turned to us.

"Well, hey, Detective Martin-ez." Her drawl turned his last name into two English words, Martin and Ez. "I saw you through the window as you drove up. Figured you could use a cup, too. Did y'all get an ID yet on that poor dead man in Rosalee's trunk?"

Martinez grabbed a coffee off the counter. He didn't say thanks.

"Yeah, we did. One of the officers recognized him." He tipped the cup to his lips, keeping his eyes fastened on my mother.

"Well, who was it?" Emma Jean picked up both remaining cups. As she handed one to me, I nodded my thanks.

Waiting, Martinez stared holes through Mama. Finally, he said, "His name was Jim Albert."

As soon as Emma Jean heard the name, she screamed and stumbled. She caught herself, but the last coffee went flying.

"Oh, Emma Jean!" Mama rushed to her friend's side. "I am so sorry."

I was confused. Shouldn't Emma Jean be apologizing, since she'd just ruined Mama's pantsuit with lukewarm coffee splotches from top to bottom?

The receptionist threw herself, sobbing, into my mother's open arms. I was afraid the impact would topple Mama, like she was the last pin on the lane at a bowling tournament. Martinez quickly stepped in as ballast.

"Am I missing something here?" He raised his eyebrows at me. I shrugged, as I helped him prop up a weeping Emma Jean.

"Oh, this is just getting more horrible by the minute, Detective." Mama leaned around Emma Jean's bulk to find Martinez. "Jim Albert was her boyfriend. And just last week, he got down on one knee and asked Emma Jean to marry him."

THREE

THE NEWS THAT HER fiancé was the dead man in Mama's convertible hit Emma Jean hard.

She was sobbing, rocking back and forth in her receptionist's chair. I thought each squeak from the wheels might be the last. If Emma Jean was to take a tumble, I feared what might fall out the top of that too-snug bustier.

Martinez leaned against the counter, watching his co-worker. I used the opportunity to scrutinize him: Except for the badge at his belt and the foam coffee cup in his hand, he might have been an ancient Roman, sculpted in marble. I pay attention to little details. That comes in handy for my part-time work, tracking animals. I can usually read people, too. But the expressionless detective offered no clues. He ought to try his luck at poker at the Seminole casino.

Mama pulled a sherbet-colored hanky from the pocket of her pantsuit. The lacy square of linen was no match for the volume of Emma Jean's tears. Mama was just returning with toilet paper reinforcements from the Ladies, when we all heard voices from the hallway.

"I demand to speak to Mrs. Rosalee Deveraux," the loudest voice said.

My big sister, Maddie, was bearing down on the lobby like a hurricane, her red hair flying like a warning flag. A uniformed officer trailed two paces behind, keeping a wary eye on Maddie and a hand ready near his gun. As soon as Maddie saw our mother sitting there safely, she lit into me.

"Mace, what were you thinking with that message on my answering machine: 'Mama's in the Himmarshee Jail. Come quick!' I nearly had a coronary. Then, I couldn't reach your cell. You have got to keep that phone turned on. If it's for emergencies, I'd say this qualifies."

Maddie has been bossing me around since she was in kindergarten and I was in diapers. I'm well into big-girl undies now, but she's seen no sense in stopping yet.

"Now, honey, don't get mad at your sister," Mama said. "It was me told Mace to call. I'm in a little spot of trouble."

"Make that a big spot," I amended. "Mama found a dead man in her convertible trunk."

Emma Jean let out a wail, springing loose a fresh flood of tears.

"Sorry, Emma Jean," I said, handing her another wad of toilet paper. "*He...*" I crooked my thumb to point at Martinez, just as he'd done to me, "*... he's* the detective who thinks Mama's mixed up in the poor man's murder."

Peeking out from behind Maddie was our younger sister, Marty. Her face went pale at my announcement. But the news just seemed to make Maddie madder. She pulled herself up to her full height, which I always remind her is two-and-one-half inches shorter than mine. Her whole body swiveled back and forth and back again between Mama and Martinez, causing the eyeglasses on the chain around her neck to spin like an airplane propeller.

"I've never heard of anything so ridiculous," Maddie finally said.

"Please, Maddie." Marty's voice was hardly audible. She bunched up the fabric of her flowered dress as she spoke. "Can't we talk about this like civilized people?" She glanced nervously at the cop with the gun.

Maddie steamrollered past, ignoring Marty. She stalked across the room, stopped beside Mama, and put a protective hand on her shoulder. "This woman has taught Sunday school to half of Himmarshee."

She turned a gale-force glare on Martinez. Maddie's a middle school principal. That glare gets a lot of practice.

But Martinez glared right back, adding an intimidating lift of his chin. I had an inappropriate urge to smile at him. I was that pleased to think my big sister had met her match.

"More daughters, I presume?" He nodded slightly at the other officer, dismissing him.

"Maddie's my oldest girl, Detective." My mother's voice was as sweet as cane syrup. She'd slipped back into that hostess gown. "The little slip of a child by the wall is Marty, the youngest. You'll always know Marty because she hardly says a word. That's not a bad thing for a librarian, is it? Anyway, Mace and Maddie never do give her a chance."

Marty had inherited Mama's debutante looks and diminutive size. She's nervous, too, flitting around like a delicate bird. Maddie is her exact opposite: tall, big-boned, and outsized in everything from voice to personality. I'm somewhere between the two of them. Not as pretty as Marty; not as mean as Maddie.

"Are you charging my mother with murder?" Maddie folded her arms over her chest, all business.

Marty went even whiter. "You shouldn't even mention muh…mur…that word and Mama in the same sentence, Maddie."

Emma Jean's receptionist professionalism resurfaced. She stopped rocking, blew her nose, and chimed in before Martinez could answer.

"No one's said anything about charging anyone with murder, girls. We're just trying to find out what your mama knows about what happened. I was recently engaged to Jim Albert, the victim." She balled up a paper towel and dabbed at her nose, struggling for control. Mama leaned over and patted her arm. Emma Jean gave her a brave, if wobbly, smile.

"Detective Martin Ez just wants to ask Rosalee some questions."

Martinez flinched a little as Emma Jean mangled his name again. He'd better get used to it. Himmarshee isn't Miami. People from up north think we have enough trouble speaking English down here, let alone Spanish.

Maddie and I exchanged a look. The unspoken message: We'll hash it out later, so we won't upset Mama. Whatever the two of us decided, Marty would go along, like always. Like Mama, Marty hates disharmony more than just about anything.

Just as we all were settling down, the sound of heavy footsteps echoed in the outside hall. Whoever it was, they were flying to get here. Soon, the familiar odor of aftershave from the dollar store wafted into the lobby. I knew who reeked even before I saw him.

16

Judging from the smile spreading across my mother's face, she recognized the Eau d' Excess, too.

"Sally, darlin', I am so relieved to see you."

That would be Salvatore Provenza, "Big Sal" to everyone except my mother, who inexplicably calls him Sally. The pet nickname bugs my sisters and me no end. It would have bugged him, too, coming from anyone but my mother. But the man loves her like the young Elvis loved Priscilla.

"Don't ... *pant* ... you worry ... *pant* ... about a thing, Rosalee." Hands on his knees, Sal was breathing hard from his sprint to the lobby. "I'm here now."

My sisters and I rolled our eyes—even Marty.

Mama was holding her hand to her chest, simpering. She plays the Southern damsel to perfection when it suits her. Of course, before Daddy lost our ranch, I'd seen her string barbed wire for fencing and wrestle a two-hundred-pound calf for branding. But that was a long time ago.

Once he stopped wheezing, Sal zeroed in on Martinez. I wasn't surprised. Emma Jean might have been the police department person in power, but Big Sal's a chauvinist with a Big C. Then again, one look at Emma Jean, all tight clothes and teased hair, and I would have pegged Martinez as the alpha cop, too.

"What's the nature of Mrs. Deveraux's confinement?" He pronounced it "nate-cha," his Bronx upbringing still lurking in his nasal passages.

"There is no confinement at this point," Martinez answered. "I need to determine the nate-cha, I mean nature, of her involvement. That's been difficult, given the constant interruptions."

Sal, all 307 pounds of him, ran a finger under the collar of his pastel yellow golf shirt. Puffing out his chest in a man-to-man fashion, he hooked a thumb into the expandable waistband of his rust-colored slacks.

"Well, my cousin happens to be a lawyer." Lore-yah, is the way Sal said it. "I can have him here in a few hours, if Rosie needs him."

I had a quick flash of Joe Pesci as the over-his-head lore-yah in the movie *My Cousin Vinny*.

"Don't worry, Mr. Provenza." I said. "We have our own cousin, who's also a lawyer, if it should come to that."

I was trying to be polite. After all, Mama may end up marrying the guy.

Maddie wasn't as restrained. "We absolutely do not need any help from you, Mr. Provenza. Or from your 'lore-yah' cousin."

Her voice was so cold, they could have pumped it into the beer cooler down at the Booze 'n' Breeze drive-thru. "I wouldn't be surprised if you and some of your New York *associates* aren't responsible for this mess our mother is in." Maddie moved real close to Sal, just about hissing in his face. "We've warned her about you, you know."

It's a cliché and an unfair stereotype to assume that just because Sal is of Italian heritage and he's from New York that he's connected with the Mafia. But that hasn't stopped my sisters and me from doing it. He's been very mysterious about his past, and we watch a lot of movies. "Maddie, you apologize to Sally this instant!" Mama said. "I didn't raise you to insult people."

My big sister towered over our mother, but she still ducked her head like a little kid when Mama used that tone.

"That's okay, Rosie." Sal patted at his impeccable hair. My sisters and I suspect he uses styling mousse. "Maddie's just proven, once again, that even educated people can be ignorant."

That got Maddie's back up. Pretty soon, we were all talking at once and nobody was listening to anybody else. All except Marty, that is. She'd edged away to the counter, where she was busy mopping up a coffee puddle from Emma Jean's earlier spill.

Just like Mama, Marty cleans when she's anxious. She looked like she wanted to stick her fingers in her ears, just like she used to do when our mother fought with Husband Number 2. Marty hates arguments and loud noise.

And our arguing was getting pretty darned loud. Until, suddenly, Martinez jammed his fingers in his mouth and whistled. It was long and ear-splitting, like the CSX train coming onto the crossing at Highway 98. Marty's fingers plugged her ears. Even Maddie had her face scrunched up, like she was in noise pain.

The room fell silent.

"This. Has. Gone. On. Long. Enough." Martinez emphasized every word, letting a dark glower linger on each of us. "I've been patient. I've been quiet. Honestly, I was thinking maybe one of you crazy characters might let something important slip out. That has not been the case. And that's an understatement. I've never heard such a load of bullshit in my life."

My mother looked shocked at Martinez's language. She was still in Southern belle mode, and damsels have such delicate ears. In fact, she could cuss a purple streak. But she always asked the Lord for forgiveness afterwards.

"You people can stand here yelling at each other until Christmas for all I care." That vein was throbbing at his temple again.

"But Mrs. Deveraux is coming with me." He grabbed Mama by the arm and yanked her none too gently toward the door. "There was a murder victim in her car."

Another wail from Emma Jean.

"Your mother's been unable—or unwilling—to explain how he got there," Martinez pressed on. "I think she's implicated. And I'm going to find out how."

We all started talking again.

"*Por favor*. Please!" Still hanging on to Mama with one hand, Martinez held up the other for silence.

"I'm arresting her," he said when we finally quieted down. "If any of you has a problem with that, I suggest you call somebody's cousin and get her a lawyer."

FOUR

Martinez made good on his threat. Mama spent the night in jail.

First thing in the morning, I tossed on some clothes and set about getting her out.

Unfortunately, I caught a glimpse of myself in the Jeep's rearview mirror on the way to my cousin's law office. I'm not much for primping, but the sight of my bed-smashed hair and raccoon eyes gave even me a scare. The shadows were so dark that, if I hadn't also seen some yellow sleep crud caked into the corner of an eyelid, I'd have thought I didn't catch a single wink over worrying about my mama.

I didn't feel a whole lot better once I pulled up to the law office of Henry Bauer & Associates. The setting didn't exactly spell success. First off, there are no Associates. Henry rents space in a strip mall, between a convenience store and a pawn shop. As hot as it's been, I could smell the garbage cooking in the can on the sidewalk. It stunk like stale beer and microwave burritos.

Next door, the pawn shop's logo showed a flattened armadillo on a highway with a word balloon over his head: *Don't Wait Too Late to Visit Pete's Pawn!*

Inside, Henry's secretary had a blonde ponytail in a pink scrunchy. She looked like a work-study student from Himmarshee High. I gave her my name and grabbed a seat.

Henry's got a small-town practice, covering all kinds of law. But his clients this morning mostly resembled pictures from a personal-injury textbook. Every chapter of pain and suffering. One poor guy was trussed into a cast from neck to groin. His bandaged arms and legs poked out like matchsticks. He leaned against the wall, looking just like a gopher turtle that some mean kids had flipped over onto its back.

"Mr. Bauer will see you now."

The secretary motioned for me to follow her. It seemed silly, since I could see my cousin at his desk behind four artificial palm trees employed as a room divider. But she stepped left to avoid the palms, so I stepped left, too.

"Mr. Bauer, this lady says she's Ms. Bauer."

A mischievous grin crept across Henry's face. "Thanks, Amber. I might not have recognized Ms. Bauer with her clothes on."

Amber blushed.

"We used to splash nekkid together in the kiddy pool in my backyard. That was decades ago, darlin', way before you were born."

Amber looked ill at the prospect of a naked Henry at any age. He'd inherited a tendency toward corpulence from Daddy's side of the family. Henry's so heavy, he gave his stomach a nickname. He calls it Dunlap, as in, "My belly dun' lapped over my belt."

22

With a final disgusted look, Amber fled past the palms to her desk.

"Do kids still have plastic baby pools, Mace?" Henry was thinking out loud. "Or are they considered too dangerous these days?"

"I'm sure if anyone can prove baby pools are fatal death traps, you can, Henry."

"Don't be snide. That's your sister Maddie's job. Where is she, by the way?"

My sisters and I had alerted Henry the night before to Mama's predicament. We'd agreed my work hours were most flexible, so the task of visiting our cousin the lawyer had fallen to me.

"We drew straws to come see you, Henry. I lost."

"Very funny, Mace. You won't be so dismissive of my legal skills when you find out what I've learned about your Mama's case."

I was still getting used to the fact that Mama had a case. And Henry was right: I needed him.

"Don't keep me in suspense, Henry."

Since we were kids, my cousin had made me grovel for information. I Spy. Twenty Questions. You're Getting Warm. I've hated guessing games ever since.

He must have taken one look at me today and refrained out of pity.

"What I've discovered about the man in your mama's trunk changes the whole character of his murder." He tapped a file folder on his desk. "This is good news, Mace. I think we can help her out." Henry reached across the desk and gave my hand a supportive squeeze.

Sometimes, I wish I was born in South Dakota, where people are direct. It's too damned cold up there to sit around squeezing a person's hand. Plus, they're usually wearing electric mittens.

"What was it you learned, Henry?" I pulled my hand away and put it in my lap.

"Well, first of all, Jim Albert wasn't his real name." Henry picked up a paper clip and tossed it from palm to palm. "That's an alias."

"What do you mean?"

"An alias is a name other than your given name that you're known by."

"I know what an alias is, Henry. I've been to college. I meant, why'd he have one?"

"The man in your mama's trunk was running away from some very bad people." As he said, "bad people," Henry rolled his neck and adjusted an imaginary tie. He shot imaginary shirt cuffs from beneath an imaginary suit. In fact, he was in a short-sleeved Madras shirt with no tie or jacket.

"What in God's name are you doing, Henry? Have you taken up yoga?"

"He was connected, Mace." His mouth twisted to a tough-guy smirk.

"Connected to what?" Did I mention I hate charades as much as I do guessing games?

"You're the most literal-minded person I know, Mace," Henry said, exasperated. "You don't even seem to try."

He peeked around the plastic palms to make sure none of his clients was listening. They all seemed engrossed in a *Judge Judy* rerun on the waiting room TV. As he leaned in close, I smelled pancakes on his breath.

"You know, 'connected.' Like Tony Soprano?" he whispered. "The *Godfather* movies? Jim Albert, real name Jimmy 'the Weasel' Albrizio, was a known member of the criminal underworld in New York. He was down here hiding out."

So Emma Jean's boyfriend was a mobster. I wondered if she'd known that detail when she'd agreed to become his wife. I pictured the getting-to-know you phase of their courtship:

Emma Jean: Tell me a little bit about yourself, Jim.

Jimmy the Weasel: Well, I'm from New York originally. I did free-lance work for The Family up there.

Emma Jean: How nice that you're close to your family…

"How'd you find this out?" I asked Henry.

He got that superior look he always got when he knew something I didn't. "I'm a good lawyer; a respected member of the legal community, Mace." He twirled his paper clip. "You may not be aware of it, but I've become a pretty big fish in this little pond we call Himmarshee. Getting information is easy if you know the right people."

"Which doesn't answer my question. Who told you about Albrizio?"

"The waitress at Gladys' Restaurant."

That explained Henry's pancake breath.

"Her cousin is married to one of the police techs who handle crime scenes. As soon as they ran the fingerprints on your mama's corpse, they knew this murder was bigger than usual."

I winced. "Please don't call that poor man in the trunk 'Mama's corpse,' Henry. We both know she had nothing to do with it. It's just a question of convincing the police she's innocent."

"I've been busy with that angle, too, Mace. The chief owes me a favor. I represented his nephew in that vandalism mess over the Confederate flag and Martin Luther King Day. I don't know what that moron was thinking, except that he wasn't thinking."

"So, the police chief…" I didn't want my aching butt parked on Henry's hard metal chair all morning.

"Well, he was pretty pissed off when he found out that new detective arrested your mama. Martinez, right? What's he like?"

"An arrogant jerk."

"Well, Miami. What do you expect? So, Chief Johnson tells me your mama taught him Sunday school when he was a kid. Said she caught him swiping a cupcake off of some other boy's tray, and read him the riot act. Said it didn't matter whether the thing you steal is big or little, wrong is wrong. 'God always knows,' your mama told him."

I swallowed a lump in my throat as I remembered similar lessons she'd drilled into my head over the years.

"Anyway, the chief said he'll look into her case personally." Henry tapped the file. "That Martinez was within his rights to arrest her. But the state attorney's office has to decide whether to file formal charges. They haven't done that yet. And they can only hold her so long until they decide one way or the other to prosecute."

"What can I do, Henry?"

"Well, Martinez is going to try to get any information that'll make your mama look guilty. You need to find something that makes it look like she's not."

"Like another suspect?"

"That'd be nice," Henry said, as he straightened out the paper clip. "Find someone else who could have done it, and Aunt Rosalee'll be out of jail and back at home before you know it."

Henry paused. "Hey, does your mama still make those lemon squares with the icing? I love those."

His mind was beginning to turn to his mid-morning snack. I started to gather my things when my cell phone rang. I fumbled in my purse past tissues, a mini-calendar, and a pack of chewing gum. No comb, of course.

When I answered, the caller was turned away from the mouthpiece, talking to someone else. Multi-tasking has meant the end of good manners.

I waited a couple of moments and then yelled "HELLO" again, hoping my screech would cause permanent hearing damage.

"Yeah, hold on." The caller mumbled distractedly, and then went back to talking to the third person.

I punched the end button on my cell. It rang again.

"I think we were disconnected."

"We weren't disconnected," I said. "I hung up. It's rude to call someone and then act like they're not there."

The caller launched into a bad imitation of a Southern matron. "Well, land's sake, where are my manners? I do declah!" He switched back to his normal voice, deep with the faintest trace of an accent. "I'm terribly sorry my behavior doesn't meet your very high standards. *Perdóname,* as we say. Forgive me. "

That didn't sound sincere, in Spanish or English.

"Hello, Detective Martinez." I made an effort to keep my voice pleasant. Neutral. He was baiting me. I didn't intend to bite.

Henry quickly scribbled a note and passed it across the desk: "*Don't talk to the police!!*"

I nodded and waved my hand to reassure my cousin. I knew what I was doing. I needed details the detective had.

"I may seem a little short because I'm kind of busy here, Ms. Bauer. I'm investigating a murder, in case you'd forgotten."

I wondered whether his accent would sound sexy minus the sarcasm.

"My memory's pretty good, Detective. Are you ready to let my mother out of jail?"

Henry grabbed the note again, added an underline and additional exclamation points, and shook the paper in my face. I turned away, cradling the phone next to my ear.

"On the contrary, Ms. Bauer," Martinez said. "Recent information has come to light."

That's exactly what I wanted from him: information.

"I'm more convinced than ever your mother is where she belongs," he said. "I need you to come by the police department. I'd like to talk to you about your mother's case."

And there was that awful word again.

FIVE

It was almost 10:30 by the time I pulled into the lot at the Himmarshee Police Department. I was getting a little too familiar with the place—a low-slung concrete block building painted a depressing shade of gray. Beside it, a chain link fence topped by concertina wire enclosed an exercise yard. Across the yard was the jail, where Mama was.

From what Henry had said, the state attorney's office still had to review her case. She hadn't seen a judge yet. So far, the only one who was saying she was guilty was the man who'd tossed her in jail: Detective Martinez.

"Penny for your thoughts, Mace."

A uniformed officer tapped at my windshield. It was Donnie Bailey, who I'd babysat once upon a time. Looking at him now, all muscles and mustache, made me feel old.

"Where you at, Mace? That look on your face puts you about a thousand miles away."

"I was just sitting here thinking of what to do next."

"Listen, I'm sorry about this mess with your mama," Donnie said. "I was on duty last night when they brought her over to the jail. I'm gonna see she gets treated good, Mace. Don't worry."

"Thanks, Donnie." I felt the threat of tears gathering behind my eyes. "That means a lot."

I shifted gears. "Listen, is there any chance of me getting in there to see her? I don't want to get you in any trouble."

"You won't get me into trouble, Mace." Donnie's chest puffed out, like a wild turkey in full strut. "I'm the one in charge this shift. I run the jail, and I say who comes and goes. Your Mama's minister already made his rounds. Family visits aren't 'til later, but we're pretty light on inmates right now."

Donnie glanced at me quickly to see how I'd taken to Mama being called an inmate. I didn't take to it too well.

"Sorry, Mace. Anyway, I don't see a problem with you checking on your mama. With her advanced age and all, I'm sure you're worried about her medical condition, right?"

"Donnie, Mama's healthier than I am."

He leveled a hard look at me, and I got a quick glimpse of how scary he might be on the opposite side of some bars. "What I said, Mace, is that you're worried about her *medical condition*, right?" Donnie spoke loud and slow, like I was a particularly thick kindergartner he was trying to teach the alphabet.

"Yeah, that's exactly right, Donnie." A-B-C. "I'm just frantic to think about how all this mess might be affecting Mama's poor old heart."

Not three days earlier, she'd run three blocks with her pet Pomeranian in her arms after the dog got a hold of a poisonous toad. She couldn't get to a hose, so she'd jumped in a creek to douse out

Teensy's mouth. Then she ran all the way back with a shovel to kill the toad. Mama's weak heart, my elbow.

"You know I'd feel awful if that poor old woman died while in our custody." Donnie did all but wink. "Y'all might get your cousin Henry to sue us and shut down the jail. And where would I be? Neither jail nor job."

Donnie hitched up his belt and shook a ring full of keys at me. I climbed out of my Jeep and followed him, through a locked gate and onto the concrete slab that serves as the exercise yard. There wasn't much to it: three rusty weight-lifting benches and a half-deflated basketball.

At the jail's back door, Donnie worked a series of deadbolts. Then he leaned into the heavy steel with his shoulder. The door inched open slowly, and he stepped aside to let me walk through.

A lingering smell of disinfectant, overlaid with spaghetti and meatballs, transported me back to Wednesdays in my grade school cafeteria.

"Lunch smells decent, Donnie."

"Smells and tastes are two different things, Mace. Let's just say we won't be winning any blue ribbon awards for cooking."

I felt a pang of sympathy. Mama loves good food.

From the movies, I'd expected the clang of bars and the catcalls of inmates. But the only thing I heard was the jangle of Donnie's keys and a faint squeak from his shoes.

"Like I said, we're quiet today. This here's the women's quarters. Men are on the other side of the building. Normally, you'd have to use the visitors' room, but I trust you, Mace. Hell, you changed my diapers."

As Donnie led the way, I couldn't help but notice how nicely he'd filled out since those diaper-wearing days.

We kept walking until we entered an open area with cells lining the outer walls. An officer sat behind thick glass, watching a console with a bunch of lights and switches. The lock-up was quite modern for a little burg like Himmarshee. But that's Florida: No money for schools; plenty of money for jails.

"Your mama's in the last spot on the left down there," Donnie pointed across the interior square. "We have space, but we have to give her a cellmate. It's procedure."

Unless it was an axe murderer, Mama would prefer the company. She can't abide being alone, which is probably why she's had four husbands.

"What's the other woman like?" I asked.

"Younger gal. Not violent, or anything," Donnie said. "She's in for check fraud. Says it was her boyfriend to blame."

"Was it?"

"Who knows?" Donnie shrugged. "Just like there's not a guilty man in jail, there's hardly a woman who doesn't claim she'd never have done it if not for some guy. I'd go crazy if I listened to every inmate who claims they're innocent."

I tried not to take offense. Donnie was as much as grouping Mama in with that guilty crowd. I kept my mouth shut and crossed to her cell. A low-pitched chuckle sounded inside.

"I swear, Ms. Deveraux, you are a stitch." The same woman laughed again. "What happened after Teensy got stuck in the road tar? Did he turn all black?"

I smiled. That was one of Mama's favorite stories, as her pet Pomeranian made a tar-free recovery. She loves happy endings.

"Is there an innocent old woman in here?" Plastering a reassuring grin onto my face, I peeked in her cell. "A gorgeous, innocent woman?"

"Oh, my stars!" Mama squealed. "It's my middle girl, Mace!"

She was dressed in a jail-issue smock and drawstring pants, as orange as the reflective vest on a highway worker. I pretended the ugly uniform just meant Mama had gone to work in the office of a doctor with bad taste in color.

"Mace, honey, I want you to meet my roommate."

I slipped my hand through the bars to grip limp fingers. Mama's twenty-something cellmate kept her shoulders hunched and her eyes on the concrete floor. If I had to guess, I'd say she'd been knocked around some. Despite a pierced nose and a wide streak of purple in her hair, she looked like the kind of woman who'd just as soon disappear.

Mama would try to fix that.

"We're becoming great friends, aren't we, LaTonya? When we get out of here, I've asked her to come visit us at Abundant Hope, Mace. Of course, our new pastor's not real popular. But we're hoping he works out."

"Donnie said he came by already this morning. That was nice," I said.

Mama pursed her lips.

"What's wrong?"

"I'm trying to warm up to him, I really am, Mace. But the man has a strange way of offering comfort. I mean, I'm sitting in jail. Do you think this is the time I want to hear about his plans for selling his DVDs and 'growing' our little church?"

I raised my eyebrows. Mama answered her own question.

"No, it is not. He's so full of himself, I barely got a word in edgewise about my situation."

I sincerely doubted that.

"Mama, if you don't like him, just tell Donnie you don't want to see him."

Her eyes got wide. "I couldn't do that, Mace. Pastor Bob is my *minister*."

"How're you getting along in here otherwise?"

Mama brightened. "Well, I've been helping LaTonya with her colors. We're pretty sure with her brown eyes and skin tone, she's an Autumn. It's kind of hard to tell, what with that interesting shade of lavender in her hair."

LaTonya's eyes flickered up from the floor for a second as she touched her purple stripe. It's just like Mama to treat jail like a slumber party, all color charts and clothing tips. I'm no expert, but those orange uniforms would flatter no one—not a Winter, Spring, Summer, or Fall.

"I'm glad to see you, Mama."

"Me, too, Mace. But what happened to your hair, honey? It looks like a possum crawled in there and dug a nest."

I ignored the criticism. A woman who cuts her own hair can't afford to be too vain. But I ran a hand through it anyway to try and fluff the flat side. "I've got good news, Mama. Henry's working hard on getting you out of here."

Alarm registered on her face. "Henry hasn't told his mama where I am, has he, Mace? That Irene will never let me forget it if he has."

By this time, the news that Mama was in jail was all over Himmarshee County, from the fish camps around Lake Okeechobee to the citrus groves that stretch to the north.

"I doubt if Henry's said a word. Lawyers have to respect confidentiality. It's a law."

I brought Mama up to date on the criminal identity of the man in her trunk.

"Poor Emma Jean," she said.

"Didn't you suspect anything funny about her boyfriend?"

"I barely knew the man, Mace. I'd only seen him once, briefly, when he dropped Emma Jean off at bingo. He never even got out of the car."

I told her about Police Chief Johnson getting involved.

"He was the sweetest child in Sunday School, Mace. Loved cupcakes."

And I said my upcoming meeting with Martinez would give us a better idea of where things stood.

"Now, don't make him mad, Mace. I know how you are. Just remember what I always say: you can catch a lot more flies with honey than with vinegar."

Maybe it was the stress, but that last part set my blood to boil. Mama's constantly on me to be more charming, to smile more. She knows I'd sooner eat dirt than flutter my eyes and flirt.

I lashed out. "Yeah, we can see where all that 'honey' has gotten you, Mama. Right behind bars. By the way, I'm glad you're having a good time in here, discussing colors and all, but I hope you know you're in serious trouble. You better start thinking about something that will help Henry and the rest of us get you out of here. You can't expect us to do all the work."

Mama recoiled like I'd slapped her. LaTonya lifted her eyes long enough to shoot me a dirty look.

"Mace, I'm perfectly aware of where I am." Mama said softly, her voice laced with hurt. "I don't live in a dream world. I know I'm in trouble. But that's the difference between us. You worry and stew and make things worse. I put on the happiest face I can. I try to make the best out of things, even the worst things. And I trust the Lord to sort things out. It's the way I've always gotten by. It's the only way I know."

I swallowed, hard. I'm an awful daughter. My sister Marty would never be so mean; though Maddie might. I heard squeaky shoes and felt a tap on my shoulder.

"Mace, you need to get going." Donnie couldn't have come at a better time. "We're about ready to serve lunch, and believe me, you don't want to be around here for that."

I ducked my head, surreptitiously brushing away tears. "It's okay, Donnie. I was just fixin' to leave anyway."

I started to walk away, and then turned back to the cell. "I'm sorry I'm so horrible, Mama. I love you. You know that, right?"

She'd always taught us, never leave mad. You never know which breath is your last.

"Mace, I'm as sure of your love as I am of the sun. Stop fretting."

"I promise you, you're going to be home soon. Teensy's going to be driving you to distraction again before you know it."

LaTonya glanced up, rewarding me with a smile.

"Detective Martinez is going to figure out this whole mess is a misunderstanding," I said. "He's going to charge in here himself and cut you loose."

I know lying is wrong. But Mama always said it's not a sin if you lie in order to save another person's feelings.

SIX

A UNIFORMED STRANGER SAT at the receptionist's desk in the police lobby. Emma Jean probably needed time to recover from the shock of finding out that A: her boyfriend had been murdered; and B: he wasn't who she thought he was.

The woman manning the desk had close-cropped hair and a husky build. A red-and-black tattoo peeked out from under her shirt sleeve. She was reading a copy of *Field & Stream* magazine. There was not a chance in hell she'd ever wear a kitty-cat pin or pour her bosoms into a pink bustier.

"Excuse me."

She looked up from the magazine, staring at me like I was something she'd dragged into the lobby on the bottom of her shoe.

"I'm looking for Detective Martinez. He asked me to stop by to see him."

Actually, he'd summoned me, like he was a medieval duke and I was a serf. But I was determined to be on my best behavior, so I didn't dwell on that.

With a monumental effort, the woman put down the magazine and picked up the phone. She punched in a few numbers, then barked, "It's Officer Watkins. Tell Martinez there's a woman up here to see him."

She waited, listening. "How am I supposed to know?" She sounded irritated.

Some more listening, then, "What's your name?"

I stared at the Bait & Tackle shop calendar on the wall.

"Hey," she raised her voice. "I said, what's your name?"

When I figured out she was talking to me, I told her.

"Have a seat." She hung up the phone. "He's busy, but he knows you're out here. He'll see you as soon as he gets to it."

She picked up *Field & Stream* again, lifting it in front of her face. I missed Emma Jean.

I was the only customer in the lobby. I didn't think Miss Police Congeniality would mind me making a call to work while I waited. I'd already phoned in sick, but I owed my supervisor, Rhonda, an explanation. We're close. I figured she should get the straight news from me, instead of the gossipy version from the Himmarshee Hotline.

"Hey, there. It's Mace."

She'd heard all about Mama's trouble, of course. Charging Mama as an accessory to murder was bull, I told Rhonda. I said we're working hard on getting her out.

"I know you've got a lot on your plate right now, Mace, and I hate to pile on." That was Rhonda's warning she was about to do just that. "Remember that lady who called all hysterical over the possum? You remember, from New Jersey. She thought she had a really big rat. She's got a new problem for you."

"What is it this time?" I asked. "A king snake in her toilet?"

"She swears she's seen a Florida panther prowling her property."

"Yeah, that's likely. What are there, like eighty of them left? And all down in the Everglades, a hundred and fifty miles south of us. It's probably somebody's pet cat, hittin' the Friskies too hard. I once had a friend with a house cat weighed thirty-one pounds. She'd toss Tiger a treat every time she walked past. That cat looked like a bowling ball with paws."

"Anyway, Mace, the woman's driving us crazy. What should I tell her?"

"Tell her the truth. Tell her my mama's in prison. It'll reinforce all her stereotypes. Go ahead and add that my man is a-cheatin' and my blue eyes are cryin' in the rain."

There was a long pause on the other end.

"Why would I want to do that, Mace?" she said, confused.

"It's a joke, Rhonda. Like a country song? Like as long as Mama's in prison, let's add on the rest of the redneck clichés?"

"Oh."

Rhonda, who's black, doesn't find anything remotely amusing about rednecks.

"All righty, then," I said. "I better get goin'. Tell the New Jersey woman I'll get out there when I can. If a panther eats her first, that'll be one fewer fast-talking, know-it-all Yankee we have to deal with."

Rhonda, a fellow native Himmarsheean, was still laughing when I hung up.

I left the lobby to visit the Ladies, where I tried without success to repair my smooshed hair. I stopped at a water fountain in the hallway, loitering by a closed door to see if I could overhear anything useful about the murder. The only sound that seeped through was the tap-tap of a computer keyboard.

I returned to the lobby, where I exhausted all the details on the calendar, including counting the dots on the large mouth bass. I took my seat again, and ran through in my mind what I'd learned about Jim Albert, a.k.a. Jimmy the Weasel. I tried to imagine who in Himmarshee might have wanted a fugitive from the underworld dead.

I moved on to wondering how I'd handle the obnoxious Martinez. I wished my sister Marty were here. People fall all over themselves to tell her things. As I weighed the best way to get information, an image of Martinez's black eyes and sculpted features forced its way into my thoughts. I tried so hard to push it aside that my head started to hurt.

I turned my attention to a dusty stack of magazines. Leafing through *Correctional News*, I discovered there's been a downturn in inmate suicides. I thought that was encouraging for Mama.

Then, I opened *Police* magazine, and read about the problem of sudden deaths in custody. I got depressed all over again. Browsing through the advertisements aimed at prison administrators failed to lift my spirits. There were no-shank shaving razors, so inmates can't make knives. There was a restraint bed for the crazy or unruly prisoner, complete with floor anchors and slots for straps. The name of the bed, I swear to God, was the Sleep-Tite.

Glancing at my watch, I realized I'd already been waiting for forty minutes. I tried not to get angry. After all, my mother's fate was in Martinez's hands. I didn't want to tick him off. I rehearsed how I'd approach him, concentrating on the flies with honey principle, like Mama advised.

Finally, Martinez walked into the empty lobby, frowning. He had a file folder in one hand and a cell phone to his ear.

Fifty-three minutes had crawled by since I'd given my name at the desk.

I started to rise from the chair. He caught my eye and motioned me to sit down. Then, he held up a warning finger. Don't speak, it said.

I counted to ten real slow, gripping the arms of my uncomfortable chair. Pretending my hands were around Martinez's throat, I squeezed until my knuckles turned white. Staring at the wall calendar, I pictured his smug face on the body of the large mouth bass. I imagined a hook grabbing hold of the soft flesh inside his cheek. I'd just formed an image of Martinez as half-man, half-fish, flopping airless in the bottom of a bass boat, when I realized he was speaking.

"I don't know what you have to look so happy about," he said.

He slipped his phone into the front pocket of his blue dress shirt. I cursed myself for noticing how snugly the shirt fit his broad chest, even as he stood glaring next to my chair.

"I was just thinking about fishing," I said. "But you're right. I have absolutely nothing to smile about. Not with my elderly mother imprisoned in a hell hole."

"Jailed, not imprisoned."

"I beg your pardon?"

"Your mother's in jail, not prison." He tucked the folder next to his chest and crossed his arms over it, teacher style. "There's a difference. Jails are locally run, and inmates are generally waiting to be tried. Or, they've been tried, and they're serving a sentence of a year or less. Prisons are run by the state or the feds. Prisoners are usually convicted felons, serving sentences of more than a year."

"Thanks, Professor," I said. "I'll try to keep my references to correctional facilities correct whenever I explain to people how my mother is rotting behind bars."

"Actually, the rotting part comes after she's convicted," Martinez said. "Accessory to murder is a felony. It can buy you a long, long time in prison."

I could have throttled the arrogance right out of his voice. But then they'd send me to jail, and probably put me in that Sleep-Tite bed.

"It must strike you as strange that you're the only one who believes my mother is involved in Jim Albert's murder." I forced a civil tone. "What evidence do you have that links her to the killing? Did you know my mother doesn't even own a gun?"

Ignoring my questions, Martinez looked down at a paper stapled to the file in his hand. "Is your mother acquainted with a man named Salvatore Provenza?" He rolled the *R's* with Latin flair.

"You know she knows him," I said, shifting my eyes away from the curve of his lips. "Sal was in here last night, raising a ruckus with the rest of us."

I didn't reveal Big Sal was in line to become Husband Number Five. I wasn't sure where Martinez was going with the question.

"So, he's her boyfriend." He made a little note on his paper. "Were you aware he had long-standing ties to the murder victim?"

I knew it! My sisters and I weren't just over-imaginative busybodies. Sal was involved in something criminal with Jimmy the Weasel.

"So?" I tried to sound casual. "That doesn't prove anything. Sal and the man in Mama's trunk were both from New York. Maybe they played on the same stickball team as kids."

Martinez looked at me like a teacher forced to flunk a once-promising student. "They played together, all right. But their game didn't have anything to do with stickball."

"Well, what did it have to do with?"

Another condescending look. "I'm not going to discuss that with you."

I thought of Henry, and the guessing games I hated. The more I wanted to know, the harder my cousin would withhold. I switched tactics.

"Whether you discuss it or not, I don't see what any of this has to do with Mama." I faked nonchalance. "Even if Sal is involved, why would you assume my mother is, too?"

"I'm not going to share the nature of my information with you, Ms. Bauer." He slipped the folder under his arm and touched the knot of his tie, as officious as a bureaucrat cutting off an unemployment check.

Had I really been thinking this smug jerk was attractive? It had been way too long between boyfriends.

"Let's just say that when your dear mother isn't teaching Sunday school, she's consorting with some pretty rough characters," he said. "The question is, 'What did she know about the relationship between the victim and Salvatore Provenza, and what did she do about it?' "

I remembered what Donnie Bailey had said at the jail. Hardly a woman behind bars doesn't claim some man put her there. I got a mental picture of Mama sobbing in a cell, trying to convince a skeptical guard she'd been double-crossed by the man she loved.

If Martinez had his way, that sad scene wouldn't play out in jail. It'd play out in prison—after he'd managed to convict my mama of murder.

SEVEN

THE BELLS ON THE glass door jangled, announcing my entrance at Hair Today, Dyed Tomorrow.

Not that Betty Taylor, shop owner and news conduit, needed that cue. She probably knew the moment I made up my mind to visit, turning left from the police department instead of right.

Inside the beauty parlor, the harsh smell of permanent solution stung my nose. Hair conditioners, as fragrant as ripe fruit, softened the stronger odor. Flickering in the corner was a carnation-infused candle. That was Mama's influence. In addition to her work with clients' color charts, she's also an aromatherapist. I'll admit, the shop smelled girly, but oddly comforting, even to a tomboy like me.

Betty stood behind a chair, a pink foam roller in one hand and a strand of a customer's wet hair in the other. Smiling at me in the mirror, she called out to her beautician trainee.

"D'Vora, c'mon out from the supply closet, girl. You won't believe who's here!"

Betty did a quick twist of her customer's hair with one hand, pulling another roller from her pocket with the other. All without breaking eye contact with my reflection in the mirror.

"Mace, toss the towels off of that chair and have a seat." Another hair twist and roll. "What in the world is going on with our poor Rosalee?"

I suppose it had been wishful thinking to imagine word hadn't reached my mother's co-workers. Gossip spreads at the shop like dark roots on a bottle blonde. It was just as well. I hadn't relished the idea of breaking the news that Mama's in the slammer.

D'Vora peeked out at me from behind the supply closet. "Mace, I'm so sorry about your mama. I just don't know what to say."

D'Vora had managed to give her purple uniform some sex appeal. It was a size too small, and the top three buttons were undone. She'd appliquéd pink butterflies along the neckline, drawing even more attention to the suntanned valley between her breasts.

"That's okay, D'Vora," I said. "We're getting the whole misunderstanding straightened out. That's what I came by to tell y'all."

Her troubled frown faded. "See, Betty? Didn't I say that? When I put that peroxide mixture on Rosalee's hair, I didn't understand how strong it was. And then the phone rang. I didn't know leaving it on for just a tiny bit longer than the directions say would cause such a mess. It was just a misunderstanding, like Mace said."

Betty left her customer in the chair, click-clacked across the lilac-and-white floor, and snapped her fingers in front of D'Vora's face. *Snap. Snap. Snap.* "Get with it, girl. That burned-up 'do you gave Rosalee is yesterday's news. I told you she got tossed in the hoosegow. Try to focus, D'Vora."

45

D'Vora looked like a puppy spanked for peeing on the carpet. "I only wanted Mace to know I'm sorry about her mama's hair. Of course, I'm sorry she murdered that man, too. Knowing Rosalee, she must have had a very good reason."

Betty shrugged an apology at me in the mirror. "You'll have to excuse D'Vora, Mace." She tapped the foam roller in her hand against the young woman's forehead. "She was behind the door when God gave out brains."

I moved the towels and took a seat. "That's all right. I just wanted to come and tell y'all that Mama's a hundred-percent innocent. And we're gonna prove it, too. She'll be back here with her aromatherapy and seasonal color swatches before you know it."

"I'm sure of it, Mace," Betty said reassuringly.

D'Vora didn't look as convinced, but she kept her mouth shut this time.

"Honey, why don't you sit right there and relax?" Betty asked me. "You look like a pair of pantyhose been put through the spin cycle."

And the day wasn't but half over. I leaned back, shut my eyes and took some deep breaths. Usually, I don't buy the aroma mumbo-jumbo, but the crisp scent was beginning to work its magic. Mama claims the scent of carnation oil reduces stress. I could use a little of that.

"Thanks, Betty. But just for a little while. I need to find some-one else who could have committed the murder. I'm going to show this jerk of a detective from Miami that his case against Mama is a bunch of manure."

I try to watch my mouth around Betty, who worships with Mama at the Abundant Hope and Charity Chapel. She doesn't cotton to cussing.

"We've heard all about that detective, Mace." Betty spoke from around a purple comb she'd stuck between her lips. "My friend Nadine's boy Robby manages the Dairy Queen. He told her that detective is as rude as can be. Nadine's boy made the mistake of asking him how long they'd have the parking lot roped off while they looked at the body in Rosalee's trunk. He didn't mean nothing by it. It's just wasn't good for business. Who wants to come in for a banana split if a body's drawing flies in the parking lot?"

D'Vora interrupted, "I heard that detective's easy on the eyes, but he's downright mean. Nadine told Betty he just about snapped poor Robby's head off at the Queen."

I knew the feeling. I think Martinez was still picking pieces of my own head out of his incisors.

"Absolutely snapped it off," Betty agreed. "Just plain rude is what that is. But what do you expect? After all, he is from Mi-amuh." She gave the word its old-Florida pronunciation. "You know how people are down there, girls. That place is worse than New York City."

I didn't believe Betty had ever been north of Tallahassee, but that was neither here nor there.

"Speaking of New York, Betty, what do you know about the man in Mama's trunk?"

She quit rolling her customer's hair and pulled the comb from her mouth, giving me her complete attention. D'Vora closed the supply closet and eased into a chair.

"We haven't heard word one yet," Betty said. "There's only been a few clients in this morning, and so far nobody who's known nothing. No offense, Wanda," Betty nodded at the woman in her chair.

"None taken," Wanda said agreeably.

Now all three women looked at me expectantly.

"It was Jim Albert," I said. "Though I've since found out that wasn't his real name."

Betty staggered theatrically, reaching out to steady herself on Wanda's shoulder. "You don't mean it, Mace," she said. "I was just talking last week to Emma Jean Valentine about their wedding. She planned a burgundy and silver theme, and a three-tier cake with butter-cream icing. She wanted me to do her hair."

I sprang the rest of the story on them, about how he was really Jimmy "the Weasel," and connected to New York mobsters.

As I spoke, Betty got animated, nodding and interjecting "You don't say!" But D'Vora got real quiet. She returned to the supply closet, where she began shifting shampoo bottles.

"Don't that beat all, D'Vora?" Betty called out, shaking her head.

"Sure does." D'Vora's tone was subdued, her head still stuck in the shampoos.

Now it was my turn to exchange a look with Betty in the mirror.

"Girl, what is up with you? C'mon out of there," Betty said.

D'Vora closed the door slowly. She held a pair of scissors. A folded purple drape hung from her arm. "I've just been thinking about your poor mama, stuck in prison," she said. "I think it'll perk her spirits if we do something about your hair, Mace. She always says how you're so pretty, but you won't do a thing to improve what God gave you."

I was curious about D'Vora's attitude shift when I mentioned Jim Albert. I could use a haircut; and maybe she'd talk. What the hell? I'd skip lunch.

Stepping behind my chair, she eyed my bed-flattened 'do. "What'd you cut it with, Mace? Gardening shears?" She lifted a thick hank of hair, letting it fall around my face. "See this jet black? It's gorgeous, like something from the silent movies. With that and your baby blues, you could be a knockout. It's a shame you go around looking like one of the critters you've dragged out from under somebody's porch."

"D'Vora, I've told you about insulting the customers!" Betty warned.

"Mace isn't a customer, Betty. She's Rosalee's kin. And I'm starting to believe she's right about her Mama being innocent."

I jumped on that. "Do you know something to help me prove that, D'Vora?"

Her frown came back. "I can't say just yet, Mace. I want to get it right."

Betty caught my eye and made a slow-down motion.

"I'll think on it while I work on your hair. No more questions 'til then," D'Vora said.

I sat, and she leaned me back until my head rested on the basin. The shampoo smelled like green apples.

"What I meant about your mama ..." She finally spoke again as she dried, rubbing so hard I feared scars on my scalp. "I'm just not sure what to say, Mace. I was taught not to speak ill of the dead. And part of it was told me in strict confidence by a customer. That's like a patient and a doctor, isn't it, Betty?"

The two of them looked over at Wanda, who'd been moved to a dryer. She sat under a whir of hot air, devouring a *National Enquirer*.

"These are special circumstances." I lowered my voice. "Mama needs your help."

She gave a little nod. "Well, first of all, you knew Jim Albert owned the Booze 'n' Breeze, right?"

"Um-hmm," I urged her along, even though I hadn't known. I wanted her to get to the part about how someone else might have killed him.

"He had a secret business, too. Loaning money. He didn't ask questions, and there was no paperwork, like at a bank. I'm embarrassed to say my husband, Leland, went to him once. He needed to borrow three hundred dollars. Leland was a week late paying it back."

D'Vora looked down, blotting at a shampoo splotch on her smock. "Jim Albert sent a man out to the house to break all the windows in our truck. He told us the next time it wouldn't just be the truck. Leland came up with the cash, and we never saw him again."

She raised her eyes to me. "That Jim Albert was a man to be feared, Mace. What if someone else couldn't pay what they owed? That would be a reason for murder, wouldn't it?"

"It sure would, D'Vora." I felt like kissing her.

"And there's more; about Emma Jean and the wedding." Her eyes darted around the shop, as if she expected Emma Jean to jump out from behind a chair. "She came in a few days ago while Betty was out to lunch. She sat right in that chair and told me she was having second thoughts about going through with it."

I jumped at that. "Did she say why? What else did she say?"

D'Vora turned her head toward Wanda. Still drying.

She leaned in close, cupping a hand around her mouth as she broke Emma Jean's confidence. "She'd found out Jim was cheating," D'Vora whispered. "She was so mad, she said she didn't know whether she wanted to marry him or murder him."

EIGHT

Maddie was pacing outside her Volvo by the dumpster at the Booze 'n' Breeze when I arrived.

It was the first time in history my teetotaler sister and the drive-thru liquor store had been forced into such close proximity. When I called Maddie to tell her I found out some things that could help cut Mama loose from jail, she insisted upon meeting me at the Booze 'n' Breeze. It was her maiden trip to Jim Albert's store, a den of sin in my sister's mind.

The store's about two miles east of the courthouse square in downtown Himmarshee. That's far enough not to offend the good citizens who gather in the square for lunch, eating out of paper bags on benches under oaks strung with Spanish moss. But it's also close enough so those same citizens can swing by for a nip on their way home from work.

In her black pantsuit, serious pumps, and reading glasses on a silver chain, Maddie looked every inch the school principal. Frowning, she glanced at her watch as she saw me drive up.

I parked on the weedy shoulder along Highway 98, and waited as a truck loaded with Brangus and Charolais cattle roared past. Then a battered pickup, its gate held shut with a length of rusty chain, clattered by. Six Latino farm workers in the back clamped their hands over their baseball caps, guarding them from the wind.

When I crossed the road and met Maddie by the dumpster, she stared at me so long I started to get nervous.

"What?" I asked her. "Do I still have sleep crud in my eyes? I know there's nothing stuck in my teeth, because I haven't had a bite to eat all day."

"What'd you do to your hair, Mace?"

I put up a hand self-consciously, and felt nothing but smooth where there had been snarls that morning. Maddie grabbed my chin and turned my head this way and that.

"It looks good," she finally said. "It really does." She sounded shocked.

"D'Vora cut it," I mumbled.

"My sister at a beauty parlor?" Maddie took a step back. "So that explains this awful foreboding I've had ever since Mama was arrested. The world really is coming to an end."

"Very funny, Maddie." I snapped at her, but secretly I was pleased. A compliment from Maddie is rarer than a three-legged cat.

I told her all about Jim Albert, including his mob ties and the fact that Emma Jean had been furious after she'd found out he was running around with another woman.

"Jimmy the Weasel, huh? That cheating lowlife was an insult to the weasel," Maddie said.

"Let's go on in," I told her, "and see what else we can learn about him."

There was no wall in front, since the whole idea of the Booze 'n' Breeze is to let shoppers motor past and get a good look at the libations. The business's motto is, you never have to leave the driver's seat to tank up.

The clerk looked at us in alarm as we stepped into the store from the drive-thru lane. She'd probably never seen a customer before from the waist down.

I smiled, harmless-like.

Maddie ratcheted up her customary frown. "Linda-Ann, tell me that's not you underneath those stupid dreadlocks! And selling liquor, too?"

So much for building rapport.

"I'm nine years out of middle school, Ms. Wilson," the clerk said to my sister. "I'm old enough to work here, you know."

I could have told Linda-Ann not to sound so apologetic. The only defense against Maddie is a strong offense.

"I happen to like your hair, Linda-Ann." I aimed a pointed look at my sister. "It's a perfect style for you, especially with those cargo pants and that peace-sign T-shirt. So few young people these days show any individuality at all when it comes to fashion."

I was afraid I'd poured it on too thick, but Linda-Ann beamed beneath her blonde dreadlocks. "Thanks," she said, smiling at me. "I like your hair, too."

"I thought you were going to college, Linda-Ann." Maddie was judgmental.

"College isn't for everyone." I was understanding.

It was becoming clear who was the good cop and who was the bad in our interrogation tag team.

We waited while a car pulled in. The driver wanted a six-pack of Old Milwaukee and five Slim Jims. Dinner. It took Linda-Ann two tries to count out the change from his twenty.

Bad cop: "Didn't you pay any attention at all in Mrs. Dutton's math class?"

Good cop: "You must be creative, Linda-Ann. Arty types are never good at arithmetic."

Maddie lost interest in creating rapport and asked Linda-Ann flat out what she knew about her late boss, Jim Albert. The clerk clammed up.

"Nothing really." She twirled a dreadlock. "My manager told me the owner got killed, but I barely knew him. I've only worked here a few months."

Linda-Ann got busy rearranging a rack of pork rinds on the counter, even though they looked fine the way they were. Appetizing, actually. She straightened a hand-lettered sign that said *Boiled P'nuts/Cappuccino*, which I took as clear evidence that the yuppies were colonizing Himmarshee. She was doing everything she could in such close quarters to avoid us.

I knew we wouldn't get anything from her—not with Maddie standing there radiating disapproval like musk during mating season. Linda-Ann was out to show my sister she wasn't a little girl anymore, quaking on a hard bench outside the principal's office at the middle school.

I dug into my purse, piling stuff onto the counter, until I found a pen and some paper. "Listen, our mother was tossed in jail because she can't explain how come your boss's body was found in her trunk."

54

Linda-Ann's eyes widened.

"She didn't kill him," I said. "We're trying to find out who did. We'd really appreciate anything you could tell us about Jim Albert that might help us do that, okay?" I jotted down my phone numbers and handed the paper over the counter.

"Let's go, Maddie. Let's let Linda-Ann get back to work."

Once we were out on the street again, I turned on my sister. "You have to learn to lighten up, Maddie. Not everybody responds to intimidation."

"Thanks for the tip, Mace. Seeing as how I've worked with young people all my life and you work mostly with raccoons, I appreciate the lesson in human psychology."

"Don't get mad. I'm just saying sometimes you can catch more flies with honey than with vinegar."

"Now you sound like Mama."

I was beginning to realize there are worse things I could sound like.

Maddie and I put our argument on hold, stepping off the street as a pickup truck with mud on the flaps made its way from the drive-thru lane. I couldn't believe my eyes when I caught a glimpse of the driver—black Stetson on his head, left arm in a cowboy shirt propped on the sill of his open window. My heart started pounding and my tongue went dry. I never imagined seeing him would send me for a loop; not after all these years.

"Jeb Ennis!" I yelled, before I even realized I'd opened my mouth.

"Oh, no," Maddie said.

When Jeb spotted me, he lit up in a smile. Maddie's face darkened. He parked his truck and waited to cross the road to where my sister and I stood. There was a steady stream of traffic—trucks carrying livestock feed and fertilizer, and the occasional tourist in a rental car who'd ventured far from the resorts on the coasts in search of the *real* Florida.

As Jeb waited for the road to clear, I had plenty of time to check him out: Blonde hair, blinding white smile, the tanned face of a man who works outdoors in the Florida sun. Tight, faded jeans fit his legs like blue denim paint. He was still long and lean; the years had added only a pound or two to his six-foot frame. First, I'd had inappropriate thoughts about Martinez. Now, seeing Jeb, my knees were as weak as a schoolgirl's. I really need to get out more.

Reaching our side of the street, he spent a long moment staring at me.

"You look great, Mace."

And he looked good enough to eat. The attraction had outlasted anger, and the passage of a decade, at least. I shoved my shaking hands into the pockets of my jeans.

Jeb removed his cowboy hat and pushed a hand through his hair, flattened and slightly sweaty where the band had rested. "You're sure a sight for sore eyes, Mace. How long has it been?"

"Not long enough," Maddie muttered.

"I think it was my first year of college," I said, surprised when my voice came out sounding normal.

Maddie stepped in front of me, getting right in his face. "That's when some horrible cowboy broke her heart. Tell me, Jeb, are you still riding rodeo?" She tossed him a smile like she'd rather it was a rattlesnake.

He nervously moved the hat in his hand to his waist, covering up the championship calf-roping buckle on his belt. "Nah, Maddie, I'm too old for rodeo." He smiled back at her. "I bought myself a little ranch west of here, out near Wauchula."

"Not far enough," Maddie said.

I bit my tongue before I echoed Mama and told Maddie to mind her manners. She was trying to watch out for me, and with good reason. On the other hand, a lot of time had passed. And the man did look mighty fine in his boots and jeans. He smelled of sweat and hay and the faintest trace of manure, which is like an aphrodisiac for a former ranch gal like me.

"I think my big sister was just leaving, Jeb."

I tried to signal Maddie by jerking my head toward the dumpster and her car, but she ignored me. "Maddie, don't you need to get back to the middle school and torture some little children?"

"I've got all the time in the world, Mace." My sister shifted her purse from her right shoulder to her left, the better to take a swing at Jeb if she needed to.

"We were just talking about the owner of this place, that poor guy who got murdered. Did you know him?" I asked Jeb.

His eyes flickered to the drive-thru. "Only to nod at."

"You're probably a pretty good customer," Maddie said. "If I remember, drinking too much was among your many flaws."

"Maddie!" I said.

Jeb glared at my sister, his green eyes cold. "I don't drink like I used to, not that it's any of your business. I just bought a couple of cases of beer for the boys who work with me at the ranch." He put his hat back on, straightened the brim, and dipped it a little toward Maddie before he turned to me. "We're having a barbecue tonight, Mace. I'd sure love for you to come."

"Mace is allergic to barbecue sauce. Gives her hives," Maddie lied.

I stole a quick look at his left hand. No wedding ring. Still, I wasn't going to be that easy.

"I've got plans tonight." I wish. "How about you ask me for the next one?"

"Is your number listed?"

"Mace doesn't have a phone." Maddie made a last-ditch effort.

"Ignore my sister. I'm in the book."

After he left, Maddie lit into me. "I can't believe you'd give that devil the time of day, Mace. When he breaks your heart again, don't say I didn't warn you."

"I'm a big girl now, Maddie. And you didn't have to be so rude. My heart's been shattered a time or two since Jeb."

"But never as bad as that first time, Mace. Never that bad." My sister glanced at her watch. "Now, I really am late. The kids will be raising a ruckus if I'm not there to supervise the school bus lines."

She got into her Volvo and rolled down the window. "I'll talk to you after school, okay? We need to decide what to do next about Mama."

As Maddie pulled away, I started looking through my purse for my cell. I wanted to call my other sister, Marty, and tell her about running into the great love of my life. No phone. I remembered pulling everything out of my purse inside the Booze 'n' Breeze, hunting for a pen.

I walked back inside and saw Linda-Ann waving my missing phone over her head.

"I figured you'd be back for it," she grinned.

"Listen, I want to apologize for my sister. She's been a principal for so long, she treats everyone like they're in the seventh grade."

"That's OK. She's just as mean as ever, though. You know how her name is Madison Wilson?"

I nodded.

"Back in middle school, all the kids called her Mad Hen Wilson."

I leaned in close. "That'll be our secret, Linda-Ann." I didn't tell her that Maddie was not only aware of the nickname, she embraced it.

"There's something else I want to tell you." She touched one of her dreadlocks to her lips. "How well do you know that good-looking cowboy who just left here?"

"Pretty well. We used to date, a long time ago."

"Then you might want to ask him what he knows about the guy who owned this place."

I got an uneasy feeling in my gut. "Why's that, Linda-Ann?"

"That cowboy's been in here a lot in the few months I've worked here. He always went back into the office to talk to Mr. Albert, and they'd always shut the door."

An old Ford rumbled into the drive-thru. I waited while Linda-Ann served a woman with three screaming kids, two of them still in diapers. I'd be buying booze too, if I had that brood.

As the Ford backfired and pulled away, the stench of burning oil filled the little store. Linda-Ann continued her story. "The last time the cowboy came in, they were back there yelling so loud I could hear their voices coming through the concrete wall."

"Could you tell what they were saying?"

"I couldn't make it out." She folded a dreadlock in two and let it spring back. "But when the cowboy left, he slammed the office door so hard it about came off its hinges. Then he kicked over a whole display case of beer. Mr. Albert came out to the counter a couple of minutes later and told me to clean it up. I thought he'd be angry."

"He wasn't?"

"His face was ghost-white and he was shaking. He didn't look mad. He looked scared to death."

NINE

I BARELY HAD TIME to process what Linda-Ann revealed about my one-time boyfriend.

I had to rush to work, where I was past late for an after-school event. Two third-grade classes were scheduled to visit the makeshift wildlife center I maintain at Himmarshee Park. A teacher from the last group of kids who came by sent me a letter, saying her students were still talking about the injured fox and scary snakes.

This latest group of kids was already there. I didn't want to disappoint them by not showing up.

I could hear the din of thirty-one third graders as I crossed the little bridge over Himmarshee Creek and turned into the park. When I walked in the office and dropped my purse on the desk, Rhonda, my boss, shot me a relieved look.

"Thank God, you're here, Mace. Those little monsters are tearing the place apart."

Within ten minutes, I had the students gathered in an outdoor amphitheater, ooohing and aaahing over the contents of a half-dozen cages. The star of the show, a bull alligator missing an eye and most of one foot, was waiting in the wings in his outdoor pool, ready to wow the kids for the show's grand finale.

"Does anybody know what this is?" I held the first cage aloft. Two dozen hands shot into the air.

"A skunk!" cried a little boy in a red shirt who couldn't wait to be called on.

"That's right. But we don't talk out of turn, do we? Anyone with the right answer today will get a special award. But you have to wait 'til you're called on to get the prize," I said.

"Now, this skunk I trapped because it was eating up the tomatoes in some lady's garden. She definitely didn't want it around because when she invited her friends over for cards, seeing a skunk freaked them out. It was probably somebody's pet, because it had been descented. Who knows what that means?"

Fewer hands went up this time. I called on the red-shirted boy so he wouldn't feel bad.

"It means he don't stink no more," he said.

"*Doesn't stink anymore.* Very good. Now, it was wrong to buy this skunk as a pet, and then let it go in the wild," I said. "You know why? Because skunks use that stinky smell as a defense against bigger animals. Without it, this little guy was as helpless as a kitten."

And so it went for the next thirty-five minutes. A demonstration with something furred or slithery; a lesson about environmental responsibility. Finally, I herded the kids to the pool holding the seven-foot-long Ollie. There, I lectured them about staying away from alligators in the wild.

"Never, ever feed an alligator, or tease it in any way," I said. "If they get too comfortable around people, it's dangerous—not just for you, but for them. That's when gators become what our state laws call a nuisance animal. And that means that someone with a trapper's license—like my cousin, Dwight—can kill them and sell them for their meat and hide."

I thought of my stuffed-head key holder at home. It wasn't that gator's fault someone built a house with a pool in his territory. But once they did, it wasn't safe for him to make himself at home there anymore. So now his head graced my coffee table, like a trophy buck on the basement wall of a deer hunter up north.

I pointed over a low concrete wall at Ollie, lolling in his pond. "Now, that gator's here because he became a nuisance to people who like to play golf. But we didn't kill him. We got special permission to keep him for educational purposes. Does anybody know what that means?"

Hands shot up. I picked a little girl in a yellow sundress. "Teaching?"

"Right," I told her. "Now, I'll educate you a little about Ollie."

Thirty-one small bodies crowded toward the pond. "Careful, now! You may peek over, but you may not climb onto that wall."

When they'd chosen their spots, I continued, "A gator's jaws are about the most powerful thing in the animal kingdom," I told them. "If Ollie were to clamp down on your arm or leg, the pressure in his bite is more than sixteen times harder than your average big dog. His jaws are even stronger than a lion's."

At this point, I tossed a whole raw chicken into Ollie's gaping mouth. Some of the girls screamed when the gator's jaws snapped shut over his meal. I took my bow.

Handing off the kids to one of their teachers, I collapsed on a park bench. I was staring up at the sky through the green-needled branches of a cypress tree when I heard a tentative voice.

"Excuse me, Ms. Bauer?"

A pretty redhead peered at me from the end of the bench.

"I'm here with the kids," she said. "They're going to want to know: How'd Ollie get hurt?"

"A fight with another male, probably over a mate. And if you think Ollie looks bad, you should have seen the other guy."

The line usually gets a laugh, but the teacher didn't crack a smile.

"Uhm ... I wonder if I could speak to you about another matter?"

With the kind of day I'd had, with her hesitation and demeanor, this couldn't be good.

"Sure." I patted the bench next to me, inviting her to sit down. "What's on your mind?"

"I knew your mother real well. I mean, I *know* her." She corrected the past tense. Mama wasn't dead; she was just accused of killing someone else. "I was in her Sunday school class."

You and half of Himmarshee, I thought. But I was silent, preparing for the punch line.

"I wanted to tell you I'm sorry about her being in jail." She sat, looking down to straighten the already perfect lines of her knee-length skirt. "I don't think she belongs there."

"We don't either."

"No, I mean it's impossible she did what the police say."

I sat up straight, fatigue forgotten.

She continued, "My mother plays bingo at the Seminole reservation, just like your mom. They were together at the casino yesterday, all afternoon. They had dinner there, and then played into the evening. At one point, before dinner, my mother got to feeling awfully cold. They keep the place air-conditioned like an ice house."

I drummed my fingers on the bench.

"Anyway, Ms. Deveraux told my mom she had a jacket in the trunk of her car. The two of them left the casino and walked way out into the parking lot to your mother's turquoise convertible. Ms. Deveraux opened up the trunk. My mother said she moved aside some fishing tackle and a cooler before she found that jacket. And there sure was no body inside her trunk."

I felt like I was Samson, the Bible strongman, and the Lord had just lifted the heavy pillars of the temple off of my hands. I wanted to hug her, but settled for grinning like an idiot.

"That's fantastic!" I jumped off the bench. "Your mother needs to tell that to the police."

The teacher stood up, too. "She already did. My mother called and told me a detective questioned her this afternoon. Spanish accent. Kind of rude, my mother said. He didn't seem all that interested in her story about bingo, until she got to the part about Ms. Deveraux and her jacket."

I grabbed her by the arm. "What'd he say?"

"Well, he wanted to know all about it. When, where, and how. My mother told him she saw clear into the back of Ms. Deveraux's trunk. He argued with her, saying your mother might have collected the body from somewhere else before she wound up at the Dairy Queen."

I sat down again, thinking about why Martinez was trying so hard to indict Mama. Did he have something against bingo-playing grandmas?

"Did your mother tell the detective anything else that could be helpful?" I asked.

The teacher rolled her eyes toward her forehead, like she was replaying her conversation with her mother in her head. She touched the hem of her skirt. "She did tell him there was no way Ms. Deveraux could have snuck away. Your mother was on a hot streak all night. All the other ladies gathered round to congratulate her when bingo was over. She wound up going home with the two-hundred-dollar pot."

And that platinum-haired imp had never said one word about winning $200.

"Listen, would your mother be willing to go to the police department with me and tell her story over again? If we can't get Detective Martinez to listen, we'll just go over his head to Chief Johnson."

She didn't hesitate a moment. "Absolutely. We'll do anything we can do to help Ms. Deveraux."

Soon, the kids and the red-haired teacher were gone.

I fed the animals and closed up the park. It was late. I'd catch up my sisters by cell phone on my ride home. I couldn't wait for a hot shower. All I wanted was that, and the fried chicken stuck in my fridge since last night, when Mama's call had interrupted my supper.

My hand was on the doorknob to leave when the office phone started to ring. I wanted so bad to head on out and let the answering machine pick it up, but I was scared it could be someone trying to reach me at work with news about Mama.

I picked up the phone, and would come to wish I hadn't.

TEN

"Mace? It's your mother's friend, Sal."

I looked with longing at the exit sign over the door in the park's office. I'd been so close.

"What can I do for you, Mr. Provenza?" He'd asked us a hundred times to call him Sal, but my sisters and I addressed him more formally because we knew it irked him. At least Maddie and I did. Marty had barely said six words to the man in the year Mama had been dating him.

"It's about Rosalee."

My heart skipped a beat. "Is she okay?"

"She's fine, so far as I know."

I let out my breath.

"But me and her aren't," Sal said. "I tried to see her today at the jail, and she refused my visit. That's why you and me need to talk." Tawk. "I don't think she loves me anymore."

I felt like Robert De Niro's shrink in the movie *Analyze This.*

"Then maybe you should have been truthful with her upfront," I said. "Why didn't you tell us last night at the police department you had ties to Jim Albert? Or, should I say, Jimmy the Weasel?"

Pause. "How do you know about that?"

"Detective Martinez told me. And I'm betting he told Mama, too. That's probably the reason she won't see you. She can't abide a liar. Martinez is very interested in how you're involved with a New York gangster, who then turns up dead in the roomy trunk of your girlfriend's car. And, frankly Mr. Provenza, I'm interested in that question, too."

There was silence on his end of the phone. I could hear him taking raspy breaths. Sal really should give up smoking.

"I'm sorry, Mace," he finally said. "I can't go into all of that. Especially not on the phone. I'm out at the golf course, just finishing up eighteen holes. I played like crap. All I could think about is your mother." Mudder. "Would you consider swinging by here on your way home?"

The golf course, the centerpiece of a posh new development along a canal off Lake Okeechobee, wasn't on my way home. I live north; the new course is south. But Sal seemed to be a key to Martinez's case against Mama. I wanted to find out why.

"Please, Mace? There are some things I wanna tell ya, face ta face." The harder Sal pleaded, the more his boyhood in the Bronx seeped into his speech.

I finally agreed to meet him at the golf course, which is out in the middle of nowhere, ten miles past the last trailer park in the Himmarshee city limits. He told me he'd wait at the snack bar, next to the pro shop.

When I got there, it was dark. Two floodlights illuminated the ornate pillars marking the entrance to the community. *Himmarshee Haven*, they said in cursive script. *Luxurious Country Living*. Talk about your oxymorons. Most of the country lives I know have very little luxury.

The Jeep bounced over a series of speed bumps as I made my way past Victorian-style homes with gingerbread trim and two-car garages. Most driveways featured golf carts parked behind white picket fences. Not a single double-wide trailer or swamp buggy in sight.

I parked in the golf course's nearly deserted lot. There was no sign of Big Sal's big car, but I decided to go inside anyway. I killed some time looking over the merchandise in the pro shop. Not that I play golf. But Marty does. I bought her a three-pack of those little ankle socks with the pom-pom that sticks out above the back of her golf shoes. The pom-poms were pink, mint green, and baby blue. Marty loves pastels.

As I handed over my credit card, I asked the college-aged kid at the register whether he'd seen a gargantuan golfer with a heavy New York accent.

"Sure, Big Sal." The kid sucked on a breath mint. I could smell cinnamon clear across the counter. "He was in here about thirty, forty minutes ago. Then he got a call on his cell phone and hightailed it outside. I heard the tires on his Cadillac squealing as he pulled out of the lot. Guess he was in a hurry to get somewhere."

He pushed my receipt toward me across the glass display case, which held dimpled golf balls and leather gloves. "Sign that, would you? And I'll need to see some ID."

I gave him my driver's license. He held it up and inspected it like he was a customs agent at the airport and I was smuggling heroin. "Hmmm, you're thirty-one? I would have pegged you as younger. It's not a very flattering picture." He flipped a sun-bleached lock off his forehead and smiled at me, showing off even, white teeth. "You're much prettier in person, especially your hair. I like the way it shines."

As he handed back my license, his fingers lingered against mine for a couple of beats too long. I couldn't believe it. The kid was coming on to me. Must be the new 'do.

"Thanks." I yanked away my fingers and slipped my ID back into my wallet. He put the socks in a little bag, and handed it to me as I headed for the door.

I was still smiling to myself as I climbed into my Jeep and started on the long drive home. Now, there was date potential, I thought: a pro-shop smoothie young enough to be my nephew. Maybe we'd drive to Orlando and I could take him on the teacup ride at Disney.

My "post-flirtus" buzz didn't last long. Soon, I started wondering what the hell had happened to Sal. Why had he stood me up? That led to me worrying about how Mama was doing. It must be just about dinner time at the jail, which couldn't be a good thing for someone who loves food. Before long, I was trying to fit together all the bits and pieces I'd discovered that day. I needed to prove to Martinez that Mama had nothing to do with Jim Albert's murder.

I tried to picture me sharing some information that might replace his customary scowl with a smile. And then my brain took a quick, unexpected detour: how would those lips actually feel against mine I wondered. I traced a finger across my mouth and felt a warm twinge. Where the hell had that thought come from?

I quickly reined in my brain, and returned to worrying about Mama.

The road wasn't crowded. I was deep in thought, puzzling out the pieces of her case. Occasionally, an unwanted image would intrude of Martinez's face, of his strong hands; of his thick hair. Then, my mind would conjure Mama in her cell, and I'd feel guilty.

I didn't notice the other car on my tail until I saw headlights flash in my rearview mirror. Maybe I'd let my speed taper off. I glanced at the speedometer. Nope, holding steady at sixty-six mph. That's fast enough that no one should be riding my tail, lights flashing crazily. Peering into the mirror, I saw nothing but a white glow with a dark blob behind it. I couldn't even say if the blob was car or truck.

Slowing, I waved my arm out the Jeep's window. There wasn't another oncoming car until next Tuesday. *Go around, fool.* He had plenty of room to pass, yet he stayed plastered to my bumper.

I eased over as far as I could to the right shoulder, giving a wide berth. It was probably a carload of teenagers, tanked up on testosterone and cheap beer. No way was I going to get into a pissing match with that mess. I slowed down some more, doing about forty now.

That's when I felt a jolt from behind. I heard a hard, solid bump, high up on the back of my Jeep. It jerked me off the road, onto the rough shoulder. I wrestled with the steering wheel, fighting to keep control. The Jeep bucked like a rodeo bronc coming out the chute. My tires spit weeds and gravel. I tried to steer left, back to smooth pavement. But the other driver blocked my path.

Like freeze frames in my headlights, a mailbox, four garbage cans, and a barbed wire fence whizzed past. Then my lights swept across the white-gray expanse of a concrete culvert. It looked enormous, looming dead center in my sights.

And then I saw nothing but black.

ELEVEN

I SAW THAT WHITE light that everybody always talks about, gleaming in front of my eyes. A man's voice called my name, softly, as if from a great distance.

"Are you there, Daddy?" I murmured. "Have you come to take me over to the other side?"

I heard knocking.

"I'm not ready to go yet, Daddy. I haven't been able to find out who really killed that man in Mama's trunk. She's still sitting in the Himmarshee Jail."

Rap. Rap. Rap. The knocking continued.

"Mace!" the voice repeated; louder and more insistent. "Are you okay?"

Masculine features blurred, and then formed into a face, peering at me from above. Worried look. Firm jaw. Full mustache.

"Did you grow that mustache in heaven, Daddy?"

"Mace! C'mon back to Earth, girl."

I could almost feel my synapses struggling to fire all the fog out of my brain. "Where am I, Donnie?" I finally asked.

Donnie Bailey, from the jail, stood in water to his waist. He was tapping his flashlight loud against the hood of my Jeep. Cracks branched out across the windshield's glass like the bare limbs of a dead pine tree.

"You're sitting in a ditch up to your wheel wells off Highway 98. Are you hurt?"

I moved my left arm and then my right; lifted and lowered each foot. I was surprised to hear them splash into the water that swirled around the floorboards. When I put my palm to my forehead, I felt something else wet. I dropped my hand and stared at my own blood.

Donnie spoke calmly: "That's a head wound, Mace. You might have banged it on the steering wheel, or caught some of that barbed wire through your open window." He blinded me, shining his flashlight into my face. "That'll bleed, but it doesn't look too deep. Do you think you can undo your seat belt and help me get you out of that Jeep?"

Barbed wire fencing was draped like Christmas garland across the Jeep's front half. Donnie used the long handle on the butt-end of his flashlight to move the wire away. Pulling open my door, he leaned awkwardly into the driver's seat.

"Put your arm around my neck, Mace. I'm gonna slip my hands under your legs and lift. Careful. You're gonna be shaky."

He swung me clear of the door. "Very good," he said. "Now, I'm going to carry you over and set you down on the hood of my squad car where I can get a look at you. Is that okay?" He was using that slow, deliberate, ABC-teaching tone.

"I understand you perfectly, Donnie. I'm not going into shock on you. Did I hit the concrete culvert?"

I could smell the muddy sediment and the grassy scent of water spinach stirring as we moved. I hoped that was all that was stirring in that dark water. Donnie slipped a little climbing up the steep bank. I'm heavier than I look.

"You missed hitting it head-on. Grazed it." He stopped at the top to catch his breath. "There's a big scratch along the culvert. Then it looks like you flew over that grassy berm, and right into the water."

We waited on the bank, as Donnie gathered strength. Mosquitoes hummed in the still air.

"You can put me down. I'm fine." I felt embarrassed that someone whose diapers I'd changed was carrying me like a baby.

"You're not walking until I know what you've hurt." He was still panting a little.

We made it the twenty feet or so to his car. He sat me down on the hood and grabbed a blanket from the trunk to wrap around me. Now, he was checking me over—noting whether my skin was clammy or warm; feeling my pulse. I'd done the same thing myself to injured visitors at Himmarshee Park. After toting me through the water and up a small hill, Donnie's heart rate was probably worse off than mine.

"Can you feel that? Does that hurt?" he asked, pressing first on my midsection and then down my legs. "How 'bout that?" he said, moving on to the rest of my body.

My head felt as big as a balloon in the Macy's parade, and my right knee ached like somebody smashed it with a mallet. "I'm fine, Donnie," I lied. "Just shaken up."

"You're lucky you didn't wind up top side down in the water," he said, moving aside my new hairdo to see if there were any more cuts. "I'd never have seen you if not for your headlights shining out over the canal. It's a good thing we've had some dry days, or that water would have been higher."

He backed up a couple of steps, the better to view all of me at once.

"Looks like you'll live." He bent down to pick a long stem of hydrilla out of his shoe. I could hear the water dripping as he held up one foot.

"Thanks for coming to my rescue, Donnie. I might have stumbled out of the Jeep, fallen underwater, and never come to. I owe you."

"You should still have them look you over at the hospital, though. I've already radioed in about your accident."

Donnie using that word triggered my recall of the frightening moments before the crash. "It wasn't an accident," I said quickly. "Somebody deliberately ran me off the road."

I told him what happened, describing how the other vehicle had chased me, finally forcing me to lose control. "I'm telling you they bumped me, Donnie. Hard. If you check the Jeep's rear end once it's on dry land, you'll probably find a scrape of paint or something from his car. I'm saying right now, this was on purpose. It was no accident."

I could see the skepticism in his eyes. "Why would someone want to do that, Mace?"

"I've been out there all day, asking questions about Jim Albert. So far, all I'm sure of is Mama didn't murder him. But maybe it's making somebody nervous that I'm going to find out who did."

Donnie swung his flashlight out to the road and then to the ditch. Aside from the bugs he picked up in the beam, we were definitely alone now. "Or maybe it was just you out here. You were tired, and you fell asleep at the wheel. That's nothing to be ashamed of, Mace. I've done it myself."

We both got quiet. I can't speak for Donnie, but I was busy trying to think of a list of suspects who might have wanted me drowned at the bottom of a canal. Frogs croaked. Crickets chirped. I slapped at a mosquito that landed on my neck. In the distance, a siren wailed.

"Don't tell me that's an ambulance, Donnie. I don't like ambulances."

"You need to go to the hospital to be evaluated," he said stubbornly. "You could have internal bleeding or swelling in your brain."

"I told you: I'm fine. And I'm not riding in the back of an ambulance. They loaded my father into one after his heart attack, and that was the last time any of us saw him. I still remember the sight of those doors closing on Daddy. My sisters and I stood there in the road, watching until that ambulance was no bigger than a dot." My voice trembled.

Donnie pulled at the collar on his shirt and looked down at the ground.

"Sorry," I said. "A narrow escape from death might make anybody a little emotional. Now," I said, shifting gears, "tell me why you can't just give me a ride back to town?"

"If it was any other night, I would. But my little boy's sick, and my wife is already late for the night shift at the nursing home. My son needs me, and those old people need her. I'm sorry, Mace."

I felt bad for being so selfish. Not to mention ancient. I couldn't believe my one-time babysitting charge was married with a boy of his own. That siren was getting closer. Even as banged up as I felt, I knew I'd rather walk to town than ride in that ambulance.

Suddenly, I had what seemed like a good idea. Then again, I might have had a brain injury.

"Could you call Detective Martinez?" I said. "I believe this might have something to do with the questions I've been asking about Jim Albert's murder. Maybe he'll think so, too. He'd want to get a look at things out here, in case it turns out this is a crime scene."

I could see Donnie thinking it over. The detective outranked him. He wouldn't want to be blamed for making a mistake. I knew if Martinez came out, I could bum a ride back with him. I'd prefer even that to being shut into the back of an ambulance.

Donnie finally agreed, putting in a call for the detective. In the meantime, the ambulance crew arrived and checked me over. They did essentially what Donnie had done, except they used various medical gizmos to gauge my vital signs. They grumbled a little when I refused to be transported to the hospital. But I know my rights. I don't have a cousin who's a lawyer for nothing.

Martinez arrived just as the ambulance was leaving. Donnie met him by the road, and the two conferred, out of my hearing. Donnie was probably telling him how I'd hallucinated a chase scene after I got knocked on the head. That, along with my daddy's visit from heaven. After Martinez stopped nodding, they headed my way.

He peered into my face. Not that I cared, but was that a flicker of concern in his eyes?

"How're you feeling, Ms. Bauer?" he asked.

"Not crazy, if that's what you want to know. Someone ran me off the road."

He put out his arm for me to grab hold of. I ignored it, and climbed down off Donnie's hood. A shot of pain from my knee nearly took my breath away. My leg buckled, but Martinez caught me firmly by the waist. I was still shakier than I'd thought. But not so shaky I didn't notice the hard muscle in his arm where he held me next to his side. Or the masculine way he smelled, like aftershave mixed with a faint trace of cigars.

"Steady, *chica*." His warm breath in my ear sent a shiver south of my stomach. I wasn't sure what the Spanish word meant, but it sounded nice. "Just take slow steps, okay?" Martinez said. "We're going to get you to the front seat of my car. We'll take our time."

He nodded curtly at Donnie, dismissing him from the responsibility of me. With a wave from the open driver's side window of his car, Donnie bid me good-bye. "Remember what I said about dozing off, Mace. It's nothing to have to hide."

I smiled and waved back. But I was simmering inside. I couldn't believe Donnie thought I was making it all up.

"I'm telling the truth, you know," I said, feeling cranky now.

As Martinez settled me into his passenger seat, I repeated what I'd told Donnie. Including how I thought my crash was linked to the murder. Every once in awhile, he'd nod, leaning against the inside of my open door, arms across his chest.

When I was done, he said, "I don't disbelieve you, Ms. Bauer."

What the hell did that mean? He wasn't calling me a liar, but he wasn't saying he believed me, either.

"We'll know more about how it happened when we can look over your car. The officer called..."

"Donnie," I said, annoyed. "He has a name."

"All right, Officer *Donnie* called for a tow truck. They'll haul your Jeep to the Florida Highway Patrol, and tomorrow we'll see what we can find. I've requested an accident investigator from the FHP. She's coming out here to check the scene for skid marks, tire tracks, and anything else she can find."

He leaned across my body and fastened the seat belt at my hip. There was that cursed twinge again. Apparently, there was nothing wrong with my nether regions. His cologne smelled spicy, but subtle. It definitely beat the ditch water stench coming off of me.

After rummaging in his trunk, Martinez returned with three roadside flares. "I'm going to light these to mark the accident scene, and then you're going to the hospital. Your friend, Officer *Donnie*, already gave dispatch the location, but these will help the investigator narrow it down." He placed the flares on the car's roof, and stooped to look at me. Brushing the hair from my forehead, he examined my wound. I was surprised at the gentleness of his touch. His hands looked so strong. I jerked away, but the warm impression from his fingers lingered.

"You were northbound when you went off the road, right?"

"When I was run off the road," I snapped at him, embarrassed by my body's response to him.

"What were you doing out here anyway? It's the middle of nowhere."

As if to emphasize our isolation, we heard the deep, bellowing grunt of a bull gator. All of a sudden, an image of Mama's boyfriend flashed into my head. I couldn't believe I'd forgotten to mention before now how he'd summoned me to the distant golf course.

"Salvatore Provenza, huh?" Martinez's attention was riveted as I related my story. "And you say he wasn't there when you showed up?"

"That's right. I didn't even want to go out to that stupid golf course in the first place. I'd been busy all day, questioning people who might know something about Mama's case."

"So I've heard. You're quite the interrogator." Did I see the tiniest smile cracking through the granite in Martinez's jaw?

"Anyway, I was tired. All I wanted to do was go home, nuke some fried chicken, and vegetate in front of my TV. But he's my mother's boyfriend. And he sounded so desperate."

"Sal's desperate all right." Martinez rose. All trace of a smile was gone. "And you'd be wise to remember that desperate people do desperate things."

TWELVE

DREAD SETTLED LIKE A boulder in my stomach as Martinez and I pulled up to Himmarshee Regional Hospital. I'm not afraid of doctors. But I am afraid of my older sister.

I could see Maddie through the plate glass window, washed in a red glow from the emergency room sign. She was sitting in a nearly empty row of chairs. The set of her mouth was as hard as the steel bolts that screwed the chairs to the floor. Marty was beside her, staring into space and worrying the tissue in her hands into shreds.

As soon as the doors to the waiting room swooshed open, my sisters jumped up as if they were stitched together.

"Thank God!" Marty ran to me and threw her arms around my neck. The tears started to flow.

"Come over here and let me take a look at you," Maddie commanded, using her middle-school principal tone.

With my knee aching and Marty still clinging to my neck, I inched across the floor toward Maddie. I untangled myself, and Maddie clasped me by the shoulders. She turned me in a complete circle. When we came face-to-face again, I thought I saw a glimmer of moisture in her eyes. It was probably just a reflection from the hospital's bright lights. She patted my arm, which turned into an awkward, one-handed hug.

"Mace, you had us so worried." She let out a sigh of relief. "Donnie Bailey called to tell me about your accident. I've been wracking my brain for a way to break the news to Mama if you didn't make it."

I expected overreaction from Marty. Mama always says her nerves are too close to the surface of her skin. But not from Maddie. "You can see I'm fine," I told her. "Didn't Donnie tell you I was okay?"

"He did. But he also told us you were on your way to the hospital. Marty and I were afraid he just didn't want to break the truth about how bad things were."

"We were afraid," Marty chimed in, sniffling into the tattered tissue.

"That's why we rushed over here to see for ourselves." Maddie patted at me again. "Lord, Mace, I'm so glad to see you in one piece."

"Your forehead is bloody." Marty tenderly brushed my hair away from the cut. "What happened? Did you swerve to avoid a possum?"

My sisters knew I'd never hit any animal, not even a possum, if I could help it.

"I didn't swerve. I was run off the road."

Alarm registered on Maddie's face. Marty looked even more scared.

Martinez had been standing by the check-in desk, studying a sign about insurance co-payments like it held the cure to cancer. I got the feeling he was more comfortable with my family arguing than with our affection. He cleared his throat, a loud rumble in the quiet waiting room.

"There'll be plenty of time for you to get into all that, Ms. Bauer. Now, you need to check in and let the doctor take a look at you."

"Y'all remember Detective Martinez," I said to my sisters.

Maddie looked at him like he'd poisoned the fundraising candy for the middle-school band. "How could we forget him? He's the man who put our poor mother into prison."

"Jail, Maddie, not prison." I figured I'd head off another vocabulary lecture on correctional facilities. "By the way, Detective." I put some ice in my voice. "I spoke to the daughter of one of my mother's bingo cronies today. I know you have some information about Mama's trunk being empty of any murder victim last night while she was playing bingo. Playing bingo all night long, as it happens."

The granite came back to his jaw. "I'm still gathering facts in relation to the investigation, Ms. Bauer. I'm not willing to go into those matters right now. Besides, I came here to make sure you get medical attention. And that's what we're going to do."

"That's true," I conceded to my sisters, "he was nice enough to give me a ride here. And he's promised to look into why Big Sal called me to meet him at the golf course, and then disappeared before I got there. If not for that call, I'd never have been way out that way in the first place, nor landed my Jeep in a canal."

My sisters started talking over each other, peppering me with questions. Maddie was louder, of course. "What does Mama's obnoxious boyfriend, have to do with anything?" she demanded.

"You were in a ditch, Mace? Were there water moccasins?" Marty shuddered.

Martinez stuck his hands into his pockets and slipped away. In a few moments, he returned with a middle-aged black woman. She had on a white coat. A stethoscope was draped around her neck.

He stepped between my sisters and me and held up his hand to interrupt.

"This is Dr. Taylor," he said to me. "She says she can see you immediately."

He turned to Marty and Maddie. "I'd appreciate it if you'd let your sister go now. The doctor's going to examine her and run some tests. You can fill the admitting clerk in on all her insurance information. Then, I hope you'll stick around to make sure she gets home safely."

"Are you saying we wouldn't do that anyway, Detective?" Maddie didn't give him time to answer. "I know you're accustomed to dealing with lowlifes and criminals, but you don't need to tell decent people how to act."

"Hush, Maddie." Marty's voice was soft but firm. "You're not acting very decent right now. This man saw that Mace got here all right. I think we owe him gratitude, not rudeness."

Maddie looked as if a rat had just run over her foot in her spotless kitchen. I was surprised, too. Marty never stands up to Maddie, not even mildly.

Maddie harrumphed, but she shut up. She turned her back on the rest of us, and put her purse up tight against her chest, like a shield. She didn't say thanks to Martinez. But she didn't say anything else nasty, either.

As I was walking into the examining room with Dr. Taylor, I saw Marty place a hand on Martinez's arm. She was gently steering him away from our older sister and toward the emergency room exit to outside.

———

Martinez was gone, but my sisters were still waiting when I came out after two hours, one brain scan, and a short argument over my refusal to wear a hospital gown. The gown fight I lost. But I won the scan, which was far more important. Dr. Taylor saw no evidence of damage to my hard head, so she cleared me to go home.

Maddie was asleep sitting up, snoring softly. It's a good thing the emergency room was empty. She'd be beside herself if she ever thought someone had seen her dozing—eyes closed, mouth open, defenses down.

Marty leaned against a wall, one tennis-shoed foot propped up behind her. Eyes cast downward, she was fending off the attentions of two handsome guys in green hospital scrubs. One offered her a cup of coffee; the other looked like he was ready to offer her his heart. Happily married or not, Marty attracts men the way honey draws bears. Always has.

"I'm back, better than ever," I called from the doorway.

Marty looked up with Mama's radiant smile; Maddie rubbed drool from her chin and frowned. "Is it time for school yet?" she asked.

"No, the kids have a few more hours of peaceful sleep before you're back to terrorizing them," I said.

We were back to normal—except for the fact that our mother was still in jail.

Marty extricated herself from her male fan club and joined us. "I'm so glad everything's okay, Mace. What are we going to do next?" she asked.

"I'm going home to a hot shower. My body's aching like those Clydesdales from the beer commercial used me as a football. First thing in the morning, I'll go back to visit our cousin Henry. I want to prod him for some idea what the state attorney's office plans to do about Mama's charges."

"I might know a little something about that," Marty said quietly.

Maddie and I looked at her like she'd grown two heads. First she'd crossed Maddie; now she was offering an opinion. We knew our sister had gotten a promotion at the library. Was this more forceful Marty a result?

"I'm not saying anything is certain." Marty cast her eyes to her shoes. "It's just that I had the chance to talk to Carlos while you went off with the doctor."

"Who the hell is Carlos?" Maddie asked me.

I gave her a shrug.

"Carlos Martinez. The detective," Marty said.

Maddie and I exchanged raised eyebrows.

"What?" Marty said. "That's the man's name. Anyway, he spent a long day asking a lot of questions about Mama. He said he heard over and over what a good person she is. He was taken by surprise at the number of people who love her for one thing or another."

"Mama's lived all her life in Himmarshee, Marty. She's popular," Maddie said. "That's not exactly a news flash."

"Let me finish, Maddie. He said he was just doing his job when he put her in jail. It was the only way he could think of to figure things out after all of us showed up at the police department. He said he's not as sure as he was that she belongs there."

If we were Catholic and Marty was a man, she could have been a priest. She's always been good at getting confessions.

"How do you do that?" Maddie asked.

"Do what?" Marty said.

"Get people to open up."

"I'm curious about that, too, Marty," I said. "I just spent a couple of hours out in the country with Martinez. I never even knew his first name, let alone that he was thinking about letting Mama go."

"I don't think I do anything special. I just sit there and people talk." Marty weighed what she wanted to say next. "But if you really want to know, Maddie, you have a tendency to judge. That might make it harder for folks to tell you things. And as for you, Mace, you give off the impression you're more interested in animals than you are in people. So they might be reluctant to bother you with personal things."

For Marty, that was scalding criticism.

"I don't mean to hurt your feelings, but you did ask," she said quickly. "There is one other thing."

"Well, go ahead and tell us, Marty. It's not like you've held anything else back," Maddie said.

"Carlos is starting to believe Mama might know things about the murderer that she's not even aware she knows. He wants to find out what they are before the knowledge brings her harm."

———

I was wound up after my sisters dropped me off at home. I stood for a long time under a hot shower, lathering with the rosemary and lemon soap that Mama claims will fight bruising. I can't attest to its therapeutic qualities, but I can say that afterwards my skin smelled exactly like lemon chicken.

I dragged out my ancient chenille robe and slipped on thin socks to sleep in. Then I had to lower the air conditioner a couple of notches. It was still September, which means full-blown summer in

Florida. In addition to the swelter, we'd already had a close pass by one storm this hurricane season. Everyone dreaded the appearance of one with better aim.

I threw back the comforter on my bed, fluffed my pillow, and climbed in. Then I proceeded to stare at the ceiling for the next fifteen minutes. The bedside clock read 2:10 AM.

The aroma coming off my body reminded me of the chicken I'd stashed in the 'fridge the night before, when Mama called from jail. It called me to the kitchen.

After I polished off the chicken, I ate some tortilla chips with a bowl of my homemade salsa. It's strong enough to blow the back of your head all the way to Guadalajara. My stomach grumbled in protest. Now, sleep really did seem a long way off.

Opening a beer, I sat down at the computer and killed off a bunch of spam. I checked tomorrow's weather—hot, but at least no new storms—and looked at some news headlines. There was an item from Orlando about a dust-up at one of the theme parks. A disgruntled parent, who'd spent too long in line under a searing sun, decked a costumed character. The last name of the man inside the cartoon-dog suit happened to be Martinez. That got me to thinking about Marty's new best friend, and what he might be planning next. His mysterious past had already made me curious. Since he opened up to my sister, he seemed even more interesting.

I found the news archives for the *Miami Herald* and typed in a search with Martinez's name and the words "police department." When the first story popped up, my heart skidded into my stomach.

Martinez's pregnant wife had been murdered in their Miami home.

THIRTEEN

I AWOKE TO THE smell of coffee brewing in my kitchen. I leaned over to make sure there wasn't a pair of men's shoes sitting under my bed. A shooting pain in my forehead reminded me that my noggin got a pretty good knock when I crashed. But even with a concussion, I think I might have remembered having sex. That'd be like forgetting your first bite of chocolate layer cake after being on a six-month fast.

Make that an eight-and-a-half-month fast.

My head was pounding. But I managed to scan under the bed and across the floor. Nope. Nothing but worn pine planks and dust bunnies. Looks like I still hadn't tasted that chocolate cake. The only footwear in sight was mine.

I got out of bed, grabbed my granddaddy's shotgun from the closet, and crept to the bedroom door. I didn't think a murderer would go to the trouble of making me coffee before he killed me, but you can't be too careful.

Peeking around the doorjamb, I spotted a familiar hand spilling three teaspoons of sugar into each of two coffee cups on the kitchen counter. As I propped the shotgun against the wall, I suddenly felt all the pains I hadn't realized I'd had. My shoulder throbbed. My knee ached like Great Aunt Ella's arthritis in December. I limped out of hiding.

"I don't take that much sugar, Maddie. Marty's the one who likes her coffee just like yours."

My older sister turned around, smiling in the sunlight that streamed through my window. "Well, hey, Sleepyhead. I wondered whether you were ever getting up."

Leave it to Maddie to sound so uncharacteristically chipper at an inappropriate time, like first thing in the morning. I mumbled a bad word, moved slowly to the counter, and waved at her to hand over the cup of too-sweet coffee.

"You'll be sorry you're being such a grump after I tell you my good news, Mace, Henry called me this morning. Apparently he tried to call you, too." She aimed me a look. "But he kept getting your answering machine."

I glanced at the clock over the sink and rubbed my eyes. Twenty 'til eleven. I must have been dead to the world.

"Henry says they're letting Mama out. The state attorney's office has decided not to charge her."

I felt tears rising. The effort of blinking really fast to stop them hurt my head, so I collapsed into a kitchen chair and just let them come.

"I know, Mace. I felt like crying, too." She pulled a paper towel from the kitchen roll and handed it to me. "Those are tears of relief, is what those are. This has all been just too much, hasn't it?

Drink your coffee now. I'll do up this mess of dishes you left in the sink. *My* kitchen is always spotless before I go to bed."

Not even my tears could deflect criticism from Maddie, who's a toothbrush-on-your-knees-type house cleaner. I'm more from the one-swipe-of-the-mop-every-six-months school.

She made a face as she picked up a bowl with hardened salsa in the bottom. "Henry says they're going to release her after lunch sometime." She shot a squirt of dishwashing liquid at the salsa and started scrubbing. "He says he'll give a call when we can go to the jail to pick her up."

Maddie mentioning jail reminded me of what I'd found on the computer about Detective Martinez. I decided to tell both my sisters at once. They'd surely have questions. And, seeing how Maddie was right in the middle of washing up for me, I didn't want to distract her.

She lifted an empty beer bottle off the counter and held it up. "Just how much of this stuff do you drink, Mace? Do you think it's smart to overdo it with liquor when you've just suffered a brain injury?"

"Beer's not liquor, Maddie. It's beer. And the doctor said my head is fine. One bottle is hardly overdoing it."

"I'm just telling you to watch yourself. You know Daddy's family had more than its share of drunks."

I had a vague memory of a family picnic that ended in a fist-fight after Daddy's brother Teddy got tossed into a jumbo-sized vat of potato salad.

"Thanks for the warning," I said. "Now, I've got to call into work and explain why I'm so late."

"I already took care of that for you. Everything at the park is squared away. I talked to your boss. I caught her up about your accident, and told her how much you needed some time off. Rhonda said to go ahead and take what you need. She did mention something about a New Jersey woman with a panther, but I didn't catch all that."

I counted slowly to five. It didn't work. "I wish you wouldn't do that, Maddie."

"Do what?"

"Step into my life and take over."

Maddie looked wounded. "I was just trying to help."

"Well, it's embarrassing. I've already got one mother. And I can manage things fine on my own."

Maddie took a long look around my little house, with the dust on the kitchen countertops, my clothes in a heap where I'd left them on the living room floor, and Paw-Paw's old shotgun leaning against the wall in the hallway.

"Hmmm." There was more meaning packed into that little sound and her cocked eyebrow than into a whole half-hour lecture.

I got defensive. "Things aren't normal right now, Maddie. Mama's been unjustly accused of murder. Someone may have tried to kill me last night. And we still don't know who murdered Jim Albert, and why they planned to let Mama take the blame for it."

Maddie dried off my beer glass. She examined it as she held it up to the light. "You're right, Mace."

I couldn't wait to tell Marty how quickly our older sister had given in. The hunt for water spots or a beer-foam mark on my glassware must have diverted her.

"Anyway, let's not fuss at one another. This should be a happy day. Kenny wants to take all of us out to dinner to celebrate Mama's release."

Kenny is Maddie's husband of nineteen years, who loves her beyond all reason.

"That sounds great, Maddie. If Mama's up to it, of course."

"When hasn't Mama been up to anything involving food?"

Just then, Maddie's cell phone rang. She walked directly to her purse, found the phone in a special pocket she'd sewn inside, and answered without fumbling on the second ring. I hated my organized sister.

Maddie listened for a few moments and turned to me. "It's Henry, Mace. He says they've let Mama out early. He's at the jail, helping her to sign some papers. But he has a court hearing in a few minutes. He can't give her a ride." She spoke into the phone again. "We're way out at Mace's, Henry. You know she lives out in the hardwood hammock with the wild creatures. I'll call Marty at work and ask her to go meet Mama. The library's only a block from the jail."

We decided Marty would pick up Mama and we'd all meet for lunch at Maddie's.

"You can borrow Pam's car until the police finish up with yours, Mace. Your Jeep will probably need work after you get it dried out," Maddie said.

Maddie's daughter, Pam, was a college freshman in California, studying film-making.

I finished my coffee, showered and dressed, and was ready to go before Maddie had put away the last of my dishes.

We were mostly quiet on the twenty-minute ride to Maddie's. I was thinking about my close call in the canal, and about everything that had happened since Mama discovered Jim Albert's body in her trunk two nights before.

"Hey, Maddie," I finally said. We were just coming up on the brick entryway to her neighborhood, with my sister driving fifteen mph under the speed limit, as usual. "Is Pam still looking for a plot for her first movie?"

"Um-hmm," Maddie murmured, careful to focus her concentration on the right-hand turn she'd made onto Whispering Pine Drive five hundred times before.

"Tell her I have a good one. It starts with a college girl's grandma who murders a man and stuffs his body in the trunk of her vintage convertible."

"Not funny, Mace."

"Lighten up, Maddie. The worst is behind us."

As we proceeded at a snail's pace onto my sister's street, I realized I may have spoken too soon. Halfway up the block, we saw Sal Provenza parked in his yellow Cadillac, taking up two spaces in Maddie's driveway.

FOURTEEN

MADDIE COULDN'T GET OUT of her Volvo fast enough. She was beside the driver's side door of Sal's Cadillac before I'd even unhinged my aching body from her passenger seat.

Our mother's boyfriend looked up, cigar in hand and a guilty look on his face. Maddie was so mad, she didn't know which of Sal's sins to seek vengeance for first.

"I can't believe you have the nerve to come here, stinking up my driveway with that cigar, after you framed Mama for murder and nearly killed my sister, Mace."

That just about covered everything, I thought.

Sal stubbed out the cigar in his ashtray and gave Maddie a long, hard look. My sister held his stare without so much as a flinch. He patted at his perfect hair. "I don't have any idea what you're talking about, Maddie. But I don't like the way it sounds. Harder people than you have tried over the years to accuse me of things. None of them has hurt me as much as hearing you say I could harm your mother." Mudder. "I love Rosie."

He looked past my sister to watch me as, wincing, I lifted first one, then the other of my aching legs over the border of Chinese juniper that lined Maddie's driveway. Sal must be a good actor, because a look of complete surprise flickered across his face as he absorbed my sorry state. Moving quickly for such a big man, he jumped from his car. The heavy driver's door pushed Maddie out of the way.

Sal offered his arm for support. "If your sister wasn't so busy attacking me, she might have realized you could use some help." He leaned me against the wide expanse of his Cadillac's hood. "What'd Maddie mean, I tried to kill you? What in the hell happened, Mace?"

"Someone ran me off the road last night, out near the golf course. Remember the golf course, Sal?" I slipped into using his given name. If someone has conspired to murder you, it seems a tad formal to call him Mister.

I continued, "That's where you called me to come all the way out there to meet you, and then conveniently disappeared before I got there."

"What are you suggesting? I set you up?" Sal looked at me like the creature from the *Alien* movie was burrowing out of my body. "I had a good reason for rushing out of there."

"Yeah? What?"

"I got a call on my cell phone yesterday that your mother had suffered a heart attack at the jail."

Maddie gasped and grabbed my hand. My own heart started racing. Then I remembered, we'd already heard from Henry this morning that Mama was fine, on her way to freedom.

"Our mother's heart is okay, Sal," I said.

"But I didn't know that then. I ran out of the pro shop so fast my shoes were smoking. I tried to call you again at the park office, but you must have already left work. I didn't have your cell number. Besides, I figured if I was getting news of Rosalee taking ill, then you and your sisters must have heard about it, too. I knew I'd see you at the jail, or maybe at the hospital."

He twisted a heavy gold bracelet around his wrist, gaze fixed on the engraving that said *Sal.* "I didn't even want to think about my worst fear: that the next time I'd see you girls would be at Rosie's funeral."

He pulled out an oversized white handkerchief with deep red the initials *SFP.* He blew his nose, loud. "Sorry," he said, blowing again. "Thinking about losing her still upsets me."

His hands were shaking. I almost felt sorry for him.

"Heart attack or not, you've already lost our mother." Maddie's voice was as cruel as a Christmas Eve burglar. "Mama believes, as do we, that you killed Jim Albert. We think you put his body in her big trunk, and then let her take the blame." Maddie crossed her arms over her chest, purse tucked in tight, and waited for his response.

Sal carefully folded and refolded his handkerchief. He looked at the ground, and then raised his face to Maddie. There was no sadness now; just a tic in his jaw and cold anger.

"You better watch yourself." His voice was a growl. "You could get into a lot of trouble making accusations you don't have fact one to support. Mace, tell her she's out of line, would'ya?"

"She'll do no such thing," Maddie jumped in. "Mace and Marty both agree with me. And so does our mother, for that matter."

When Sal looked at me, I saw hurt, not anger in his eyes. "Is that true, Mace? Does Rosalee think I'm a murderer? Do you?"

I paused, considering what to say. The truth was I didn't know what to think.

"It seems suspicious, Sal. We find out you have ties to Jim Albert, ties of the criminal kind. You're dating my mother, who just happens to have a spacious trunk in the back of her old Bonneville. She's playing bingo at the Seminole reservation. The car is parked way out in the hinterlands."

He ran a finger around his collar, sweating in the full sun on Maddie's driveway. "Anyone could have had access to that car, Mace."

He addressed the car, but avoided the topic of his ties to the murder victim.

"Everyone in town knows your mother and her turquoise convertible," he continued.

"Yeah, but how many other people have an extra set of keys to the car?"

From the flush on Sal's face, I could see my comment hit home.

"She gave you a set, didn't she?" I asked.

"You know she did. Rosalee's always losing her keys. I have a set for safekeeping."

"Humph!" said Maddie.

"You both know I'm not the only one. A few extra sets are floating around town."

"True," I conceded. "But how many of those other folks with Mama's keys have also drawn the suspicions of the detective investigating Jim Albert's murder? Just you."

Oddly, Sal smiled. "I wouldn't be so sure you know everything Detective Martinez has up his sleeve," he said. "Policemen play things close to the vest. They don't share everything they know, especially not with civilians."

"That's neither here nor there, Mr. Provenza." Maddie put her hands on her hips. "On top of everything Mace just said, you also seem to be the most likely suspect in her near-fatal crash last night."

"Now, that's where you're a hundred percent wrong, Maddie." Looping his thumbs into his waistband, Sal leaned against his Cadillac, the picture of confidence. "Why haven't I heard you making accusations about the person who called me to say your poor mother was at death's door, that she'd collapsed at the Himmarshee Jail?"

My sister and I looked at each other. It was a good question.

We would have gotten the answer, too, if Marty hadn't chosen exactly that moment to pull up in front of Maddie's house. She was beeping her horn like Himmarshee High had just won the homecoming game. And there was Mama, grinning and waving from Marty's front seat.

FIFTEEN

It's kind of hard to pretend you don't see Big Sal Provenza. But Mama was doing her best.

"Rosalee, I just want to talk to you," Sal begged, placing his palms on the rolled up window on the passenger side of Marty's car.

Mama climbed out of her seat, pushed around Sal with a withering glance, and then immediately turned a big smile on Maddie and me. "Girls, I'm so happy to see y'all. I thought I'd never get out of that place. Oh, my Lord, the food. And then a visit from that talky Pastor Bob Dixon. And those horrible cots. Mace, you saw those inmate smocks. Remind me never to wear orange again."

"Please, Rosalee." Sal ran his hands through his hair, messing up his careful styling. "I can explain everything. I just can't do it right now."

She didn't say a word to Sal. The look she gave him said enough. Then she turned to us again, grinning as she squinted in the sun.

She was like a swivel-headed doll with two expressions: ecstatic for us; furious for Sal.

"I can't wait to have some real food, girls. Maddie, I hope you have something good in your fridge. You and Kenny aren't still on that low-cholesterol kick, are you?"

Sal tried again. "Rosie, honey…"

"Enough!" Mama cut him off. Then she glared at him for a full ten seconds.

Sal seemed to shrink in his Big-and-Tall-Man ensemble as the moments passed.

The tense silence was making Marty uncomfortable. She shot an apologetic glance at Sal, then stooped to pick a stem of juniper from the driveway border. Maddie, with her arm around Mama's shoulders, bored a hole through Sal with her own version of laser vision. Watching the two of them staring at Sal, I could see now where Maddie had inherited *The Glare*.

Finally, Mama spoke: "I know you want to talk to me, Sally. I'm not ready to listen. That detective told me you lied to me about Jim Albert. I don't know what all else you lied about. I don't know whether I trust you anymore. I do know that right now, I'm as mad at you as a wasp with a ruin't nest."

"But Rosalee…"

Mama put up a hand. "Now, why don't you climb back into that gaudy car of yours and give me some time to visit with my girls? I may cool down some, and we can talk later. Or maybe I won't. You'll just have to wait and see."

I had to credit Mama's finesse. Though I did question how a woman who drives a turquoise convertible the size of a cruise ship could call someone else's car gaudy.

She turned her back on him. "C'mon, girls, let's go inside."

Maddie's hands were at her hips, the better to stare down Sal. Mama looped one arm around Maddie's elbow. Marty dropped the juniper and took Mama's other arm. Then the three of them trooped off toward the house.

Sal and I looked at each other over the hood of his car.

"Well, you're in some deep shit now," I said.

"I can't believe I've lost her, Mace. She's my whole world." Wold. Sal leaned his elbows on the roof of his car and dropped his head into his hands. "What am I going to do?"

"You could start by telling her the truth."

He rocked his head from side to side, his crowning glory a complete fright now. "I can't do that, Mace." Misery filled his voice. "I can't talk about the murder victim; can't discuss how I knew Jimmy Albrizio. Don't you think I would if I could? I'd do anything to get Rosie back."

Sal might be macho, but love was bringing him to emotional meltdown. As big as that man was, if he started crying I feared a flood.

"Well, what about me, then?" I changed the subject. "What about how I was run off the road into what could have been my grave? Can you talk about that?"

He raised his head. "I had absolutely nothing to do with that, Mace." His tone was honest, not evasive. His eyes met mine and held there, no darting about. Either he was telling the truth or he was an Olympic-caliber liar.

"It's just that I'd have never been out there on that lonesome road if not for you, Sal."

"And I'm sorry about that. But I explained about the phone call."

"Not completely. You never said who called you with a story so terrifying that you ran out and left me swinging in the wind. You could have left me a message at the pro shop."

The junior Don Juan flashed into my mind. He had a message for me all right; but it wasn't from Sal.

"I told you I wasn't in my right mind when I left there, Mace. I was frantic."

"So, who called?"

When Sal told me who'd scared him off our meeting, I just about fell down and cracked my one good knee.

———

Opening Maddie's front door, I smelled cold fried chicken. Mama was laughing.

"What's so funny?" I said, limping into the gleaming kitchen. The place was so clean, you could perform surgery on Maddie's stainless-steel countertops.

"I was just telling your sisters what my neighbor Alice said about taking care of Teensy for the last two days. That dog can get into more trouble than ..." The smile died on Mama's lips. "C'mere and let me take a closer look at you, Mace." She hunted in her purse for the glasses she was too vain to wear. "What happened to your forehead? Why are you hobbling?"

Maddie shot me a panicked look. "Mace hurt herself at the park, Mama."

"That's right," Marty echoed quickly. "At work."

We weren't going to reveal that someone—possibly Mama's recently departed former true love—had forced me off the road into a canal.

"Actually, it was after work," I improvised, slowly closing the distance to the table. Maddie pulled out a chair for me. "You remember that crazy New Jersey lady I told you about, Mama? The one who moved to the country, even though she's scared of anything that slithers, creeps, or flies?"

She nodded, a frown on her face. I sat down and let her brush away my bangs to examine my head.

"Well, last night, I crawled into her attic after a possum. The crazy thing jumped right out at me. It startled me, was all. I slipped and hit my head on a rafter. Then I took a spill and smacked my knee pretty good."

It scares me how easily I can lie. But I figure if the Lord knows Mama, he must know that a little deception is for the best.

She sighed with relief, resting her hand on my cheek. "Is that all, Mace? A trapping mishap? You'll be fine."

I heard Marty let out the breath she'd been holding. Crisis averted.

"Now, tell me about this beautiful haircut." Mama lifted my thick hair, watching it fall. "Maddie says you actually sat still for D'Vora. Lucky for you that girl's better with the scissors than she is with peroxide."

Her fingers went to her own ruined hair, sending platinum strands with gray roots onto Maddie's glass-topped table. Lips pressed into a disapproving line, Maddie swept the hairs into a napkin, held it by two fingers, and dropped it in the garbage.

"I saw that disgusted look." Mama slathered butter on a piece of white bread. The bones of two chicken legs already littered her plate. "I can't believe I endured fifteen hours of difficult labor to bring Maddie into the world, yet a couple of hairs off my poor head gives her fits."

"I've got news." I cut short the oft-told story of Maddie's painful delivery. "You'll never believe what Sal just told me."

"I don't want to talk about that man." Done with her bread, Mama was delicately licking butter off her fingertips.

"Don't you want to know why he rushed over to the jail last night, frantic?" I asked.

"I didn't know he was frantic, and I wouldn't care anyway. Donnie Bailey came back to my cell and asked if I wanted to see him, and I told him absolutely not. Donnie didn't say why Sally was there."

"He came because Emma Jean Valentine called him up and told him you'd had a heart attack."

SIXTEEN

"Close your mouth, Maddie," I said. "You're gonna draw flies."

It's so rare I get the chance to surprise my older sister. I was taking full advantage.

"Emma Jean told Sal I had a heart attack?" Mama lifted a fork load of banana cream pie to her mouth. "I'm healthy as a hog, girls. What was she thinking?"

"That's what we need to find out," Maddie said, handing our mother a napkin to wipe meringue off her chin. "This isn't the first time Emma Jean's name has arisen since you found the body in your trunk, Mama. I, for one, would like to know why."

Marty darted in like a sparrow after a crumb, snatching the half-bite of pie crust Mama left on the plate. "You can't suspect Emma Jean of anything bad, Maddie," she said. "She's so nice."

Maddie and I looked at each other.

"Even nice people can have guilty secrets, Marty," I said.

I repeated what Emma Jean told D'Vora, that she was mad enough to kill over Jim Albert's cheating.

"Funny she never told me he was cheating," Mama said. "She was likely embarrassed, planning that big wedding and all. Emma Jean's life has had some real heartache, girls."

Maddie snorted.

"Don't be mean, Maddie. The poor woman lost her little boy; and there's no heartbreak like that. He ran away when he was just thirteen. They never did find him, neither. It just about tore Emma Jean up. She and the boy's father divorced. She just couldn't get over the loss."

"How sad." A tear rolled down Marty's perfect cheek. "Poor Emma Jean."

"You might have noticed that picture on Emma Jean's desk at the police department," Mama continued. "That was her son."

All of us were silent, even Maddie. She got up to return the sweet tea pitcher to the refrigerator.

I finally said, "Emma Jean's not the only one with a secret, Mama. Your man-of-mystery boyfriend has been at the top of our list of possible murder suspects."

I ticked off on my fingers everything we knew—or suspected—about Sal: his criminal ties to Jim Albert; his evasiveness; the fact he had access to Mama's car trunk. The only thing I didn't mention was his possible role in my crash, since we didn't want to scare her.

"I don't know, girls." Mama opened the refrigerator and took out the pitcher Maddie had just put away. "It's true Sally's lied to me. But I just can't believe he's a killer. I've always been a good judge of character."

"That's true," Marty said, using a napkin to sop some tea Mama spilled on the floor.

"Please!" Maddie said. "The woman has had four husbands. How good a character judge can she be?" She wiped Mama's fingerprints off the door of her stainless-steel fridge.

"Now, Maddie, you know that's not fair." Mama took a swallow of sugared tea. "Only that second one was what you'd call a failure as a human being. And I blame that on me still being in shock over your daddy's dying. The last two were good men, just bad matches."

Mama was right. One of those exes still lives in Himmarshee, and brings carnations and chocolates every year on her birthday.

Marty changed the subject. "Speaking of men, did Mace tell you she saw Jeb Ennis the other day?"

"Talk about a suspect," Maddie muttered.

I hadn't told my sisters what the liquor store clerk said about Jeb. For some reason, I felt protective of him. I wanted to talk to him first before I told about his temper and Jim Albert.

"That boy sure knew how to handle a horse," Mama said dreamily. "I liked him."

"Proving my point," Maddie said. "Jeb Ennis broke your daughter's heart. I'd say his character leaves something to be desired."

Mama got up to clear her plate. "Sometimes it's nobody's fault when a romance fails, Maddie. Jeb was wild and free; Mace is cautious and careful. She was in college; he was in rodeo. Those buckle bunnies on the circuit wouldn't leave him be. Maybe it was good man, bad match."

"He sure was good-looking." Marty sipped from Mama's glass.

"Still is," I added, and left it at that.

Mama turned the toaster on the counter so she could check her lipstick in the reflection. "Maddie, I don't know what possessed you to get this silver finish on all your appliances. You're forever wiping off prints," she said.

Maddie bit her tongue, and moved on to the toaster after scouring chicken grease and a ring of Mama's sweet tea off the counter.

Hearing Mama say "prints" reminded me of fingerprints which reminded me of jail, which reminded me of the man who'd sent Mama there.

"I can't believe I forgot to tell y'all something." I slapped my injured forehead, which stung like crazy. "I did some research on the computer about Martinez."

Three sets of eyes turned toward me, as intent as my animals at feeding time.

"Remember when Emma Jean said something bad happened to him in Miami, Mama? He was a hotshot detective. A real star. Then his wife was murdered."

Marty gasped.

"It was during what they call a home invasion robbery. The bad guys push their way in, right through the front door, and then kill anyone in the house who might be a witness."

Mama's eyes widened and her hand covered her mouth.

"How did it happen, Mace?" Only someone who knew Maddie like a sister would hear the quiver in her voice.

"Well, that's the thing. Once I read the article, I understood why Martinez was so ready to believe Mama could be a killer."

"That doesn't make sense," Marty said.

"It will." I folded my hands on the table. "Patricia Martinez had also been a police officer, until she quit to start a family. Like any good cop, she was suspicious and careful."

"But not this time," Maddie said.

"Not this time." I shook my head. "The police found out later she'd opened the door because a sweet-looking old woman was on the stoop, crying and appearing confused. When Patricia started out to see if she could help, the old lady's accomplices pushed her back through the open door. They shot her right there. Martinez found his wife's body when he got home from work. She was seven months pregnant."

Marty gasped again.

"They ultimately caught the robbers, because another home-owner they'd shot survived to describe them." I shifted in the chair to ease the pain in my knee. "He told the newspaper the old woman looked so harmless, he never suspected a thing. Want to know why?"

All three heads nodded.

"She reminded him of the sweet old lady who used to teach at his Sunday school."

SEVENTEEN

MAMA HAD ONE HAND on her head and the other holding on to the dashboard of Pam's old VW convertible. The wind was blowing the yellow pansies flat on her Sunday hat.

Actually, it was Wednesday evening. But we were on our way to church, which explains the fancy headwear. After what Mama had been through, I figured the least I could do was accompany her to mid-week services at Abundant Hope and Charity Chapel, like she's always asking me to.

I was driving my niece's car. Maddie had owned it a hundred years ago in high school, and she'd kept good maintenance on the engine. Of course. But the top had rusted into the down position. Maddie didn't see any reason to waste the money to fix a car that Pam only drove when she came home from college two or three times a year. If it rained, Maddie always said, Pam could put on a slicker.

"How you doin' over there, Mama?" I yelled into the warm night air.

She nodded she was okay, but that might just have been the pansies trembling on her hat.

"Just hold on, we're almost there." I stepped on the gas.

I learned to drive over rough terrain in orange groves and across fields rooted up by wild hogs. To me, a smooth, paved road seems like an open invitation to exceed the speed limit.

Within minutes, we were whipping into a parking space. The church, a converted convenience store, is unfortunately situated right next to a rib joint called the Pork Pit. Whenever I attend church, the scent from the Pit makes me think more about getting barbecue than getting saved. I turned off the key, and the old engine shuddered to a stop.

"Here we are. Safe and sound."

"Remind me to take a tranquilizer the next time I have to ride with you, Mace." Mama unclenched her hand from the dash and turned the rear view mirror in her direction. "You were driving so fast, gnats were hitting me like buckshot. I think I still have bug parts embedded in my face." She bared her teeth, checking for black dots.

"You look fine, Mama." If I told her she'd actually lost a clump or two of pansies to the wind, she'd insist on going home to get another hat.

"Well, you do, too, Mace. But you could look so much better than fine. I don't know why you put on all those dark colors when I asked you to wear that beautiful pink pantsuit your Aunt Irene gave you. The woman can be a pill, but you can't fault her taste in clothes."

"I told you I wasn't gonna wear the pink, Mama. That suit makes me look like an Easter egg on stilts. Marty's the one that likes pastels, not me."

"But the pink looks so pretty with your dark coloring, Mace. You don't even try to look nice."

"Evening, Rosalee." I was saved by a middle-aged woman in a blue-flowered skirt and a sleeveless sweater. She dipped her head at Mama as she passed in front of the VW.

"Hey, Delilah. C'mon over here and say hello to my middle girl, Mace. Honey, this is Delilah Dixon. She's Pastor Bob Dixon's wife."

Delilah walked to Mama's side of the car and extended her hand over the absent top. I took it, grateful for the interruption in Mama's long-running critique of my fashion sense.

"Well," Delilah said in a sugary tone, "we haven't seen you here before, have we, Mace?"

No, Ma'am, I'm a sinner. That's what I felt like saying, but didn't. "I'm not able to make it to church as much as I'd like."

"Mace is one of those Christmas and Easter Christians, Delilah. You know, the ones who crowd the pews on the holidays? They think the Lord will forget He hasn't seen them the rest of the year."

"Well, I'm here tonight and I'm looking forward to the service," I said, heading off a tangent on my church-going habits. "What will your husband be preaching on, Ms. Dixon?"

"Oh, I never know until the moment Bob starts his sermon." Delilah's drawl-free accent sounded Midwestern. "I like to enjoy hearing it for the first time, along with the congregation."

I thought I noticed the tiniest smirk on Mama's mouth.

"Well, I better get along inside." Delilah started for the church door, then turned at the halfway point. "We're sure happy to see you tonight, Rosalee," she said in a voice that carried clear to the Pork Pit. "I wasn't sure you'd have the nerve to show up, considering."

113

Mama's back stiffened in the car seat. "Why wouldn't I 'show up,' Delilah? The only thing to consider is I had the bad luck to discover some poor soul's body in my trunk."

Delilah traced a finger along the spine of the Bible she carried. "Well, we did hear you'd been hauled into the Himmarshee Jail." Her voice was loud enough to wake the crows roosting across the street in a magnolia tree. "All of us were worried you'd never get out."

Heads turned as other congregation members filed past.

"As you can see, I'm out. I wasn't charged with a thing," Mama said sharply. "It was a misunderstanding, is all. By the way, Delilah, you might want to reread the Gospel of Matthew in that Good Book you're carrying. He writes all about the evil nature of false accusations."

I'd planned to jump to Mama's defense, but she seemed to be doing fine on her own. Sputtering, Delilah flounced into church, her skirt a floral swirl around her sturdy legs.

"I know it's not very Christian of me, but I sure don't like that woman," Mama whispered to me. "And did you see her in a sleeveless sweater? She's built like a truck driver. With those big arms of hers, a three-quarter length sleeve would be much more flattering."

I aimed a sanctimonious look to the passenger seat. "Doesn't Proverbs address gossiping, Mama? If I recall, the Bible says guard your mouth and tongue to keep yourself from calamity."

I couldn't resist the jab. But I was secretly glad Mama was focused on Delilah's fashion *faux pas* instead of mine.

"You're absolutely right, Mace." She looked contrite. "It isn't nice to gossip. But I almost busted out laughing when she said how the congregation enjoys her husband's sermons. The only thing that keeps most of them awake is the promise of the Pork Pit when it's over."

I patted her on the arm. "Don't worry, Mama. The people who really know you would never believe you had anything to do with the murder. The Dixons are fairly new, aren't they?"

"Just since this year." She formed an O with her lips in the mirror, and painted them with her favorite shade, Apricot Ice. "Bob Dixon replaced Pastor Gooden, who everybody loved. And that wife of his doesn't help his case. There's something a little off about the two of them, Mace." Shaking her head, she tossed the lipstick back in her purse. "At least half-a-dozen members have quit since they arrived."

Making our way inside, we were forced to step around a card table stacked high with homemade DVDs. The covers showed a dark-suited man, looking reflective in a beam of light from a stained glass window. *Walking the Path with Pastor Bob*, the title said. I turned it over. Fifteen bucks, according to a bright red price sticker on the back. I returned it to the pile.

Mama's minister must have found a fancier church than Abundant Hope to stage his DVD photo. This one just had the store window, and not a pane of stained glass in sight.

Several people waved and smiled. But a few stared with cold eyes as we found two seats halfway down a row of folding chairs. Mama fiddled with a stack of church books under her seat, looking for a hymnal. Fortunately, she didn't seem to notice the nasty looks before the music minister hit the first chord on a portable organ.

A young man in the front row lifted a video camera to his eye. The red *Record* button lit. The choir burst into *What a Friend We Have in Jesus*. As Mama warbled along, I counted the fake lilies in pots lining a raised wooden altar. I'd gotten to twenty-two, and

115

started in on studying the Ten Commandments on three big panels against the wall, when a commotion broke out behind us.

"I told you, I WILL NOT sit down." It was a woman, and she sounded on the verge of hysterics. "I have something to say, and I'm going up there to say it."

There was some quiet murmuring and shushing from behind us.

"People should know. *They should know!*" She let loose a wail, which sounded familiar.

I turned around to see Emma Jean Valentine being corralled toward the exit by a short man in a dark suit. Pastor Bob? Emma Jean's green skirt was two inches too short. A kitty-cat pin shone on the lapel of her neon blue jacket.

Delilah Dixon stepped in, trying to help steer her out the door.

"*Take your hands off of me!*" Emma Jean's eyes were wild. She raised her hand, and along with it a threatening-looking tire iron.

Mama clutched my elbow. "Oh, my stars and garters! Emma Jean is fixin' to murder Delilah and her husband, the preacher."

Emma Jean backed up, knocking over the card table display. The DVDs clattered to the floor. As the guy with the camera moved in for a closer shot, Pastor Bob swiped his hand across his throat, yelling "Cut! Cut!"

Now every head in the church was turned to the rear. Even the choir had quit singing to stare. Delilah and the reverend backed off a few steps. Emma Jean lowered the tire iron a fraction. She raised her other hand to her head to straighten a straw hat decorated with green-and-white daisies.

"Most of you know me." Her voice rang out in the pin-drop silent room. "I suffered a terrible loss this week when Jim Albert was murdered. And now I've discovered something that hurts almost as bad as losing him. I've been looking into a few things. Jim was cheating on me. And the woman he betrayed me with is a member here, supposedly a good Christian."

Shocked gasps rippled through the seats. A loud clap sounded on the floor by the choir. I turned in time to see a pretty blonde soprano stoop to retrieve the hymn book she dropped.

"I just wanted y'all to think on something, sitting here in this church: People aren't always what they seem. There's a woman here who tried to take away someone I loved. She's here among you, pretending to be pious and holy. But really she's just a common whore."

Mothers covered their kids' ears. The Reverend Dixon put out a hand to silence Emma Jean. She shook her tire iron at him, and his hand dropped like he'd touched a hot stove.

"God gave Moses the commandments." Emma Jean's voice rose like a preacher's. "All of you know the one about coveting thy neighbor's wife. Well, someone here coveted the man who was going to be my husband."

She walked halfway up the aisle and stopped, tire iron raised like a staff. All eyes followed her as she looked slowly around the church, pointing her arm like a weapon toward any woman under seventy. For a long moment, her gaze held on the soprano. The young woman cast her eyes down as she fidgeted with a barrette holding back her hair.

Finally, Emma Jean broke her stare, speaking again to the full congregation.

"I'm not going to rest until I find out which one of you is the adulteress who seduced my Jim," she said. "And when I do, I may break one or two of God's commandments myself."

117

EIGHTEEN

MAMA AND I SPUN on our stools in Gladys' Diner, listening to the mechanical hum of a plastic cylinder with six shelves of revolving pies. The scent of sizzling hamburgers wafted from the open kitchen behind the counter. More than half of the dozen tables in the restaurant were filled. A harried waitress rushed by. Barrel-sized tumblers of sweet tea crowded her tray, and her forehead glistened with sweat.

"I'll be with y'all just as soon as I can," she said.

"Take your time," Mama said. "We're in no hurry."

We'd headed to the diner after services at Abundant Hope. Once Emma Jean dropped her bombshell, Delilah hustled her out the door. Pastor Bob immediately took to the pulpit, and signaled the cameraman to start rolling again. Aiming a pious smile at the lens, he acted like there'd been no interruption from an unhinged churchgoer, screaming about adultery and murder.

With a rich tenor he launched into "Are You Washed in the Blood?" and nodded to the choir to join in. I thought the hymn was a poor choice, given the circumstances.

I'd jiggled my leg and tapped my fingers through at least half of his long sermon. Mama pinched my arm and promised me pie if I stopped squirming.

So I did. And here we were, reviewing Emma Jean's outburst as we waited to be served.

"Who was that girl in the choir she kept staring at?" I asked.

Mama had her churchgoing hat on the counter, looking for missing pansies. "That's Debbie," she said. "She's as sweet as a sugar beet, and she has an adorable boyfriend. He was the one with the long hair, playing guitar on the stage. I can't imagine Debbie cheating on him with someone like skinny ol' Jim Albert."

"You never know what some women find attractive." I didn't add, *just look at Sal*.

"More likely, Emma Jean zeroed in because she's the prettiest girl at Abundant Hope. Being pretty is a curse, Mace." Mama patted her hair, preening like a beauty queen.

"I'll keep that in mind."

With a squeak from her rubber-soled shoe, the waitress slid to a stop in front of us. She pulled an order pad from the pocket of a forest-green apron, then licked the dull tip of a pencil. "I'm busier than a horsetail in fly season, Rosalee. Did ya'll decide?"

Charlene, her name tag said. There'd been no Gladys at the restaurant since the namesake died, but the sign stayed as a memorial to the grande dame of Himmarshee dining.

Mama caressed the pie case like it was a lover. "I know what I want." Her fingers traced the path of a butterscotch slice, rotating inside.

I ordered a hamburger and coffee. So did Mama. We each wanted pie. As Charlene hustled off, my eyes roamed the diner. It was all fake-wood paneling and country-themed knick-knacks. A butter-churn decorated one corner; a spinning wheel another.

"Who's that sitting with Ruth Harris' grandson?" I whispered to Mama, as Charlene returned with our coffees. "They look like refugees from a Metallica concert."

"What's a Metallica?"

"They're a heavy-metal … never mind. I was just wondering how come he and the girl are dressed like that."

Mama answered in my ear. "Ruth says that's the fashion among the teenagers these days. Black, black, and more black. Black hair, black fingernails, black clothes." She leaned way back on her stool and gave my own dark ensemble a meaningful look. "They look like they're going to a mortician convention."

I was gazing into the mirrored wall across the room, trying to convince myself I looked more sophisticated than mournful in black, when I saw Jeb Ennis walk through the door. A Western-style denim shirt covered his broad chest. The snap buttons gleamed like rare pearls. My hand flew to smooth my hair, knocking my coffee cup off the counter and right into my lap.

"Ouch! Ouch, ouch!" I yelped, hopping to my feet. Every head in the diner, including Jeb's, swung my way.

Unlike the police station swill, this coffee was nice and hot. I clamped a hand over my mouth as I pictured red blisters bubbling like lava on my thighs.

"Charlene, fetch my daughter some ice," Mama yelled. "She's drenched in coffee."

I wondered if it was possible to be any more embarrassed.

"And hurry, honey. Mace might hurt herself again before you get here."

At least I had my answer about exponential embarrassment.

I watched in the mirror as Jeb pulled a white handkerchief out of his jeans pocket. He grabbed a glass of ice water off a table and dunked it in.

"Here you go, Mace." Easing me back onto the stool, he tenderly placed the wet handkerchief over my lap. "That should feel better."

He scooped a handful of ice from the pitcher Charlene held, and rubbed the cubes across the tops of my thighs.

Now my face felt hotter than the coffee burn.

I thanked Jeb and swiveled to the watching diners: "I'm fine, everybody," I announced. "That'll be my last performance of the night. Y'all can go back to eating now."

Laughter lit the flecks of gold in Jeb's green eyes. "I think the patient's gonna live." He bowed to the room, to scattered applause.

He placed his hat over his heart, and said in a lower voice, "Mind if I join you, ladies?"

Mama returned his smile with a dimpled grin and an adorable eyelash flutter.

I could practice in the mirror every day for a year, and never manage that flutter without looking like something was stuck in my eye. But when Mama does it, men swoon.

"Mace, honey, move over a seat so it'll be girl, boy, girl."

Ignoring her request, I slid my purse off the empty stool to my left. I patted the green-and-brown-striped plastic, giving him a wide smile. "Yes, do sit down, Jeb." My voice was banana-pudding sweet.

Mama raised her eyebrows. "Maybe you two young people would like to chat. I'll just go powder my nose."

As soon as she left, I wiped the smile from my face. "I've got a couple of questions for you."

Jeb cocked his head at me. I'd been distracted by shiny shirt buttons and scalding coffee. But I hadn't forgotten what I'd learned at the Booze 'n' Breeze.

"I had a nice little chat with somebody about your visits to Jim Albert at the drive-thru," I said as he sat down.

He gave me a puzzled frown. "What are you talking about? Who'd you talk to about me?"

"I'm not going to say where I got the information. But it seems you two were a lot better-acquainted than you let on. Why'd you lie to me, Jeb?"

His eyes darted to the counter. He lined up a napkin holder shaped like a horseshoe. He straightened a place mat with a red star for our little town above Lake Okeechobee on the map of Florida. Picking up a fork, he stared at it like the words he wanted might be written there.

"I didn't lie, Mace." He finally looked into my eyes. "I just left some things out. I hadn't seen you in years, and you ask me out of the blue did I know a man who'd just been murdered. I did know him. But I really didn't want to get into how, especially standing in a parking lot with your sister firing dirty looks my way."

"You could have said something, Jeb."

He pointed the fork at me. "To get right down to it, I didn't think it was your damned business, Mace."

I batted his hand away, getting angry now. "Not my business?"

A trucker at the end of the counter glanced at us over the top of his menu. I lowered my voice. "I suppose you didn't know the cops believed my mother killed Jim Albert. I suppose the news of her being jailed never reached that ranch of yours."

Surprise flickered across his face. It looked genuine.

"Maddie and I were trying to find out who else might have had a reason to murder him. Then I hear how the two of you had a big fight."

Jeb clenched his jaw hard. "Did you tell anybody else about that?"

"Not yet. I wanted to give you the chance to explain first."

My mind flashed back more than a decade, to the night I'd caught Jeb with another girl at a popular lookout over the lake. I'd given him the chance to explain then, too. I should have cracked his truck's windshield with Emma Jean's tire iron instead.

"I'm gonna tell you the truth, Mace. I borrowed some money from Albert. The man was bleeding me dry. We argued, yes. But I swear to you, I never laid a hand on him."

"I heard different."

"And I'm saying I never hurt the man." His warm hazel eyes went cold. "I don't know where you got that. Did that girl behind the counter tell you something?"

"No," I lied.

"Well, whoever it was is wrong. And why would you believe them over me? We've known each other since we were kids, Mace."

I thought about that long-ago night at Lake Okeechobee. Jeb had rushed after me, telling me I'd misunderstood everything. The girl meant nothing. It was the first time he'd even kissed her. It was a mistake. He begged me to forgive him.

I did, and found out later he'd been seeing her on the side for five weeks.

"Mace?" he said again, jarring me back to the present.

I took my time before answering, looking around the restaurant. Mama had taken a seat with Ruth Harris' grandson. She and the girlfriend-in-black were sharing a slice of butterscotch pie.

In a quiet voice, I said, "You don't have the best track record with me for being truthful."

Jeb picked his hat up and stood. "All you can see in me is that stupid twenty-something kid, cheating on you with another girl. I was a scoundrel, Mace. I'm sorry I broke your heart; but that was a long time ago. I've grown up. I've changed."

He placed the hat on his head, and tapped the brim as he looked at me in the mirror. "My regards to your mama. I think I'll skip dinner tonight. It seems I've lost my appetite."

He started to walk away, then turned to whisper in my ear. "I'd appreciate it if you wouldn't go around spreading lies about me and Jim Albert."

"What?" I whispered back. "Like you owed him money and now he's conveniently dead? That's not a lie, Jeb. That's a fact."

He straightened, staring at me for a long moment. His eyes looked just the same as the night I'd accused him of cheating. Hurt. Bewildered. Angry that I could believe something so awful about him.

I couldn't help but remember how convincing Jeb had seemed back then. And all the while, he'd been lying like a tobacco company bigwig testifying to Congress.

NINETEEN

"WHAT IN THE NAME of Mike was all that about?" Mama slid her coffee cup back onto the counter and climbed up on the stool in front of the hamburgers Charlene had finally delivered.

"I don't want to talk about it." I stared straight ahead at the stainless steel wheel above the kitchen. So many white order slips were clipped up there, it looked like laundry day for a race of tiny people.

Mama reached over to straighten my bangs. "Well, I'm not surprised. You seem just about talked out after that scene with Jeb. What were you two whispering about, Mace? I could hear you all the way over to the table with Ruth's grandson. The way you were hissing, it sounded like somebody stepped into a mess of snakes."

There was a snake, all right; and its name was Jeb Ennis.

"Mama, did you know Jim Albert loaned money to people?"

"I didn't know too much about him, Mace. But what I had heard, I didn't like. Truth is, this whole marriage came up awfully fast. I don't believe they dated for more than a few months. And I always thought Emma Jean could do better. I think she sensed I disapproved of Jim, because we didn't talk much about him."

I took a bite from my burger and watched the order slips flutter in the breeze from an air conditioning vent. I was thinking about how Jeb was linked to Jim Albert, who in turn was linked to Emma Jean. And then there was Mama's boyfriend, Sal, and his ties to everything. The whole mess was looking exactly like that nest of snakes Mama mentioned.

"Honey." Mama tapped my shoulder. "Your purse is ringing."

I fumbled in my purse for my phone, past some packages of beef jerky and a jar of peanut butter, which I use to bait animal traps. By the time I found it, it'd quit ringing. I've got to get Maddie to sew me one of those little cell phone cases.

I went to the phone's log and called back the last number that called me.

"Where are you two?" Maddie said. "Marty's waiting for y'all. Mama left her things from the jail in the car this morning. Marty decided to run them by on her way home from her meeting at the library. You know that promotion she got? She's running the whole show now." My hamburger and fries awaited, salt crystals sparkling like diamonds on hot grease. I longed to take a bite, but I knew Maddie would yell at me for talking with my mouth full.

"How was church?" she asked.

"Just about like usual," I lied. "We'll tell you all about it tomorrow."

"I should have been there, too. But I couldn't move a muscle after Kenny went and got us barbecue from the Pork Pit for supper. I ate so much, all I could do was unzip the waist of my slacks and lie there on my couch like a big, fat hog."

I got an image of my normally proper sister stretched out with her undies exposed, and smiled for the first time since Jeb sat down.

"Thanks, Maddie. I needed that. Listen, we'll finish here and head over to Mama's in about a half hour. Can you tell Marty? Tell her I want to hear all about the promotion."

"Will do," Maddie said. "She already opened a bottle of Mama's white zinfandel and she's watching *Cops* on TV. It's a good one, too, Mace. They caught this guy who got stuck in a hole he made in the ceiling when he was trying to burglarize a store. So far, I haven't seen any of your old beaus."

Once, while watching the show, we'd spotted a boy I ran with during my wild period. Drunk and shirtless, he was being hauled out of a trailer on a drug charge. Maddie, of course, had never let me forget it.

After I rang off, Mama and I polished off our burgers, split the check, and headed home.

———

Teensy was running in circles and yapping at Mama's front door. We could see Marty through the sheer curtain at the window, trying to navigate around the dog to let us in.

"Teensy, hush!" Mama shouted, which just pushed the Pomeranian over the top. He hurled himself at the door, intent upon breaking through the wood frame and hurricane-resistant glass to reunite with his mistress.

Marty finally got an ankle in between the dog's chest and the door and pushed the little ball of fluff out of the way. She had one foot off the floor, a glass of wine in her hand, and the other arm wrapped around Mama in a welcoming hug. Marty was so graceful, she could pull that off. If I tried it, I'd be out flat on Mama's hallway rug, covered in sweet wine and dog fur.

"Ooooooh, is this Mama's little boy? Is this her itty-bitty boy?"

Teensy launched himself straight up and levitated, like a Harrier fighter jet. She caught the dog in his skyward orbit, planting a big kiss on his head.

"Have you girls ever seen a more adorable little angel than this one?" She waved one of Teensy's paws at us.

Marty and I exchanged a look. All that Teensy lacked was a bonnet and a bassinet.

We escaped to the kitchen, entering a veritable barnyard of gingham. Mama had a thing for cute animals in country checks: Her cookie jar was a pig in a gingham cap. Her canisters pictured ducks in gingham ribbons. Bunnies frolicked in gingham bowties along a wall border.

Marty hiked up her knee-length, linen skirt and climbed onto a step stool. She removed a wine goblet from the shelf, and poured me half a glass. I motioned her to keep going. We could still hear Mama murmuring sweet nothings to the dog in the living room. Teensy's frantic barking had mellowed to an annoying whimper.

"God forbid anything should ever happen to that creature," I said, lifting the pig's gingham hat to help myself to two macaroons.

Her eyes widened. "Oh, Mace, don't even think about it. She loves that dog beyond description."

"How was *Cops*?"

"Funny, but sad. As usual. Where on earth do they find those people?"

Unlike Maddie, Marty was too nice to mention my intimate knowledge of someone who'd had a starring role

"I saw Jeb Ennis again tonight."

Marty's face lit up and she sat down at the table, ready for a good story.

"It didn't go well."

I leaned against the counter and filled her in on what I'd learned about Jeb's ties to Jim Albert. I told her how he'd tried to cover up their big fight.

"I need to find out how much he owed him, Marty. Money is an excellent motive for murder."

"You can't suspect Jeb, Mace." Marty shook her head, blonde hair shimmering in the wagon-wheel light hanging over Mama's table. "You dated the man."

"Yeah, Jeb and that handcuffed suspect on TV. My taste in men seems a little iffy."

"What would his motive be for putting the body in Mama's car, Mace?"

"I'm not sure. I haven't figured that out yet." I topped off my wine glass, and grabbed a third macaroon. "But Jeb's not the only one who seems suspicious, Marty."

I told her about Emma Jean's scene at the church, and her threat of committing violence.

"Emma Jean said that bad word, right there at Abundant Hope?" Marty spoke around the hand she'd clapped over her mouth. "Maybe I was wrong about her being so nice."

We could hear Mama moving toward her bedroom, probably going in to change to something more comfortable than her pansy hat and pantyhose. Teensy followed, tags jingling on his collar.

"Marty, why didn't you tell us about your promotion?"

She blushed. "I didn't want to make a big deal of it, Mace. Not with everyone so worried about Mama and the murder."

"Well, it is a big deal." I clinked my glass against hers. "I've always known you had it in you. You've proved you don't have to be bossy to be boss."

I'd made a small pile of macaroon crumbs on the counter. I was just about to get another wine glass from the cabinet for Mama when Teensy shot out of the bedroom like a rocket. The dog was going nuts, barking and scaling the couch by the window like it was the Pomeranian version of Everest.

Mama called out, "Mace, see what in the world is wrong with that dog. He hasn't been the same since I went to prison."

"Jail, Mama."

A loud thump sounded from the wooden porch outside the front door. I grabbed Mama's grandma's heavy, carved cane from the hallway umbrella stand.

"Marty," I whispered. "There's someone out there."

Within seconds, my sister was right behind me, clutching a cast-iron pan.

Teensy was yelping and jumping, a Pomeranian pogo stick.

As I crept toward the window, I heard a car door slam in the distance. Outside, I saw nothing but dark, empty, street in front of Mama's house. From down the block, an engine raced. Tires squealed. Whoever had been out there was now roaring away. Or, maybe that's what they wanted us to think.

Mama, her face a white mask of Ponds cold cream against a red satin robe, joined us in the hallway. "What in heaven's name is all the fuss, girls?"

I shushed her, and motioned for her to grab hold of her crazy dog.

Cracking the front door, I peeked out. What looked like a bundle of rags tied to a heavy brick sat on the porch, next to a potted Boston fern. Mama held a wriggling Teensy. Marty sidled up beside me, frying pan shaking in her hand. We stepped onto the porch.

The rag bundle was the only thing out of the ordinary. I stooped to pick it up. It was a white toy dog. Deep slashes crisscrossed synthetic plush, spilling stuffing from the head and sides. A collar dangled from the nearly decapitated stuffed animal.

I held the collar to the light spilling out the front door. Marty and Mama each crowded in over a shoulder. Together, we read the name in crude letters on the mutilated dog tag.

Teensy.

TWENTY

I HEARD A SHARP gasp and then another thump on the wooden porch, much louder this time. I whirled around to find Marty collapsed in an unconscious heap. The frying pan had missed my foot by about an inch and a-half.

"Oh, my stars! Would you look at my poor baby?"

I glanced at Mama, and was relieved to see she was referring to Marty, not Teensy. She'd put down the stupid dog and was focused on her youngest daughter.

"Mace, let's get her up and onto the couch. You know Marty can't take shock of any sort. Then run get a cold cloth for her forehead. We'll lift her feet up on two pillows to get the blood flowing. Better bring that bottle of wine, too."

Mama's tone had turned all-business. She might flirt and fuss and swan about like a Southern belle, but if the crisis involves one of her girls, there's no one better than Mama to have in your corner.

Marty didn't weigh much more than the sacks of puppy chow I lift to feed the abandoned wildlife babies at the park. If it'd been

Maddie who fainted, we'd have been in real trouble. Mama and I easily carried Marty off the porch and into the house. We settled her on the living room couch, printed with salmon-colored roses.

"Get down off of there, Teensy!"

The dog, ignoring Mama, was busy climbing across couch cushions and onto Marty's chest. He'd moved up to her head where he was sniffing at her ear. He looked shocked when, none too gently, Mama swept him off her youngest human child and onto the floor.

By the time I returned with the items Mama had ordered, Marty was coming around.

"How'ya doin', darling?" Mama murmured softly, stroking Marty's baby-fine hair.

"Uhmmmm … uhmmm," Marty answered.

"That's all right, honey. You just rest right there. Mace and I have got things covered, don't we Mace?"

Not exactly, I thought, considering that someone had just tossed a brick and a decapitated stuffed dog at the house.

"What … what? That … the porch …"

"Hush, Marty." Mama put a finger to my sister's perfect lips. "Everything's going to be all right."

I moved a crystal candy dish full of butterscotch toffee so I could sit on the coffee table. Mama perched on the couch, next to Marty. I watched closely as her eyes focused. Then they clouded, worry taking the place of the confusion evident a moment before.

"That dog, Mace," Marty said.

"It's just a stuffed animal, a toy. It was someone's idea of a joke."

"Teensy's always getting into things, honey," Mama said. "That little dickens probably chased a cat up a tree or tore up a neighbor's flower bed. It's just a message to keep my dog inside."

Even Mama didn't look like she believed that.

I headed outside to the porch. Now that Marty was safely prone, I wanted to bring that stuffed dog inside for a better look.

I slipped my hand into one of the plastic grocery bags that Mama keeps by the door to remove Teensy's messes from her lawn. Using the bag, I picked up the white dog. I wasn't sure if the police could get fingerprints off a fluffy fake dog or a brick, but I was taking no chances.

Once I had the hallway light on and the stuffed dog displayed on Mama's salmon-colored carpet, I noticed a slip of paper taped under the brick. I turned it over with the toe of my boot. The misspelled message was in the same crude letters as the dog's name on the collar.

Stop questons on the murder or the real dog gets it. Then your next.

I raised my voice to carry to Mama and Marty in the living room. "I think we'd better call Detective Martinez."

——

Mama's house smelled like a field of lavender flowers in Provence. Not that I've ever been to France, but it's how I imagine it, anyway.

After she changed out of her robe, Mama had gotten busy with her candles and essential oils, intent upon easing our anxiety through the miracle of aromatherapy. She dabbed lavender oil on the warm bulbs in her lamps. She lit two candles for the coffee table. Dried lavender and ylang-ylang petals simmered in a pan of water on the stove.

We might have a stuffed-animal-tossing psycho stalking us, but at least we smelled good.

"How long before he'll get here, Mace?"

That was Marty, sitting up now, crumpling and smoothing the hem of her beige-and-brown floral blouse in nervous hands. Her leather loafers were tucked neatly under the couch.

"He said he'd be here as soon as he can," I answered.

We sat quietly, listening to the hips on Mama's Elvis clock swinging back and forth. Tick-tock. *Jailhouse Rock.*

Only fifteen minutes had passed since I phoned the police department to find Martinez. He called back quickly. But it seemed like the wait was going on hours. We stared at each other, trying not to let our eyes roam to the mutilated toy dog on the carpet.

Mama finally got up from the couch and rubbed her hands together. "Well, I don't know about you girls, but all this activity has made me hungry. I think I'm gonna have me a bowl of vanilla ice cream with butterscotch topping. Anybody care to join me?"

Marty turned green. But, nerves or not, I've never been one to turn down ice cream. Teensy and I followed Mama into the kitchen. She was spooning out the dessert when the dog did a double take, its little head twisting from the ice cream carton to the door and the outside beyond. Finally, Teensy's territorial nature beat out his sweet tooth. He ran to the living room, barking like he believed he was a Doberman. I followed.

"Hush," Mama yelled at the dog, to no discernible effect.

Headlights reflected through the windows out front, as a late-model white sedan swung into the driveway. Marty jumped up from the couch and flew into our old bedroom. I heard her lock the door from the inside.

Looking out the curtains, I yelled at my sister: "You can come out, Marty. It's Detective Martinez."

The bedroom door opened slowly. I saw Marty's pert nose and a curve of lip peek out. "Carlos Martinez?"

"One and the same."

I watched from the window as he walked to the door, dressed in a white button-down shirt and gray slacks. Open collar. No tie. His hair was wet, like he'd just had a shower. I slammed shut the mental door on an image of him stepping out of the bathtub, water droplets clinging to his bare chest. The fact that he was frowning, as usual, helped end my inappropriate fantasy.

The doorbell rang, the dog started doing flips, and Mama came into the living room juggling three bowls of vanilla ice cream.

"Evenin', Detective," she said, as I opened the door for him. "You may as well have some ice cream before you have a look at the victim." She held out the biggest serving, swimming in butterscotch.

Stepping inside, Martinez looked at the bowl like he suspected strychnine.

"Go ahead," I said. "She's already forgiven you for throwing her in jail. I can't say the same for the rest of us."

Mama pushed the ice cream toward him.

"She's not going to quit until you eat some," I told him. I dipped my spoon into his bowl and took a bite. "See? Nothing but a frozen dairy treat."

He took it, mumbled a thank-you, and stood with his bowl over the stuffed dog.

"So it was just this toy and the note?" He carefully placed one of Mama's *Guideposts* magazines on the hall table so he could set down the ice cream. I liked the fact that he was worried about leaving a ring on the polished wood.

He stooped down for a closer look. "Any idea who might've thrown it?"

All of a sudden, I felt cranky over everything he'd put us through by arresting Mama.

"Oh, gee, I don't know," I said. "Could it have been the real murderer? The one you didn't catch while our mama was sitting in jail?"

"Listen, Ms. Bauer." His eyes darkened ominously. "I did what I felt was necessary with the situation and information I had at the time. I'm not going to apologize, or explain myself to you."

"Well, of course not. You're arrogant. God forbid you should apologize."

"Mace, that's enough. Please ignore my sister, Carlos." Out from her bedroom fortress, Marty carried the quiet authority of someone who rarely spoke out. If she was moved to criticize, I knew I'd gone over the line.

"I'm sorry," I said, chastened. "We appreciate you coming over here to check this out."

Martinez looked at me, raised eyebrows registering his surprise.

"We were all just so upset about Mama." I tried to excuse my bad manners. "And now, this stuffed dog. We don't know who tossed it. But I can tell you we have some suspicions about who might have killed Jim Albert."

He shifted, sitting cross-legged on the carpet to listen. I filled him in on Emma Jean's threat in church. I told him about Jeb Ennis owing money to the murder victim. And I mentioned the mysterious Sal Provenza, again.

"That's outrageous, Mace! Sally would never threaten Teensy. He loves him like his own." Mama stroked the flesh-and-blood Pomeranian.

"In case you hadn't noticed, the stabbed dog is a replica." I crooked a thumb at Teensy.

The dog was splitting his attention between wary regard of the detective, an alpha-male threat in this female household, and pitiful begging for a bite of ice cream.

"I'd just die if anything bad happened." Mama shoveled ice cream onto Teensy's pink tongue. "Don't worry," she said, when she saw our disgusted looks. "He has his own spoon."

Martinez pulled a pair of gloves and a zip-top plastic bag from his pocket, slipped on the gloves, and picked up the stuffed dog. "I'm not sure how much we can get from this." He dropped it with the note and brick into the bag.

"I hope I don't need to tell you to keep your doors locked," he said as he stood. "It may be a prank. But maybe it isn't. And that's a chance you don't want to take."

TWENTY-ONE

MARTY BEGGED OFF, HEADING home with the beginnings of a migraine.

Mama managed to convince Martinez to sit for a spell at the kitchen table to finish his ice cream. I caught him checking out a family of porcelain mice in gingham bonnets cavorting across a display shelf. He dabbed with a gingham napkin at a tiny drop of ice cream on his white shirt. If that'd been my spill, vanilla on white cotton, it wouldn't even merit action. When you go crawling around in the dirt after nuisance animals, you can't be too fussy about stains.

"Mace, honey, why don't you show Detective Martinez where the bathroom is, so he can get some soap and water on that spot?"

Like a trained investigator would get lost traversing two rooms and a hallway to the toilet. Mama's ploy was transparent. But I was too tired to point out he could find soap and water right there at the kitchen sink.

We pushed back our chairs, leaving Mama to place our bowls on the floor for Teensy to lap up the leftovers. Thank God her dishwasher water is good and hot.

Martinez stopped in the hallway on the way to the bathroom. Pictures of my sisters and me in various stages of development decorated the walls. I saw him grin as he looked at a circa-nineties shot of me in a starchy white dress, leaning against a tree. What had I been thinking with that 'do? I looked like Billy Ray Cyrus, with his mullet cut, in drag.

Martinez gently grasped my elbow, pulling me near. "Listen, I didn't mean what I said before." He lowered his voice so Mama wouldn't overhear. "I do feel bad about putting your mother in jail. I wasn't sure about the extent of her involvement. I'm new here. I've never had a whole family show up for what seemed like a party in the police lobby. And then no one would shut up. I could barely get in a word edgewise."

"We do tend to get a little rambunctious," I allowed.

"It's just that the police do things more formally in Miami."

I shook off his hand, crossed my arms, and leaned against the opposite wall. I wasn't quite ready to forgive him. "Um-hum."

"You don't give anything up, do you, Ms. Bauer?" His lips had formed into a half smile. "Maybe you should get a job as a detective." He was standing so close, I could feel heat from his body. I caught the scent of cologne. Exotic, like sandalwood mixed with ginger. He smelled all male, and damn sexy. I took a step sideways along the wall.

"You've found out quite a bit in these last couple of days." He stepped with me, staying close and keeping his voice low.

"It helps to know who to ask." Mama always preaches modesty. She says there's nothing worse than tooting your own horn.

"I'll definitely follow up on your tip about that man with the cattle ranch. Jeb Ennis, right? And he lives in Woochola?"

I had a guilty twinge about steering Martinez in Jeb's direction. "Wauchula. We say, *WAH-CHOO-LA*." I opened my mouth wide, like a speech therapist coaxing a stroke victim. "Mispronouncing these old Indian words will mark you as an outsider quicker than just about anything."

"I've had enough trouble with Himmarshee," he said. "What's it mean anyway?"

"It's supposed to mean *new water*, from an old Seminole legend about how Himmarshee Creek sprung up overnight. And don't worry about your pronunciation. We're probably all mangling the original Indian name anyhow. Just wait until you have to question somebody at Lake Istokpoga or Lake Weohyakapka."

"Thanks for the warning." He bent in a little bow. "*Gracias.*"

"No problem-o. You set me straight on the grammatical difference between *prison* and *jail*, remember?"

He had the good grace to look embarrassed. "Pretty obnoxious, wasn't I?"

"You said it, not me." I softened the criticism with a smile. Mama would be proud. "Anyway, the bathroom."

I gestured to the open door. The toilet, with its pink tulip seat cover, was perfectly visible through the frame. Even a bad detective could have discerned it. And from what I'd read in the *Miami Herald,* Carlos Martinez was a good detective.

I returned to the kitchen to find Mama feeding Teensy a doggie treat right at the table.

"Gross."

"Just ignore Mace, baby. You are not gross. You're Mama's little darlin' dog, aren't you?"

I stood near the trash can, in case I needed to vomit.

Just about then, Teensy's ears perked up and he leapt off Mama's lap. The little nails on his paws scrabbled on peach-colored tile as he ran from the kitchen to the living room, barking all the way.

Before we had the chance to follow, we heard the front door jiggling. And then a loud knocking.

"What in the blue blazes? Open up!" More door-shaking, and a voice full of impatience. "Mama! Since when do you lock this front door?"

Maddie's irritation seeped right through the sheer curtain at the window.

By the time Mama and I made our way to the living room, Martinez had already opened the front door. "She locks it since I told her it was the safe thing to do."

Maddie's mouth gaped open so wide, you could have docked an ocean liner inside. But all those years of dealing with whatever junior high-school kids can dream up had served her well. She recovered quickly.

"Detective Martinez." With that inflection and the look in her eye, she might just as well have said "Detective Dog Poop."

"Happy to see you, too, ma'am." Martinez matched Maddie's insulting tone, syllable for syllable.

"Judging from the absence of handcuffs, may I assume you're not here to arrest our mother again?" she asked.

Mama chimed in, "Now, before you say something you'll regret, Maddie, we called the detective to come over. We've had a little spot of trouble."

"I know. I talked to Marty. She was in bed in migraine pain, with the lights out. I could barely hear her voice when I called. We only spoke a minute, but she told me about the dog."

"It could be simple vandalism," Martinez said. "But we're not taking any chances."

"Marty didn't mention *he* was here." Maddie pointed a long finger at the detective. She looked like the *Wizard of Oz*'s Wicked Witch, directing the evil monkeys at Dorothy and her pals.

But unlike the movie's scarecrow, Martinez had a brain.

"I don't want us to be enemies, ma'am." His voice was warm and polite. "I hope your mother isn't in any danger. But if she is, I really need your help."

Maddie was wearing flip-flops and her post-barbecue fat pants, but she still straightened to her school-principal posture. My sister loves nothing more than being needed.

"Well, of course, Detective. All of us want to do anything we can to help find out who really killed Jim Albert. For some reason, the murderer has involved Mama in this nasty business. Who knows what kind of message he's sending with that stuffed dog?"

"I'd like you to take a look at it." Martinez was so respectful, he might have been seeking help from Scotland Yard. "Maybe something will strike you that didn't strike the rest of us, ma'am."

"Lead the way, Detective. And please, call me Maddie."

"I'll do that." As Martinez turned to escort her to the stuffed dog, he threw me a wink. "And Maddie? Call me Carlos, *por favor*. Please."

———

Martinez left Mama's a half-hour or so later. By that time, the compliments were flowing between my sister and him like floodwaters into Lake Okeechobee during the rainy season. I thought he was going to pin her with a special deputy's badge at any minute. I actually saw Maddie bat her eyelashes. My sister being swayed like a schoolgirl was a sight to behold. Martinez must have studied with those Eastern mystics who are able to charm cobra snakes.

Maddie and I only stayed a little while after he left. We all were tired. And I had a long drive ahead to get home.

The streets of downtown Himmarshee were just about deserted. The yellow light blinked at Main and First. The sign at Gladys' Restaurant was dark. A few cars were still parked at the Speckled Perch restaurant, where the bar's open past midnight. Behind the wheel of Pam's VW, I replayed in my mind some of the odd events of the evening: Delilah's cutting remarks before church; my fight with Jeb; the mutilated toy dog.

As I sped past the courthouse on my way to State Road 98, I caught a glimpse of a familiar car from the corner of my eye. I slowed and peered toward the far end of the government lot, where the light is dim. Sal Provenza's big Cadillac was parked next to a light-colored sedan. The two vehicles sat driver's-side-to-driver's-side, like squad cars sometimes do.

As I passed, Sal torched a fat cigar. I could clearly see his profile in the flickering glow. But who was in that other car, parked in a deserted spot for a clandestine meeting near midnight?

TWENTY-TWO

WHEN SAL'S LIGHTER FLARED a second time, I nearly ran Pam's car into the war memorial on the courthouse square.

Carlos Martinez leaned from his driver's window with an equally large cigar between his lips. Sal, smiling, fired him up. The detective puffed, and settled back in his seat with a contented look. As he exhaled, a smoke cloud swirled around the two men.

Sal relit his own stogie. Martinez said something. They both laughed. From my vantage point, now getting more distant in the rearview mirror of the VW, it looked like the investigator in Jim Albert's murder and the man we all thought might be the killer were the oldest and best of friends.

I slammed on my brakes and did a U-turn.

The putt-putt-putt of the ancient VW made a stealth approach unlikely. By the time I navigated off the road, into the police department lot, and all the way to their corner in the back, Sal had started his car and gunned it. Pedal to the metal, he screeched out the exit like Dale Earnhardt Jr. in the last lap at Daytona.

As I sputtered up, Martinez got out of his car and leaned against the driver's door. He looked completely relaxed; casual. Just an average, hard-working cop, enjoying a cigar at the end of a long day. Of course, his smoking pal happened to be the very same man Martinez had said was criminally linked to the dead mobster. And that wasn't the least of it. He'd all but told me Sal was a suspect in that mobster's murder.

I brought Pam's car shuddering to a stop, and turned off the key in the ignition. Martinez walked over to the VW to greet me. "We meet again so soon, Ms. Bauer."

"Oh, can the act, Detective. It's been a long day. I'm as tuckered out as a plow horse after forty rows. Why were you just sharing a smoke with the man you implied might have murdered Jimmy the Weasel?"

"I like a woman who cuts to the chase." He smiled down into the driver's seat.

"I'm thrilled," I said. "And I like a man who isn't a pathological liar. What the hell is going on?"

He looked right then left, like there might be someone lurking in the vast rows of vacant parking spaces. He turned around and peered behind us. Then he took a step around the front of my car and scanned the road I'd just come from. Unless someone was hovering over our heads or hiding underneath one of our cars, there wasn't a soul to overhear him.

"I can't really talk about the investigation." He pressed his lips together like a crooked cop on the witness stand who'd just invoked the Fifth Amendment.

"That's it?" I asked. "You can't talk about it? That's all you're going to say?"

"I wish I could say more. I really do."

I started counting, but only made it to two.

"Maybe Chief Johnson will be more forthcoming when I share with him that I saw you chumming around with a murder suspect," I snapped. "What do you think he'll say about that?"

His big brown eyes filled with disappointment. "Do whatever you have to do, Ms. Bauer. I will say this: the situation with Sal Provenza is a very delicate one. You going around spreading tales when you don't understand what you're talking about could compromise the investigation into Jimmy Albrizio's murder. You're not Agatha Christie, you know. The last thing the police need is some half-cocked civilian, meddling in crucial matters and trying to solve the Big Case."

My hands squeezed the steering wheel. My knuckles were white. This man had a way of getting on my last nerve. "I get your point, Detective. You don't have to insult me while you're at it." I turned the key. "Now, if you'll excuse me, I'm going to take my dumb civilian self home and get some rest."

The car stalled. So much for a dramatic exit. I pumped the gas again. It finally started on the fourth try.

"Good night." I raised my chin and stared straight ahead, trying to appear as dignified as possible for a woman who was driving the Little Engine That Couldn't.

I glanced into the rearview mirror as I pulled out of the police lot. Martinez was leaning against his car, puffing away on that stupid cigar and watching me disappear.

———

As the VW rattled down the dirt drive that leads to my cottage, the outline of three masked bandits flashed in the headlights.

I cursed. "Stupid raccoons!"

The creatures seemed to be struggling to get the tops off my garbage cans. A smart-ass detective from Miami might put me in my place. But, by God, I'd shown those raccoons. I'm not an experienced animal trapper for nothing. My garbage was trussed up tighter than Fort Knox. The lids on top of the cans were snapped down; bungee cords secured the tops to the handles.

I was feeling pretty good, until I got a little closer and saw the 'coons had busted the vault. They were picnicking on leftover chicken and cantaloupe. The biggest one looked as pleased as a fat man at an all-you-can-eat buffet.

I flashed the brights and blew the horn. They just looked up and blinked. Most of my country neighbors would have simply shot the varmints. But I'm soft about animals. I parked the car, headed to my shed, and picked out a rake. Then I turned the hose on them, holding the rake ready in case they ran at me instead of into the woods. As they scampered away, I swear that biggest one aimed a look out of *Terminator* at me over his shoulder.

I'll be back.

"Just try it, you little bastard," I yelled.

Hump-backed, they loped toward the line of cypress trees and Sabal palms that mark the edge of my property. "I'm getting out the smelly stuff," I shouted after them. "We'll see how y'all like it when you come sniffing around for dinner and the stench of laundry bleach knocks you over instead!"

So this is what I'd descended to: a crazy woman living alone in the woods, warring with raccoons. I grabbed my purse from the car, tossed a tarp over the seats in case of rain, and headed for my cypress-wood cottage.

From the front porch, I took a moment to appreciate what I love about living so far out. The stars lit the black sky. Cattle lowed in a distant pasture. The scent of orange blossoms from a grove hung in the air. There was also a whiff of manure, fortunately faint, from the Big Lake Dairy. It had drifted over Highway 98 and across the marshes of Taylor Slough, traveling west on a slight breeze.

Inside, the gator jaws gaped on my coffee table, waiting for my keys. The answering machine light blinked. I wanted to ignore it and hit the sack instead. But given all the recent crazy events, I figured I'd better not.

You have one message, an electronic voice intoned. *First message.*

"Mace, honey? It's your mama."

Like I couldn't tell. I started sorting mail as she carried on her conversation with my machine.

"You will never believe who called me up here after y'all left. None other than Pastor Bob Dixon, from church. Abundant Hope, that is."

Like there's another Pastor Bob.

"I may have been wrong about him, Mace. He seemed awful sweet on the phone. He went on and on about how Delilah told him you'd come to church with me, and how nice that was. Said it sure would be wonderful if you'd come more often."

Nice try, Mama.

"Anyway, he said the real reason he called is he wants to talk to me about Emma Jean. I told him we were really more acquaintances than friends. But he told me that didn't matter; she needs a friend right now. Pastor Bob said I should stop by the church sometime tomorrow to see him and Delilah. They're hatching a plan to see if we can't get poor Emma Jean some help."

I kicked off my boots, opened the refrigerator, and got a beer. If Mama had a point, I may as well get comfortable while I waited for her to find it.

"After she threw that fit at church, he said it's obvious she's hurting. I never would have believed it of Emma Jean, Mace. But with all that's happened in her life, it seems like she's gone plumb crazy. First, her little boy disappeared, like I told y'all. Then she finds out Jim was cheating. And now he gets killed."

Thirty seconds remaining.

"Well! These machines sure don't give you much time, do they? Anyway, I was wondering whether you'd run me by church in the mornin', about 8:30? I'd ask Maddie, but she has a sixth-grade assembly. And Marty will still be feeling poorly. I worry about her so much with those awful headaches, Mace. And now she's got the responsibilities of that new job. What do you suppose we can do about her migraines, Mace? Anyway, I'd sure appreciate the ride. I wish you'd wear that sweet Kelly green blouse with the bow at the neck. You look so…"

Beep. End of message.

I look so … so … what? So much like the wife of the Jolly Green Giant in a ruffled collar? So much like a leprechaun on growth hormones?

I knew how poor Teensy must feel, having to suffer the humiliation of Mama dressing him in a yellow slicker when it rains and a reindeer sweater at Christmas. He even has a tiny set of antlers to match the sweater. Fortunately, I get to choose my own clothes.

The Kelly green horror would stay at the back of my closet, where it belongs.

Finally, I was able to peel off the jeans I'd been wearing for what seemed like a week. I dropped them on the floor, changed into my PJs and fluffed the pillows on my bed. Suddenly, the phone shrilled, sending my stomach somersaulting around the burger and fries and ice cream.

In a country town like Himmarshee, people turn in early. When the phone rings past midnight, the news is never good.

TWENTY-THREE

THE CALLER WAS A woman, her shaky voice so soft I could hardly hear it.

"Mace? I'm awful sorry to call so late."

My heart thrummed. "Is my mama okay? Has anything happened to my sisters?"

"Oh, honey, I'm sorry I scared you." She took a long breath. "They're all fine, so far as I know. This isn't about anybody but me."

The acrobats in my gut took a break. The bass drum in my chest slowed to a normal beat. I waited, trying to let her proceed at her own pace. She was clearly in distress. But my compassion extends only so far at 12:44 AM.

Then I heard a familiar wail.

"Hey there, Emma Jean." I raised my voice to compete. "Don't cry now. It's going to be all right."

"I didn't ... *sob* ... know who else ... *sob* ... to call, Mace. Your mama always talks about how smart you are. I liked the way you handled yourself at the police department. Not too bossy, like your older sister. And not too much of a scaredy cat, like that younger one." Emma Jean paused to blow her nose. "I need someone with a good head on her shoulders to tell me what to do."

I gazed with longing at my fluffy pillows. They looked like two white clouds that had floated down from heaven to carry me off to a blessed sleep. On the other hand, we all wanted to know what the hell was up with Emma Jean.

"How can I help?" I sat at the foot of the bed, turning my back on the pillows.

"Mace, I found out who was cheating with Jim."

I sat up straight, sleep forgotten. "Who?"

"I don't want to say over the phone. You never know who might be listening in." No sobs now; not even a sniffle. "I couldn't sleep, as you can imagine. I'm out driving around. I know this is a big favor, but I really need to talk this out with someone, Mace. I saw on *Oprah* that when something is bothering you, you need to get it out in the open. You need to confront it, or it'll fester."

"That's good advice, Emma Jean, depending on what you mean by confronting." I thought of the ruckus at the church. Her threat of doing harm to the Other Woman. "If you could say who's involved, it'll help me know how to handle this."

She lowered her voice to a whisper. "Not on the phone, Mace. Please."

It seemed pretty paranoid, but I didn't want to upset her. I remembered that tire iron.

As if she'd read my thoughts, Emma Jean said, "I know I made a fool of myself at Abundant Hope. I need somebody smart like you to tell me how to go about settling things. I'm out on Highway 98 now, only a few minutes away from the old Raulerson cottage.

Your mama told me you bought that old ruin, and fixed it up real nice."

I looked at the clock. It was 12:51. No, 12:52. What the hell? I'd sleep tomorrow night.

"C'mon over. I'll put on a pot of herbal tea."

Tossing a robe over my pajamas, I went into the kitchen. I lit a couple of Mama's carnation candles. The water boiled, and I poured it into a pot over three chamomile teabags. After choosing some pretty flowered cups, I set out two spoons and a plastic bear full of honey. By the time I'd washed up a few dishes, read the headlines in the *Himmarshee Times*, and turned on the TV, I began to wonder what was keeping Emma Jean.

I'm too cheap to pay the phone company an extra monthly fee for caller ID. But I can usually discover the last number that called me by punching in *star-69* on my phone's keypad.

The display panel flashed: *Number Unavailable*.

I cursed the fact there'd be a charge for the service, even though it failed to retrieve Emma Jean's cell number. Then I reminded myself to stop being a petty cheapskate. A fellow woman was in crisis, after all. And it was only ninety-five cents.

Clicking channels on the remote, I found an ancient rerun of *The Andy Griffith Show*. Sheriff Taylor was teaching some kind of life lesson to his boy, Opie. Deputy Barney Fife was wreaking havoc on an otherwise peaceful Mayberry.

And that's the last thing I remember, until my alarm went off from the next room at 7:30 AM.

The sun streamed through the living room window. The glare bounced off one of the gator's teeth, hitting me dead in the eye. I lifted my head from the couch, which was wet where I drooled in my sleep. The TV blared. One candle flickered, weakly. The other was burned out.

And Emma Jean Valentine was nowhere in sight.

———

I microwaved the leftover chamomile tea. No sense in wasting it. Along with a sliced banana between two pieces of buttered wheat toast, that was my breakfast. After last night's pig-out, I wanted to get something wholesome down my gullet for a change.

Within fifteen minutes, I showered, dressed, and was out the door. My second cup of honeyed tea was still steaming when I shook the rain puddles off the VW's tarp, and headed for Mama's house.

On the way out, I saw the aftermath of the raccoon fiesta. It was worse than I thought. My yard looked like the picnic grounds at Himmarshee Park after the Fourth of July: beer bottles, paper scraps, and chicken bones gnawed clean. I'd clean up after work.

The VW bounced under a canopy of live oaks. The air smelled clean from the rain. The downpour had revived the resurrection ferns that grow on the trees' branches, turning them from dull brown to deep green.

No sooner had I pulled onto Highway 98 than my cell phone started to ring. It was in my purse, which was on the floor. Of course. Bracing the steering wheel between my knees, I placed the mug of tea on the dashboard's least perilous spot and reached for the phone with my free hand. Thank God there was no other traffic on the highway.

"Hey, Mace. I've got some interesting news for you."

At a bump in the road, the tea started to topple. To rescue it, I had to drop the phone. I played it safe and dumped the rest of the hot chamomile out the window.

"I'm sorry," I said, jamming the phone back to my ear. "Who is this?"

"Donnie Bailey. From the jail?"

I flashed on a massive chest and manly mustache.

"Of course, Donnie. How are you?"

"Pretty good. I hope you don't mind me calling you on your cell. When your mama stayed with us, she listed you as her emergency contact. She gave us both your home and cell numbers."

I dabbed with a napkin from my purse at a small puddle of herbal tea on the dashboard. "Did you say something about news, Donnie?" I was an advertisement for dangerous distractions behind the wheel.

"I thought you might want to know you were right."

"About?"

"The other night on the road, when you said there was another car there? You were right and I was wrong. I owe you an apology. I just saw the report."

Now Donnie had my full attention. Driving was on automatic pilot. The road to Mama's rolled past, nearly unnoticed.

"They found a second set of tire imprints where your car went off the road, Mace. Both tracks veered off the pavement onto the shoulder. Yours kept going, on into that ditch. But the other vehicle steered back onto the roadway. The investigator took a bunch of black-and-white pictures and made an impression with casting powder."

"What's that?"

"It's kind of like pancake batter, except you'd never want to eat it. You pour it into the track, it gets real hard, and then you can lift it out. You can use the impression to compare to the bad guy's tire. That's the good news. The bad news is you have to find the bad guy's car first, so you can compare."

"Can they tell what kind of tire it is?"

"The impression wasn't the greatest. They know the tread was worn, and it's a big tire, like for a pickup."

"Great. That means it could have been just about anybody in Himmarshee. Trucks are as common here as taxicabs in New York. Everybody's got one; or knows someone who does."

"Guilty as charged, Mace." Donnie laughed. "I've got a brother drives a pickup."

"See? That's my point."

"That's not all, Mace. They couldn't find any usable paint chip evidence, either. The other driver must have just tapped that spare tire that sticks out where it's mounted on the back of your Jeep. It would have been better if they'd really hit you hard, painted metal to metal. That would have left behind something to analyze."

I remembered my terror on that dark road; the black water swirling around my legs. All that from a tap.

"Yeah, well, a harder impact might have made me flip. And we probably wouldn't be having this talk right now."

"Oh, Mace … I'm … I'm … sorry." Donnie was flustered. "I sure didn't mean that the way it sounded. Of course it's better that you're alive."

"That's all right, Donnie." I thought of babysitting him. Teary eyes on the floor, he'd stammered out an apology for breaking his mama's vase. "I know what you meant."

I was approaching Himmarshee. I'd been so intent on talking to Donnie, I could barely remember getting there. Luckily, it wasn't an auction day, when the traffic on the highway would be busier.

"Listen, I better get off the phone. You being in law enforcement, I'd hate to tell you how little attention I've paid to my driving this morning."

Donnie chuckled. "You're not the only one, Mace. Have you seen all the things people do in their cars these days? I saw a girl yesterday with a hamburger in one hand, putting on her mascara with the other."

"Did you bust her?"

"Nah. She poked herself in the eye and dropped the hamburger in her lap when she saw me in my uniform. Nobody pays attention to the road anymore, Mace."

Donnie was right about that. And, on this morning at least, that wasn't a good thing.

TWENTY-FOUR

MAMA STOOD ON THE walkway in front of her house, tapping her foot and staring at her watch. The color of the day was yellow, from the chiffon scarf around her neck to the sling-back sandals on her feet. Standing in the bright morning sun, she looked like a four-foot-eleven-inch lemon slush. Her white puff of platinum hair could have been a straw, peeking out over the rim of the slushy cup.

Teensy was barking, spinning like a circus dog, on the other side of her living room window. Mama turned to blow him a final kiss, and rushed to the car. "I thought you'd never get here, Mace."

I looked at my watch. "Mama, it's only twenty-five minutes after eight. I'm early."

Settling into the seat, she glanced again at her wrist. "So you are, Mace. I'm sorry. I'm as nervous as a long-tailed cat in a room full of rocking chairs. I barely know Pastor Bob. I can't imagine why he'd call me for this meeting about Emma Jean."

I told her about my own strange call.

"She never even bothered to show up, Mama, after calling past midnight."

"That's nice, honey." She turned the rearview mirror to apply more lipstick. Fishing a tissue from her purse, she blotted. "Now, what do you suppose Pastor Bob is going to want me to do about Emma Jean?"

"I have no earthly idea," I said sharply. "And there's no sense in worrying about it now. Why don't you wait the five minutes it'll take us to drive over? Then you can ask him yourself."

She aimed a glare at me. "You know, little Missy, you're not too old to spank. No one likes a girl with a smart mouth."

I punched on the radio. They'd just started a news break. We arrived at Abundant Hope before they'd even finished the weather. Temperatures in the nineties. Afternoon thundershowers. Not exactly news in central Florida in September. Still, it was the height of hurricane season, and the northern edge of the county was still recovering from a relatively weak storm in June. So the fact nothing new was gathering strength in the tropics was a hopeful sign.

Someone peered out of the mini-blinds of the storefront church's window, following our progress into the parking space. All I could see were heavy eyebrows and dark eyes. Within moments, Pastor Bob opened the front door and walked out to greet us. His eyebrows needed a trim, but his smile was as blinding as a Hollywood actor's. And just about as authentic. The work in his mouth had surely financed a brand-new luxury car for some dentist somewhere.

The pastor raised his hands skyward. "Isn't this a beautiful morning, ladies? It's a gift from God."

Not to be sacrilegious, but if God had asked me what kind of day to send, I'd have requested a break from the summer swelter. It wasn't even nine o'clock, and already the sun was baking the VW's roofless interior. The temperature on the Big Lake Bank sign read 94 degrees. We peeled ourselves off the sticky car seats and joined Pastor Bob on the sidewalk.

He escorted us through the entrance, by the card table of DVDs, and past folding chairs now stacked against scuffed walls. When we came to a small office to the side of the pulpit, he motioned us into two steel-frame chairs, thinly upholstered in a black, scratchy fabric. Then he took his seat behind a tidy desk, his small frame nearly disappearing in a leather chair befitting the CEO of a Fortune 500 company. He leaned toward us, elbows on the desk, and straightened the monogrammed cuffs on his powder blue dress shirt.

"Now," he said, showing us a mouthful of teeth, "what can I do for you this morning?"

Mama and I looked at each other. Maybe he had us confused with a mother-daughter counseling appointment. Not that we couldn't use it.

"We're here about Emma Jean," Mama said. "You called and asked me to come by?"

"Oh, my goodness gracious! Rosalee! I'm sorry. I wasn't expecting you to bring someone else along."

"This is Mace, my middle daughter."

I nodded hello as I tried to place his accent. Flat, Midwestern, a bit nasal. Ohio, maybe, or Illinois.

"You'll have to forgive me, ladies. Last night was such a muddle. And I'm still having a bit of trouble placing everyone in the congregation."

Mama smiled sweetly and said, "Perhaps you should ask your lovely wife for help. Delilah seems to know all the lambs in your flock quite well."

I pinched her on the leg to stop her from being catty. She pinched me back.

"By the way," Mama continued, "where is Delilah? I was expecting her."

Pastor Bob pressed his lips together. He started fidgeting with one of his silver cufflinks. His eyes did a quick scan of his desktop. Then he looked at the ceiling, like maybe his wife was hanging up there behind the fluorescent light. Before he got up and lifted the Persian rug to look, I figured I should say something.

"My mother's just asking because we spoke to her last night before all the trouble started. And then the two of you seemed to work together as a team, the way y'all got Emma Jean quieted down and hustled out the door. We're a little surprised Delilah's not here, too."

He leaned back and turned his fingers into a steeple, which he rested against his chest. "Well, it's always something when you're a minister's wife," he said. "She was called away suddenly. A member of the church has taken ill."

"Really?" Mama asked. "Who?"

"You've got me there, Mrs. Deveraux." He showed his teeth again. I thought of fairy tales and wolves. "I'm just awful with names. But even so, it's a confidential matter. I'm sure you'd appreciate the same treatment if you came to us about a health issue or for counseling."

Mama looped her wrist through the strap of her purse and set it squarely on her lap. "I'm not much for counseling." She held onto the purse with both hands, like she was afraid Pastor Bob might ask her to pony up for psychotherapy.

"Well, people seem to want that kind of thing these days. I'm going to offer another DVD: *Ending Emotional Pain with Pastor Bob*. What do you think, Mace?"

I thought he wasn't setting any sales records with his first DVD. The only time I saw them move was when Emma Jean stumbled into the display table.

"I don't know much about marketing," I answered.

He flushed. " 'Marketing' sounds so crass. I'm talking about helping people."

"In that case, why don't we see how you can help in this situation?" I put my hand on Mama's shoulder. "You may have heard my mother was briefly detained in connection to the murder of Emma Jean's boyfriend. We've been trying to find out who really killed him. But somebody doesn't seem to want us to do that. Some strange things have been happening."

I filled him in on the stuffed dog and the warning note. I mentioned there'd been another threat, but kept things vague since we still hadn't told Mama about my narrow escape on the highway. She thought my Jeep was just in the shop—again. I summed up Emma Jean's behavior.

"You both know her. Do you think Emma Jean could be behind any of this?" I asked.

The minister tapped together his fingers. Mama picked at a piece of lint on her pantsuit.

"Is she violent?"

Pastor Bob said, "She did look awfully comfortable with that tire iron."

Mama scowled at him. "Well, I don't believe it." She shook her head. "I think what Emma Jean needs right now is some proper Christian charity, not condemnation."

"I'm perfectly willing to render that charity, if only I could find her, Rosalee." More teeth. "Delilah and I called several times after services last night, and again this morning. We didn't reach her. I was hoping you had."

That's when I repeated what I'd said in the car about Emma Jean calling, but not showing up. This time, I had Mama's complete attention.

———

A half hour later, we'd about exhausted the topic of Emma Jean's troubles. Sitting on that itchy black chair in the pastor's office, my mind started to wander to work and the day ahead. I needed to stop at the poultry plant and buy a dozen whole chickens for Ollie. That alligator was about to eat up the annual operating budget for Himmarshee Park.

I shifted my wrist to get a look at my watch. Pastor Bob caught me. He must get a lot of practice at that from the pulpit. Clearing his throat, he stretched his toes to the floor and pushed back the leather chair.

"Ladies, it's been a pleasure speaking to you both. I only wish the circumstances were better. I'm praying for Emma Jean. I hope you are, too."

He seemed to stare extra hard at my lapsed self as he said that. It was my turn to look down at his desk.

He walked around and enfolded Mama's right hand in both of his. "Don't worry, Rosalee. When we find Emma Jean, we're going to take care of her. The Bible tells us to help up a companion who falls." He pulled Mama up from her chair, acting out the verse.

"*Woe to him who is alone when he falls and doesn't have another to lift him up. Ecclesiastes 4:10,*" he recited.

He turned to me. "You're certainly a good daughter, a companion for your mother."

Placing one of his boy-sized hands on my shoulder, he gazed at me. His green eyes were piercing, especially against those white teeth. His hand lay there so long, I started feeling uncomfortable. His clammy fingers wriggled. I shifted my shoulder, trying to get out from under what felt like a flopping catfish. Then, just before he removed his hand, he kneaded the bare skin on my upper arm like it was dough and he was a baker.

Could I have imagined it? I searched his eyes, and saw the slightest flicker. "C'mon, baby. I'm ready if you are," it said.

Ewww.

Grabbing Mama's elbow, I moved her as a barrier between Pastor Bob and me. I backed out the door of his office and into the church.

"PleaseCallMamaIfYouHearAnythingAboutEmmaJean," I said, the words squirming out like tadpoles in a creek. "We'veGottaGo. INeedToGetToWork."

I rushed Mama past plastic lilies and pulpit, across dark blue carpet and out the door.

"My stars and garters ..." she protested as I pushed her onto the sidewalk. "What in the world?"

"Don't ask questions, Mama. Just get in the car."

Pastor Bob stood in the church's front window. He pulled open the blinds, watching us go. He looked just like Ollie the alligator—right before I toss a raw chicken into his waiting jaws.

TWENTY-FIVE

MAMA'S HEAD SWIVELED LIKE a one-eyed dog in a butcher shop.

I was telling her all about Pastor Bob's stroking and come-hither stare. She'd look at me for a second, then snap her head toward Abundant Hope, disappearing in the distance behind us. Me, the church. The church, me. I think she expected the minister to jump in his car and chase me down for some nookie-nookie.

"Well, I never!" Mama's lips formed a disapproving line. "That is just about the awfulest thing I ever heard, Mace. I knew there was something off about that man. He's a predator in pastor's clothing, plain and simple."

"Oh, c'mon, Mama." I laughed a little at how naïve she seemed. "It's not the end of the world. He thought he saw the chance for a little somethin' on the side, and he decided to go for it. He's not the first man to do it. He won't be the last."

Once I'd put a few blocks between me and the lecherous Pastor Bob, I eased off the gas. Unclenching the grip she'd had on the window crank, Mama snapped her seat belt shut.

"He's not just a man, Mace." Her face was as serious as a sermon. "He's a man of God. There's supposed to be a difference."

"Tell that to Jim Bakker and Jimmy Swaggart. I seem to remember they were famous ministers, and they had a little trouble with the ladies, too."

She ran a hand through her hair. I imagined stray strands scattering in the wind. "That's not fair, Mace. Those scandals happened a long time ago. And the majority of religious men are good, righteous leaders. They're not out to jump the bones of anything that moves."

"Thanks for the compliment, Mama. Maybe my knockout looks and sex appeal tempted that poor pastor, just this once. Did you ever think about that?"

She took a long look at me: sleeveless collared shirt in park-department green; shapeless matching trousers in olive drab. I wore heavy-soled black boots, laced up past my ankles. No lipstick or blush. No perfume, either. The park's animals don't like it, and it draws mosquitoes.

"Honey, I love you to death." Mama put her palm on my cheek. "You can be an awful pretty girl, when you try. But let's face facts. You're no Marty."

Mama had a point. My little sister draws men like flies. Usually, I just draw the flies.

Mama put her hand over mine on the stick shift and patted. "I feel guilty, Mace. If I hadn't dragged you to church, you wouldn't have had to put up with that awful man attacking you. Just disgusting, that's what he is. And how about those DVDs? It's not right for a pastor to be so intent on selling himself."

I turned on the radio. Another weather report. Still hot.

"Maybe he wants to be a celebrity, like everybody else in America," I said. "And he didn't really attack me, Mama. Honest. It was no big deal. We'll tell my sisters, and it'll give us something to laugh about. Lord knows we haven't had too many laughs these last few days."

"I like that idea, Mace." Another pat to my hand. "Now, I've already put you out more than enough this morning. Why don't you let me out of the car, up there at the corner? Right there by the pawn shop and your cousin Henry's law office. I can walk the rest of the way to the beauty shop."

I glanced down at her sandals with their three-inch heels. My feet felt sore just looking at them.

"That's four blocks, at least. You are not walking to work in those shoes, Mama."

"It's okay. I don't want to put you out."

I rolled my eyes at her. "Mama, asking me to drive a hundred and seventy-four miles, round-trip, to the airport in West Palm Beach to pick up a relative I barely know is 'putting me out.' Dropping you off at Hair Today on my way to work is not. Still, I don't know why you insist on wearing heels. It's not like people don't already know you're short."

"Easy for you to say, Miss Five-Foot-Ten." She put her foot up on the dashboard to admire her lemon-hued shoe. "These *are* ridiculously uncomfortable. But haven't you ever had a shoe that you loved just for the way it looks, Mace?"

I ran mentally through my footwear inventory: leather ropers for riding, waterproof boots for work, sneakers or loafers for any other occasion.

"Nope. Can't say that I have." We passed Pete's Pawn, with its roadkill armadillo sign. "Now, are we agreed that it's not too much trouble for me to drive you what's now three remaining blocks to work?"

She straightened herself in the seat; her hair barely grazed the headrest. "I'm just trying to be considerate, Mace. You don't need to get snippy."

"I could use some of that consideration the next time Cousin Whatever-her-name-is flies in to visit, and you volunteer me to pick her up at the airport."

She crossed her arms over her chest and stared out the windshield.

All of a sudden she reached out, turned down the radio, and yelled, "Stop! Stop right there, Mace. Stop the car!"

"Mama, I can't stop. I'm doing forty miles an hour. I've got cars in front of me and cars in back of me."

No wonder she had that fender-bender that started everything at the Dairy Queen.

"Okay, slow down, then. That next street there, with the used car for sale on the corner? That's Emma Jean's street. I remember from one time Sally and I gave her a ride from bingo."

As we approached, I read the street sign out loud: "Lofton Road."

"That's it, Mace." She leaned forward, peering out the windshield. "Let's drive by to see if she's okay."

I downshifted to take the corner.

"I'm worried about her, Mace. She sure didn't seem right when she was swinging that tire iron at church."

Who would?

"There it is, Mace. The blue one. About half way down, on the left."

I slowed, and turned into Emma Jean's driveway. Her cat-shaped mailbox was painted in Siamese colors. The cat's black-tipped tail was the flag, which was flipped up straight.

I continued up the drive, noting a gaggle of yard gnomes. The rose bushes needed attention. Only the most dedicated gardeners can grow roses in the Florida heat and mucky soil around Lake Okeechobee. Judging from the mold-spotted leaves and sparse blooms, Emma Jean lacked the necessary dedication.

There was no car in the open, metal-roofed carport. I pulled in and parked. Mama and I got out.

The sun had faded the house's blue paint almost gray. The window curtains were drawn. Her screen door was shut, as was the solid wooden door behind that. Pink and white impatiens wilted in a pot on her porch. Mama leaned over to feel the soil. Shaking her head, she picked up a watering can and poured the contents on the flowers.

I knocked at the door. No answer. I pounded.

"Emma Jean? Are you there, darlin'?" Mama called at the window.

"Well, we know she was here fairly recently," I said. "If that tail on her mailbox was up yesterday when the mail carrier came, he would've taken Emma Jean's outgoing letters and flipped it back down."

Mama glanced out to the cat-shaped mailbox. "You know, I didn't even think about that. There's a reason you were top in your class at college, Mace."

I opened the screen door and tried the knob on the door inside. Locked.

A Siamese cat, live, not the mailbox one, minced its way up the porch steps. It sniffed at Mama's lemon-colored sandal, and then made a beeline to me. I'm an animal lover, but I've never been able to warm up to felines. And don't the cats always know that? In a crowded room, they'll bypass a dozen cat-lovers; ignore every outstretched hand; fail to recognize a chorus of "Here, kitty-kitty's." Then they'll decide to make friends with me.

The cat entangled itself around my ankles, rubbing against my slacks. I lifted my boot to gently push it away. Meowing, the critter stared up with big blue eyes.

"I'll be sneezing in about two seconds, Mama." Did I mention I'm also allergic? "I'm going around to check the back."

The cat leapt off the porch and followed.

I looked in a big kitchen window, where the curtains were tied back. Dirty dishes sat in the sink; an afternoon *Himmarshee Times* was closed on the table. It had to have been there at least a day, since it was still too early for today's delivery. The silent house looked empty, but undisturbed, like Emma Jean just ran out to do an errand.

Turning from the window, I nearly stumbled over my new best friend. The cat looked up as if to say, "Careful, Clumsy."

I scanned the backyard.

"Hey, what kind of car does Emma Jean drive?" I yelled around to the side garden, where Mama was pinching sooty leaves off the rose bushes.

"It's a little one," she shouted back. "Something foreign, like a Toyota or a Honda. Why?"

"Because there's a pickup parked back here, next to her shed. It's white, and it looks old."

I stepped closer. The bed was rusted. It was empty, except for three crushed beer cans. I looked through the driver's window. There wasn't anything personal inside. Just a blue bench seat, upholstered in plastic with the stuffing showing through. Kneeling on the grass, I ran my hand over well-worn rubber tread.

"What are you doing down there, Mace?" Mama joined me, stepping as delicately as the cat across grass still wet with dew. Beads of water clung to the reinforced toe of her knee-high stocking.

"Nothing, really." I trailed my fingers again over the tread before I stood and brushed off my pants. "I was just noticing how big the tires are on this old truck."

TWENTY-SIX

Bump-bump-bump-bump-bump-bump.

My tires thumped over the wooden bridge at Himmarshee Park. No matter how bad the day, or how much work waits, driving over the little bridge always gives me a boost. Below, dark water swirled. Above, sunlight slanted through the feathery branches of cypress trees. I inhaled, breathing in the woodsy, organic aroma of the swamp.

Newcomers crinkle their noses and complain of the rotten-egg smell. It comes about as bacteria break down dead plants and animals in the water. That allows them to be consumed by other creatures; which in turn are eaten by larger critters. And so it goes.

To me, the muck and mud of the swamp smells like life itself.

I love the outdoors, but even I'll admit there are better spots to be in the summer. The nearest coastal breeze is an hour east. If heat stroke doesn't get you, the mosquitoes will. And park in the full sun, and your car seat will reward you with third-degree burns upon your return. Not surprisingly, our parking lot was nearly empty.

I pulled into the shade of a clump of Sabal palms. Grabbing my purse and two plastic bags full of Ollie's chickens, I headed in to work.

The park's office is built of cypress, with tall windows and a wrap-around porch. The designer did a good job of making the structure look like it grew up in the woods. But to me, being stuck for too long inside any kind of building anywhere still feels like a trap.

Inside, a phone was affixed to my boss' ear. Rhonda drummed the pink-polished fingers of her free hand on the arm of her chair. When she saw me in the doorway, she flexed her hand into a yak-yak-yak sign next to the phone cradled on her shoulder.

"Yes, Ma'am. I will tell Mace you called." Rhonda's fingers hovered over the phone, ready to hang up. She leaned back again, listening. "No, as I mentioned to you, she's had a bit of family difficulty in recent days." She paused. "No, Ma'am, I don't know what it's like to have a panther stalking the pretty red birds that come to your bird feeder."

The New Jerseyite! I signaled frantically, pointing at my chest and shaking my head no, no, no. The last thing I needed was her tale of woe about what I suspected was a neighbor's fat cat. If it was a panther, it'd be after bigger prey, like her obnoxious poodle.

I was tuckered out, mentally. All I wanted was some peace and quiet to try to make sense of recent events: The come-on by the DVD-peddling pastor. The truck at Emma Jean's. The possible connection—beyond cigars—between Martinez and Big Sal.

I went back outside to the storage room to dump Ollie's food in the freezer. Rhonda was just hanging up when I returned.

"You owe me." She rubbed at a phone-related crick in her neck. "You owe me big."

She stood up to stretch. Not many women are as tall as me, but Rhonda had an inch and a half on me. Nearly six feet, she should be wearing designer clothes instead of government-uniform green. She's as beautiful as any model, and at least three times as smart.

"I know I owe you, Rhonda. I'm taking you to dinner at the Speckled Perch when all of this is over."

She sat back down, a smile spreading from her mouth all the way up to her angled cheekbones. The Perch is famous for its fried hush puppies. Blessed with the metabolism of a marathon runner, Rhonda devours the round corn-meal morsels by the dozen.

"I'll handle *all* your unpleasant details for dinner at the Perch, Mace."

"Believe me, boss, you don't want that burden right now."

I sat at my desk and attacked some paperwork, separating letters and messages into *Soon*, *Later*, and *Never* piles. A call from a retirement home in Highlands County went into *Soon*. Sometimes, I'll take an orphaned possum and a few snakes and give a talk for the old people. They get nearly as big a kick as the kids do out of seeing the animals. A request to speak about wildlife at the country club, not exactly my natural audience, I filed in *Later*. An invitation to attend a fashion-show? Mama must have gotten me on that mailing list. *Never*.

When I'd cleared enough paper to see some of the daily squares on my desk calendar, I stood up and stretched. I'd been at it for fifty-five minutes. That was long enough. I needed to breathe some outside air.

"I'm gonna take a look around the park, then hit the vending machine. Want anything?"

Rhonda looked up from a towering pile of permit cards and requisition forms. If that was management, she could have it.

"No, thanks. Take your time. I can tell from the way you've been jiggling your leg that you're itching to get outside. Say hi to your animals for me."

"Will do."

"And, Mace?" Rhonda's shift to her supervisor tone stopped me with my hand on the doorknob. "If you see any visitors, please say hi to them, too. It wouldn't hurt you to be a little friendlier to the park's humans."

Some guy had complained to Rhonda that I was rude to his girlfriend. She was whining about how the brush and the bugs on the nature walk had eaten up her legs. All I said was it was plain stupid to come to the woods in short-shorts and high-heeled sandals, so what did she expect?

"Got it, Rhonda." I pulled open the door. "I promise not to use the S-word, even when people *are* stupid."

Outside, I headed straight for the far corner of the park, where I keep the injured and unwanted animals. I could see Ollie on a sloped bank. He was sunbathing, with his body half in and half out of the water. I leaned over the concrete wall that encloses his pond.

"Hey, buddy," I called down to the gator. "How's it hangin'?"

I talk to the animals. A lot. Maddie says it's a clear sign I need more friends.

"Listen, I just put a dozen plump hens in your freezer. You're going to be dining fine."

Ollie blinked his good eye.

With a brain a little bigger than a lima bean, he's not much for conversation. I started to push myself away from the wall, when I heard a distant rustle in the brush behind me. I've spent a lifetime in the woods, and rarely been afraid. But something about that movement didn't sound natural. A wild hog will crash through the undergrowth, not caring who all's around. A deer will pass by, as quiet as a sigh. But the movement I heard sounded different: Sneaky. Stealthy. Big.

Maybe the New Jersey woman was right about that rogue panther.

I turned slowly, straining to hear the sound again so I could try to place it. The woods grow all around the animal area, close enough for the tallest hardwood trees to throw shadows across half of Ollie's pond. A mockingbird sang. Dragonflies hummed. Whatever else was out there was silent now. I turned back to the gator.

"You didn't hear anything, did you, buddy?" My voice sounded unnaturally loud and hearty, like I was trying to sell something.

Ollie wasn't buying. He was so still, he might have been an alligator-hide duffel bag with a head. But he can move plenty fast when he's motivated.

I peered into the dark shade of the woods. Laurel oaks lifted their branches. Air plants nestled in the crooks of the trees. All of it looked ordinary. Yet, I sensed unseen eyes watching me. A clammy rivulet of sweat worked its way past my waistband, rolling down the gully of my lower back.

Then, I heard the rustle again, nearer now. Something was moving toward me through the trees. I backed up, hard against the concrete of Ollie's wall.

The rustle got louder. Moving faster. Coming closer.

My heart pounded. Every nerve cell screamed, "Run!" but I had nowhere to go.

Whatever was in those woods was in front of me. Ollie's pond was behind. And I was frozen in between, as motionless as a rabbit in the moment before its predator strikes.

TWENTY-SEVEN

LOUD, ANGRY VOICES SUDDENLY rang out from my left.

"And I say it's this way!"

"Is not!"

I turned from the woods. A sunburned man with a camera and a woman in a Hawaiian-print shorts-set were arguing at a fork in the trail. The debate: which path to follow for the parking lot.

I'd never been so happy to see two human visitors. My slamming heart slowed. My lungs clocked back in on the job. I gulped in a big, shuddery breath.

For the first time, the woods had seemed like a threat, not a comfort. I was afraid. That must be how my sister Marty feels all the time, I thought. I didn't care for it much.

The rustling in the woods was fainter now, moving harmlessly away. Scanning the shadows, I saw nothing but trees and palmetto scrub. Feeling somewhat foolish, I hurried into the bright sun of the clearing.

"Hey, there! How you folks doin'?" I called to the tourists, as friendly as a Wal-Mart greeter. "Parking's to the right. But why don't y'all have a look at the alligator first? Ever seen one up close?"

The woman started tugging on her husband's Hawaiian shirt, dragging him at a run toward Ollie's pond. "Oh, Hal! An alligator! Get the camera ready, honey!"

I joined the visitors at the concrete wall. I could smell coconut-scented suntan cream.

"Where's Bobby, Hal? He really should be here to see this," the woman said.

"The last I saw, he was stalking off through the forest to get his Nintendo game out of the car." Hal looked at me and shrugged. "Kids. What're you going to do?"

Judging by the size of his dad, whose flowered shirt could have been the tablecloth for a party of six, Bobby could be big enough to make the sounds I'd heard in the woods.

I asked, "Would your son normally stay on the nature path?" We'd groomed it, clearing away brush, after the woman in the tiny shorts complained her legs got scratched.

"He's thirteen. What do you think?" Hal's voice had an aggressive edge. "Bobby's not so good with rules."

He held up his camera. "I'd love to get my wife in the picture, too. Is there any way Ev can climb down and get close to the alligator?"

Rhonda's warning about the S-word ran through my mind.

"I don't think that's a good idea," I said evenly. "Ollie hasn't been fed today."

"Oh, that's something we could do, Hal!" Ev took an excited little hop up and down. "Alligators are supposed to love marshmallows. A man at the RV camp where we're staying says one in the canal will climb right onto shore. The alligator opens his mouth, and the man just tosses in the marshmallows, one after the other."

No S-word. No S-word. No S-word.

"I hope your RV neighbor's not too attached to his arm," I said. "A couple of years ago, fishermen in Lakeland found the body of a man who'd been missing for a while. A gator got 'em. In the same lake, trappers killed a three-hundred-pounder. All the residents had been feeding him. That's illegal, by the way. They opened the gator up, and there was the poor fisherman's forearm. It was still intact, in the alligator's stomach."

Ev ran a hand down her own arm, glancing nervously over the wall at Ollie.

"Alligators are wild, unpredictable creatures." I could hear the annoyance seeping into my voice, but I plowed ahead. "You have to realize, they're dangerous. They're not costumed characters at Walt Disney World, ready to pose for tourist pictures."

"We get it, we get it." Hal stuck out his chest. "We're not stupid. You don't need to take that high-and-mighty tone with us. You don't have to be rude."

Uh-oh.

"Sorry." I backpedaled. "I didn't mean to sound nasty." I flashed them a smile that would make Rhonda proud. "It's just that people who feed alligators cause a lot of problems, both for the people and the gators. They're naturally skittish of humans. But if someone feeds them, they learn to associate people with food." We all looked down at the gator in the pool. "Missing one eye and part of a foot hasn't done much to slow Ollie down. And it hasn't done a thing to diminish the power of his jaws and tail. He's here because he got a little too close for comfort on the eighteenth hole at the new Kissim-mee Links country club."

Hal let out a low whistle. "That's a hell of a water hazard."

"Did he kill someone?" the woman asked.

"Not yet."

I recited the facts I knew by heart from my lectures to the kids: Biting strength more fearsome than a lion's; eighty razor teeth; a tail that can break a man's—or a woman's—leg.

Then I agreed to take a picture of the two of them leaning against the wall. I climbed onto a step stool I dragged over from the shed. With that and my height, I could angle downward to get Ollie in the background and the stupid couple in the foreground. I took four or five shots from different angles. The visitors left with all their limbs. Everybody was happy.

Being friendly is hard work.

Giving my little talk about alligators had just about erased the uneasiness I'd felt at the noise in the woods. But with the visitors gone, a twinge of fear came back. What was it moving toward me, pinning me between the woods and Ollie's wall? Was it just the couple's son, stomping around in a teenage sulk? Or was it some-thing more sinister?

I decided to try to find the Nintendo-addicted Bobby, and ask him some questions. Normally, I'd cut through the woods, reduc-ing by half a fifteen-minute walk to the parking lot. Today, I stayed in the clearing as long as possible. Then, I chose a wide, well-marked path.

The parking lot held just three vehicles in addition to the VW and Rhonda's car. One was a burgundy Mercury, with Pennsylvania plates. A bumper sticker on the back said: *My son can beat up your honor student.*

I pegged that one as Hal's car.

Another was a rental, with a Florida map and a bird-watching brochure sitting open on the front seat.

The third, a white pickup, was the only one parked in the shade. Squinting through the heat rising from the lot, I thought I recognized the black cowboy hat on the man in the driver's seat. I quickly closed the distance to the truck.

Engrossed in a cell phone call, the driver was alone in the truck. He didn't notice as I approached from the rear. The driver-side door was open.

"I told you I'm good for those cattle, Pete." I could hear his half of the conversation. "How long have we known each other? All I'm asking for is a little more time."

It sounded like Jeb Ennis' business troubles had taken a turn for the worse.

Silently, he listened to whatever Pete was saying on the other end of the line. Then he shook his head and looked like he was ready to start arguing, until he caught me from the corner of his eye. "Listen, I'm going to have to call you back, Pete." He paused. "If I say I'll do it, I'll do it. I've got someone here just now."

He cut off the call and slipped the phone into his top pocket. His face was shiny with sweat.

"Kind of warm to be out here sitting in your truck, isn't it?"

"Hey, Mace. I just pulled up a little while ago. I was headed to the office to see you when my phone rang." He swung his long legs out the door and stood on the asphalt lot. When he turned and leaned in the back to grab something from the truck's cab, I saw his shirt was soaking wet and stuck to his back.

"You look like you've just chased a coonhound through the woods, Jeb."

When he straightened, he was holding a bouquet of daisies.

"Yeah, I'm sweatin' buckets." He looked embarrassed. "The AC's out in my truck. Never happens in December, does it? It feels like a sauna in there."

He held out the flowers. "Anyway, these are for you. I figured I owed you an apology for being so rude at the diner. Your mama must have heard an earful after I left."

As I took the flowers, our hands brushed. His fingers were strong, work-callused. I fought myself over the little shiver of desire I felt.

"Daisies are your favorite, right? I remembered."

I couldn't even think of the last time a man had given me flowers. I smiled my thanks. That didn't mean I wasn't still suspicious.

"So, you just drove up." I took a couple of steps to the front of the truck and put my hand on the hood. The metal was as hot as Hades. The engine still ticked. "I had an interesting experience a little earlier this morning."

He raised his brows in a question.

"I felt like something was watching me from the woods by the alligator pond. Then, I heard something big coming at me through the brush."

Jeb's face lit up. "Was it a black bear? Remember that time we spotted that cute little cub over in Highlands County? And then its mama came on the scene, and she didn't look near as cute."

I laughed. "I remember you were just as scared as me, and I almost peed my pants."

He looked at me, and the golden flecks in his eyes shone. "We had some good times in those days, didn't we, Mace?"

"Some real good times," I agreed. "And a few bad."

He took off his hat and shifted his eyes to the ground. He ran a hand through his hair, which curled in sweaty clumps. Then he looked up at me again. "Do you think we could talk somewhere, Mace?"

"We can. But first I have to ask you something. You wouldn't have had any reason to be running around in the woods out here this morning, would you?"

He cocked his head "Mace, it's hotter than a pepper patch. The mosquitoes are as big as B-52 bombers. I can think of about twenty places off the top of my head that I'd rather be than in the woods. And that would include sitting in the chair at my dentist's office. I told you, I just got here. The only reason I came at all is to apologize to you."

He slapped at his neck, then flicked a dead mosquito from his palm.

I glanced into the trees surrounding the parking lot. Nothing but the insects stirred.

"It's just that I had a ..."

My voice trailed off as I tried to figure out how, without sounding weak or crazy, to explain what I'd had. The sense of threat. The paralyzing fear. After all, it was just some rustling in the brush.

"You know what, Jeb? It's no big deal." I held up the flowers. "Let's head to the office, where I can get these in some water. We can sit out on a bench in the breezeway. At least there's shade, and ceiling fans to keep us cool."

He put his hat back on. "Give me a minute to throw something over the feed I've got in the truck. I don't want it to get wet if it rains."

I stepped aside to let him get to the truck's bed. I took the opportunity to admire the view as Jeb leaned over to secure a tarp. His sweaty shirt was tucked tautly into his narrow waist. The W's on the back pockets of his Wrangler jeans lay just right. My eyes traveled all the way from his well-shaped rear, down his legs, to the heels of his dusty cowboy boots.

That's when I noticed something small clinging to the bottom of his pants leg. In the back, where it'd be hard to see, a burr from the woods' brushy undergrowth was stuck to the fabric of Jeb's boot-cut jeans.

TWENTY-EIGHT

"WHAT THE HELL IS this?" I leaned over and plucked the burr from Jeb's pant leg. Pinching it between my thumb and forefinger, I thrust it inches from his face.

"How should I know, Mace? You know plants a lot better than I do. Why don't you look it up in a plant book?"

"It's a beggar's tick, Jeb. And I don't mean, What is it? I mean, How in the hell did it come to be hitching a ride on your Wranglers?"

He cocked his boot up to examine the back of his pant leg. Then he repeated it with the other leg. "I thought I got all of those off before I headed over here to see you. I worked this morning, but I did clean up. Not that you'd be able to tell it from the stink of me, after I drove all the way from Wauchula in my sweat box of a truck."

I tucked the beggar's tick into the pocket of my work pants. You never know what you might need as evidence.

"What are you so freaked out about anyway? Is that from some nasty plant you don't want taking hold here at Himmarshee Park?"

His eyebrows raised in a question. And then, as he realized what I was implying, they V-ed down to a frown. "You're not serious, Mace."

"As serious as a heart attack." I took a step back, my hands on my hips. "Which is what I almost had this morning, when I was convinced something in those woods was stalking me. Now I find a burr from the brush on a man who claimed he'd rather be anywhere else than out stomping through some swampy woods."

"You've lost your mind." He inched away, like he was afraid to catch crazy from me. "Your mama getting arrested for murder has sent you clear round the bend." Staring at me, he shook his head. "Do you think Himmarshee Park is the only place in Florida with brush?"

He waited for an answer. I didn't give him one, staring off into the trees.

"Well, it's not." Jeb answered his own question. "I was tearing through it on my own property early this morning when a calf got tangled up. He ran off, trailing some barbed wire into the woods."

I thought about that for a moment. It seemed logical. I was beginning to feel stupid.

"Are you gonna suspect me of everything, just because I made one of the biggest mistakes of my life when we were kids? How many times can I say I'm sorry I lied to you? I'm sorry I cheated on you. I was young and stupid. I didn't know how to handle the attention from the girls who hang around the rodeo."

He put a hand on my wrist. My skin felt hot where he touched it, and it wasn't just the outside temperature.

"Look at me, Mace."

I slowly shifted my gaze from the tree line to his face. He was staring into my eyes. His hand still burned a palm print around my wrist.

"Sorry," I mumbled.

Jeb cupped his other hand to his ear. "Can you speak up a little? I didn't quite hear that."

"I said I'm sorry." I shook off his hand. "This case has got me as skittish as a colt in a pasture full of snakes."

I looked down to where he'd held my wrist. I was surprised to see no outward sign of how his touch had affected me. But I did notice the daisies were starting to wilt. "Why don't we go on in and get out of this oven?" I said.

I led the way across the lot and onto a wood-chip trail. We don't waste much in Himmarshee. If a hurricane or lightning storm takes down a tree, workers with chain saws cut it up, feed it into a chipper, and truck in the chips for pathways. Jeb and I turned at the fork, heading away from Ollie's pool and toward the office.

"Look at that," I whispered. As we rounded a bend near Himmarshee Creek, a great blue heron startled into flight. The woods were so quiet; we heard his big wings beating the heavy air.

At the office, I went inside to put the daisies into water. Jeb stopped to buy sodas at the vending machine. He didn't need to ask what I liked. A Coke for me; an orange drink for him. He was just settling onto a bench in the shady breezeway when I returned to join him.

"When did you find out about Mama getting tossed in jail?" I asked, as I popped the top on my can of Coke.

"I already knew that night at the diner, Mace. One of my hands at the ranch dates a gal who works at the Dairy Queen. I didn't let on when you told me. I didn't want to embarrass you. And I didn't think it'd be too nice to greet your mama after ten years by saying, 'Glad to hear you're out of the slammer, Ma'am.' "

He took a long slug from his soda. Staring at the spot where his lips met the can, I felt memory waves wash over me. Lying on three folded blankets in the bed of his truck, watching shooting stars. The feel of his lips on mine, soft yet insistent. My first time, and how Jeb kissed away the tears that came from the realization that I wasn't a virgin anymore.

"Can I ask you something, Mace?"

I nodded, hoping it wouldn't be "What are you thinking?"

Jeb said, "They let your mama out of jail. But you said the case is making you nuts. Why are you still involved?"

Good question, I thought.

"Well, for one thing, someone has made it pretty clear they don't want us looking into Jim Albert's murder." I told him about Mama's stuffed dog, and about my close call in the canal.

"That sounds pretty dangerous. Yet you're still fooling around, trying to figure out whodunnit."

"You've known me a long time, Jeb. Tell me I can't do something, and that's exactly what I want to do. Besides, Mama's name hasn't been cleared." I outlined how her fellow church-goers had stared and whispered. Martinez might be busy right now, I said, trying to build a stronger case against her. I didn't mention I'd tried to steer the detective off my mother by telling him about Jeb's troubles with Jim Albert.

I watched a drop of condensation roll off my can and onto my thigh.

"I also want to know how Mama's boyfriend figures in, Jeb. What if he's responsible? Mama could be in danger. I'd toss myself into Ollie the alligator's pond if something happens to her, and I could have prevented it."

"It just seems like you're putting a lot of pressure on yourself, Mace."

"I'm not alone. Both my sisters are involved. We're all trying to find the real murderer. You don't think Maddie would let anything happen to me, do you?"

He smiled, and put an arm around my shoulder to draw me close. "Your sister Maddie's like a mama gator with a clutch of babies. She smacked her tail, showed her teeth, and hissed at me. And all I did was invite you to a barbecue."

I thought of a gator's head, with huge gaping jaws, on my sister's body. It was such a fitting image that I laughed out loud.

"Now, that's what I like to hear, Mace. I always did love your laugh." He traced a finger around my lips. "It's not a girly giggle; you bring it up from deep down in your belly." He touched my belt buckle. "I like that in a woman."

"Whatever happened to Cindy?" I said, shifting away from him.

I'd heard Jeb was involved with a girl we both knew in high school, a cheerleader and homecoming queen. I was pleased when a classmate told me she'd gained forty pounds since senior year.

Jeb took off his hat and began working the brim with his fingers. He studied the pointed toes of his boots. The way he was acting, I

191

hoped he wasn't going to say she was dead. I'd feel awful after the way I crowed about her putting on weight.

"I screwed up, Mace," he finally said. "Cindy left me."

"Were you cheating on her?" I figured we two gals could form a support group for women Jeb had done wrong.

"No. I learned my lesson about that a long time ago, when I lost you."

I looked at him sideways, not sure whether to believe him. "Well, what happened?"

"Remember how I told you at the diner that I'd borrowed money from Jim Albert?"

I nodded.

"I couldn't pay it back fast enough to suit him. That bastard sent men out to the ranch, and they busted the place up. Cindy was there, alone. They didn't hurt her. But she was terrified. It happened again, and this time they knocked me around. She packed her clothes and left the next day. Said she couldn't live like that, wondering what they'd do the next time they came."

Jeb looked like a little boy who'd just seen his dog hit by a truck. My heart went out to him. Then I realized owing money *and* losing his girlfriend gave Jeb a doubly good reason to want Jim Albert dead.

Leaning toward him, I brushed the hair out of his eyes. I wasn't exactly faking concern. But I did have an ulterior motive. I wanted to see if I could lead Jeb to reveal anything more. I edged a bit closer again, thigh to thigh. His sweat had dried in the breeze from the fans. But he still had the salty, hard-work smell of a man who handles horses and cattle. I breathed it in, remembering the thrill I'd always gotten from watching him ride and rope.

"Do you still have that horse you were breaking when we were going together, Jeb? What was his name? The big bay, with the white blaze?"

"Cheyenne." The smile returned to Jeb's lips. He draped an arm casually around my shoulders. "He's getting old, but he's still going strong. Why don't you come out and ride with me, Mace? I'd love to see you on a horse again. I'll never forget the sight of you barrel-racing in that white outfit with the fringe, your black hair flying from underneath a white hat. You were a sight. Just beautiful. Still are."

I looked at him, and the plan to work him for information flew out of my brain. The flecks in his eyes were liquid gold. He leaned down a bit to kiss me. I lifted my chin. I couldn't wait to feel again the touch of his lips; the heat of his body.

I closed my eyes...

And heard a harsh cough. Someone was standing not two feet away, interrupting our moment with an infernal hacking. They were quite insistent. Loud, too. How rude, I thought.

Reluctantly, I put a hand on Jeb's chest and pushed away. I opened my eyes.

There stood Detective Martinez, clearing his throat and staring cannon-ball-sized holes into Jeb and me.

TWENTY-NINE

A DOOR SLAMMED. I heard the *clomp-clomp* of school-principal pumps on the wooden deck between the office and the breezeway.

"What do you mean they're Mace's daisies, Rhonda?" A familiar voice boomed, scaring any wildlife within a hundred yards. "Who brought my sister daisies?"

Martinez's respiratory distress had already spooked me. Now, Maddie's approach finished the job. I scooted away, like Jeb's thigh was the campfire and mine was the marshmallow. I moved too slowly: The sight of me cozying up to my former boyfriend stopped my sister so fast that Rhonda ran into her from the rear. *Clomp-clomp-smack.* Maddie looked from the two of us to Martinez, the eyeglasses on her chain bouncing on her generous bust.

"I let you out of my sight for one day, Mace." Maddie shook her head. "And you go and get yourself into all kind of mess with Jeb Ennis."

Rhonda looked uncomfortable. An only child, she was unused to the goings on of dysfunctional siblings. "I'll just excuse myself."

She edged backwards toward the office. "I've got a mountain of paperwork."

It was the only time I ever envied my boss her forms in triplicate.

Jeb stood up. "Howdy, Maddie. Nice to see you, too." He put his hat back on and brushed his hands along the front of his denim-covered thighs. "Even though I'm enjoying this little reunion, it's time for me to hit the trail."

"Hold your horses, Cowboy." Martinez's voice was a command.

Jeb looked at him, a question on his face. Martinez took his time with the answer. He extracted a cigar from his top pocket. He sniffed it, then held it up like it was a piece of art he was inspecting for a museum. Finally, he put back the cigar and stared at Jeb.

"You're not saddling up just yet, *hombre*."

Maddie just about licked her chops in anticipation. "That's Carlos Martinez. He's a police detective," she said to Jeb. "Carlos, it appears you already know who Jeb Ennis is."

The two men looked at each other, measuring. Long and lean, Jeb might've had a few inches in height. But the burly detective outweighed the cowboy by at least twenty-five pounds. They stared across the breezeway like two bucks do, just before they crash antlers to see who gets to mate with the female deer. I couldn't help but wonder if the doe ever gets her say.

"Could you ladies find something else to do for a little while?" Martinez spoke to us, but he never took his eyes off Jeb. "I have a few questions for Mr. Ennis. I was going to visit Ms. Bauer here, to see if she could put me in touch. But it looks like I've been saved the trouble of traveling all the way to Wah … Wash … Watch …"

"Wauchula." Maddie helped him out. "I believe Jeb's cattle ranch is over in Wauchula, Carlos."

"Thanks, Maddie. But your sister here already filled me in with quite a bit of information on her good friend, Mr. Ennis."

Jeb shot me a look. I stared at the ground, too late to avoid seeing the betrayal in his eyes.

"By the way, I'm not sure what you've got going on here, Ms. Bauer, but you need to stay out of this investigation. I've told you it's dangerous. Leave police work to professionals."

The superior tone in his voice propelled me to my feet.

"If I did that, Mama would still be in jail, where the *professional* tossed her. I'd say the *professional* has made a few missteps. Wouldn't you agree, Maddie?"

My sister examined the links on her eyeglass chain.

"Maddie?"

"Well, Mace, I'm thinking maybe we should let bygones be bygones."

My own sister, a Judas!

"It *is* dangerous. During the course of a murder investigation, there's no telling what kind of people you might come in contact with." Maddie stared straight at Jeb.

"You better not be meaning what I think you're meaning, you old rattlesnake." Jeb's voice was low and menacing.

"All right, all right." Martinez held up a hand. "Maddie, would you mind taking your sister for a walk? I think everyone needs to cool down a little. I'm just trying to get to the bottom of things. I'm hoping Mr. Ennis can help me do that."

"Absolutely." Maddie sounded just like the teacher's pet she always was. "Mace, why don't you take me to your compound, and show me the animals? Marty told me Ollie's getting as round as a barrel on all those chickens you're feeding him."

Maddie's false enthusiasm didn't fool me. She likes animals about as much as she likes seventh graders, which is to say not much. She touched my elbow. I shook off her hand. I might go, but I wouldn't do it graciously.

"Fine." I could hear the pout in my voice. It sounded ridiculous. But something about my bossy big sister makes me act like a six-year-old.

As Maddie and I left, I glanced over my shoulder. I wouldn't have wanted to wander into the open space between Jeb and Martinez. It would be like stepping into standing water charged by a downed power line.

———

Lifting a forty-pound bag of puppy chow to my shoulder, I edged past my sister in the tight quarters of the animal compound's storage room.

"Good Lord, Mace. You're as strong as a man!"

"You make that sound like a bad thing, Maddie."

I rested the feed sack on the slatted wood floor. Any number of animals, including skunks and raccoons, can eat moistened dog or cat food. At feeding time, I supplement the dry chow with everything from fish and eggs to fruit and yogurt, depending on the critter.

"Drag that garbage can over here, would you, Maddie?" I nodded toward a fifty-gallon pail against the far wall. "I need to fill it with this chow."

Maddie looked at the pail like I'd asked her to move a mountain.

"Go ahead, Maddie. It's empty. I wouldn't ask you to exert yourself. I know you're not used to lifting anything heavier than that paddle you use to scare the sixth graders."

I took a pocket knife from my work pants and sliced a hole into the top of the bag. A meaty, cereal smell wafted from the sack.

"You know corporal punishment is outlawed in the public schools." Maddie couldn't keep the note of regret from her voice. "The kids know it, too; even the sixth graders. I don't have a lot of tools in my threat kit anymore."

"I'm sure you manage, Maddie."

"Maybe so. Still and all, I haven't managed to scare you off that devil, Jeb Ennis."

I looked up from the sack. Maddie was wearing her serious face.

"You didn't fool me for an instant, Mace, jumping away on that bench. Your face was flushed. The blood was pulsing at that spot on your neck, the way it does when you're upset or excited."

I poured the feed into the plastic can without a word. The small chunks filling the bucket sounded like rain on a shingle roof.

"I'm not gonna deny it," I finally said. "I'm still attracted to the man. He was my first real boyfriend, you know."

"Oh, I remember. But you're looking at those days through rose glasses, Mace. Because I also remember you sobbing for hours on your bed the night you caught him cheating. I remember you couldn't choke down a thing but water for three days after."

My stomach lurched at the memory. Even the smell of food had made me want to throw up. Finally, on the third day, Maddie came into my bedroom with a bowl of mashed potatoes. She stretched out next to me on the bed, propping me up with an arm around my shoulders. Then she fed me spoonful after spoonful until I could eat no more. I still remember the texture of those potatoes on my tongue, mixed with some salt and a tiny bit of butter.

It sounds overly dramatic now. But at age nineteen, sick with a broken heart, my first indication I wanted to keep living was Maddie feeding me those mashed potatoes.

I emptied the rest of the bag into the pail and snapped the lid shut to keep out the rats.

"People can change, Maddie."

She wiped the dirt off a shelf, leaned against it, and folded her arms over her chest. "A tiger doesn't change its stripes, Mace. And a devil doesn't trade in his pitchfork and horns for a harp and angel's wings. That man is bad news. He was back then; he is now."

It wasn't a conversation I cared to continue.

"Do you want to see the animals?"

Maddie curled her lip.

Most of them are nocturnal anyway, so they were asleep. Not that Maddie minded.

"Not even Ollie?"

"Mace, I've seen enough of those overgrown lizards to last me a lifetime. Just because this one's got a name doesn't make him any different. I wouldn't mind a bit if they turned every alligator in Florida into a handbag." She brushed her hands together. "Let's just go back to the office where I can clean up. I'm coated in puppy chow dust."

Walking along the nature path, we heard a truck engine rumble from the parking lot. We got there just in time to see Jeb pulling out, hat on his head and a hard line to his mouth. His pickup tore over the wooden bridge. He must have been doing at least triple the park's posted speed limit of fifteen mph.

Maddie and I stood watching as he raced to the exit.

"There goes the devil, running off like a scalded hound." My sister's lips tightened with disapproval.

"He better be careful, or Martinez will cite him for speeding," I said, as Jeb's brake lights briefly flickered at a curve.

"A speeding ticket would be the least of your friend's troubles right now, Ms. Bauer."

I jumped at Martinez's voice, so close I could feel his breath on my neck. "You scared me." I aimed an accusing glance at him. "Do you always sneak up on people?"

"I would have warned you of my presence, but I didn't think you could hear me over the squealing tires." Martinez pulled a pen from his top pocket. He dug out his wallet and extracted a business card.

"I have a favor to ask of you." He rested the card on his billfold and scribbled on the back. "Please take my advice and stop trying to solve this murder."

He slipped the card into the pocket of my T-shirt, and his fingers lightly brushed against my breast. Inadvertent or intentional? I searched his eyes. Of course, they revealed no clues. I hoped my own eyes didn't show that I wanted him to touch me again.

He continued, "If you ignore my advice, as you've done so far, you'll likely find yourself in trouble. You can call me at any of those numbers. I'll do my best to rescue you, unless it's too late."

Rescue me? Smug bastard. The desire I'd felt for him fled.

"I can take care of myself. I don't need some man riding to my rescue ..."

He held up a hand to interrupt. I hate that.

"Excuse me. I'm running late, and I'm not in the mood for an argument. Just use the card, *por favor*. Please." He pulled his car keys from his pocket. "Maddie, could you talk some sense into your sister?"

"I'll do my best, Detective," Maddie called after him, the teacher's pet left in charge of a difficult student. "Take care, now."

As he left, I read the card. "What a jerk."

Maddie leaned over my shoulder. I held it up so she could see what Martinez had written:

More beaus who are murder suspects? If so, pls. call.

I thought of Jeb standing in the breezeway, looking hurt when he discovered I'd ratted him out to Martinez. I pondered on that for a while, feeling guilty, until a different mental picture came into view. It was Jeb, gunning his truck out of the park. Remembering now, I realized his windows had been rolled up tight.

And wasn't that odd, after how he'd complained his pickup was a hot box with no air conditioning?

THIRTY

HEADING HOME FROM WORK, I was thinking about a hot shower and a cold beer.

The day had been a scorcher, the kind of heat that makes you wonder what those early Florida pioneers had been drinking. I could just picture it: They struck out in energy-sucking temperatures, through swamps with sawgrass so sharp it'll draw blood. They continued on, through clouds of ravenous mosquitoes. They suffered heatstroke. They endured hurricanes. And through it all they said, "Hey, why don't we settle here? This looks like a nice spot."

It had to be something stronger than beer.

It was almost six-thirty, but the sun still blazed. It burned against my bare shoulders as I downshifted Pam's VW around a truck hauling hogs. That's a stench you don't want to trail too long, especially in a convertible with no top.

The old car shimmied a bit as I punched it, but it rose to the occasion.

I passed the sign for the Big Lake Dairy, and then the grand entranceway on Highway 98 for the Flying J ranch. Skeet Johnson, who owned the Flying J, had the delusion that he was J. R. Ewing and his place was like Southfork on old reruns of *Dallas*. In reality, he never got much past sinking the concrete pillars and attaching some fancy wrought-iron gates. Inside, he only had a hundred acres, a few mud holes, and about sixteen crossbred head. All hat and no cattle, as they say in Texas.

Cattle started me thinking about Jeb Ennis' visit to the park. A little sweet talk, a few soulful looks, and I'd been willing to take up almost where we'd left off all those years ago. Of course, that was before I watched him speed away from Himmarshee Park, looking cool as an ice cube in his supposedly sweltering truck.

I came to the little bridge over Taylor Creek, which meant home was only a mile or so away. I always look to the right for the sign that says *Turkey Buzzards on Bridge*. Is it a warning, or a notice to the tourists taking the back roads to Disney to get out their cameras?

As I looked today, my eye caught a glimmer of sun on metal in the high weeds that lead to Taylor Slough. I was nearly over the bridge before it registered that something didn't look right about that silvery shine.

I slowed on the other side, pulling off onto the shoulder. Backtracking on foot, I peered over the bridge's railing. From this angle, a dark-colored compact car was visible. Clambering down the incline I waded into the brush.

The car was a Toyota. There was no one inside, though the driver's door stood wide open. I pushed through mucky soil and fetterbush, grateful for my slacks and boots. With brush pricking at my arms, I wished I'd slipped into long sleeves before striking out into the swamp.

I looked around the car for someone who was hurt or lost. But the only sign was a long trail of flattened grass, corresponding to the path the car made off the road. At the rear, there was a Florida tag and a bumper sticker. *Beef: It's What's for Dinner.* Probably a local. You don't see many pro-vegan messages on bumpers in the state's cattle belt.

Back at the driver's side, the headlight button was pulled out. But if the lights had been on, the battery was now dead. Not even a gleam came from the headlights or the interior light. The keys were in the ignition, which was turned to the off position. I leaned in, careful not to touch anything. Something dangled from the keys in the shadow of the steering wheel.

It was a small plastic doll with pink fluorescent hair, just like the Troll family I'd seen on Emma Jean's desk.

———

Martinez answered on the first ring.

"It's Mace Bauer."

"That was fast." He spoke before I got out more than my name. "Don't tell me you're already dating someone else who might have killed Jim Albert."

I ignored that. "I'm out here along Highway 98. I think I've just found Emma Jean Valentine's car, abandoned in the swamp."

His voice was instantly serious. "Where are you?"

I filled him in, and agreed to wait until he arrived.

Sunset was still a good hour away, but you couldn't tell it by the bugs. Waving one hand around my ears, I searched with the other through the VW's front trunk. My fingers clasped a metal canister. Success! Bug spray is something no native Himmarsheean should ever be caught without. And my can was still in my waterlogged Jeep.

I sprayed my palms with repellent, then rubbed my neck, my ears and across my face. I donned a long-sleeved shirt from the trunk, smelling of spare tire and mildew. The mosquitoes marshaled their forces, seeking entry to an unprotected spot. I thought I heard a whine of frustration as they flew off in search of a less experienced opponent.

A swollen thundercloud darkened the horizon. I retrieved the tarp, just in case the skies opened. While I waited, I called my home answering machine. There were messages from Marty and Mama. I returned the calls, leaving my own messages on their machines. Just as I was wondering whether anyone actually speaks to anyone else anymore, I spotted Martinez's police-issue sedan approaching the bridge.

As soon as he got out of the car, he started dancing and slapping. I handed him the spray.

"DEET," he read off the side of the can. "Isn't that stuff toxic?"

"Only to the bugs. You need something strong here. Our mosquitoes will wipe the floor with their puny cousins from down in Miami. Coat your hands, then wipe it on. Don't get it in your eyes or mouth." I'd seen more than one newcomer with teary vision and a stinging tongue.

"I'm not an idiot." He sprayed, then handed back the can. "Where's the car?"

I looked down at his pressed dress slacks and shiny leather shoes. Not an idiot, huh?

"It's pretty wet down there," I said. "Don't you carry a pair of boots?"

"Don't you think I'd be wearing them if I did?"

"Just asking."

"What makes you think the car is Emma Jean's? Did you find a purse?" Martinez spoke as I led the way down the embankment and into the brush.

"I recognized her key chain. Mama told me she drives a dark green compact, which is what this is. Plus, my house is only about a mile from here."

I told him about her late-night phone call. "She never showed."

"Did she seem distraught?"

"Yes, but no more so than when she appeared waving a tire iron at church." I stepped around a mucky spot. "Watch that..."

"*Mierda!*" I don't understand Spanish, but that had the ring of a bad word. I turned to see him release his dress shoe with a sucking sound.

I itched to say I told you so. "I might have spotted the car this morning if I'd been paying more attention."

"What do you mean?"

"Well, I was distracted. Donnie Bailey called my cell to tell me about what they found when they checked out my Jeep. Or, more like what they didn't find."

"That's police information." I could hear the scowl in his voice. "Officer *Donnie* shouldn't share those kinds of details with a civilian."

"Even if it's the civilian's Jeep, and the civilian was the one who was run off the road? Get real, Detective. What do you think I'm gonna do with what Donnie told me? Run to the media? We're just a little town. But not even the *Himmarshee Times* would run a story that lame: *Local Woman Veers off Road; Big Vehicle Might Be Involved.*"

The only response was brush moving and Martinez breathing.

"Anyway, there's the car." I stopped and pointed ahead. "I walked around a bit, trying to make sure no one was out here hurt. But I didn't do a real search, and I didn't touch anything. I figured I'd better call you first."

Martinez had whipped out his phone. "That's the first smart thing I've seen you do." He studied the display panel as he scrolled, searching for a number. "You can go now. I radioed in earlier with your report. Now, I'll call in the tag number. We'll take over from here."

Right. The *professionals.* "All righty, then. Y'all take care." I injected a pleasant, polite tone into my voice.

Martinez stopped peering at the telephone and looked at me. "What the hell does that mean?"

"Y'all is the way we say 'you guys' in Himmarshee."

"That's not what I mean, and you know it. Why are you giving in so easily? Why haven't you insisted on combing the swamp? I thought you'd want to be the one to find Emma Jean, maybe carry her to safety on your back. *La heroína*, the heroine."

"Nah." I didn't tell him I had other plans. "But I hope you find her safe. She seems pretty strange to me, but she's a friend of Mama's. I hope nothing bad has happened to her."

He nodded, looking down at the phone again.

"I'll just leave you out here with the mosquitoes and the mud." I looked at his pant leg, with muck up to the shin. "You better get those slacks in water when you get home. That muck stinks like crap. And you ought to get yourself a good pair of boots, too."

"Thanks for the advice." He didn't sound grateful.

"No problem." I started back toward the road, and then turned around. "Detective?"

He looked at me, phone to his ear. I tossed him the bug repellent I'd stuck in my pocket. "You'll need to use some more of that. You'll sweat out here like an asphalt worker in August, and everything you sprayed on will drip off. Not to mention, it'll be dark soon. That's when these baby bugs out here call in their big brothers."

He caught the toss and rewarded me with an almost-warm smile. "Thanks, Mace."

I couldn't ignore the thrill I got when I heard him use my first name. No doubt about it: I had feelings for Detective Carlos Martinez, and that signaled trouble.

THIRTY-ONE

MEOW. MEOWWWW.

The cat was doing curlicues around my ankles as I climbed the stairs of Emma Jean's front porch. It slunk behind me; then in front. "Go on, kitty. Move." I gently nudged the cat's hindquarters with the toe of my boot.

It looked at me over its shoulder as if to say I had my nerve.

I knocked at the door. No response. It was a long shot, but I still hoped to find Emma Jean home, embarrassed at the fuss she created. I pictured her in a bathrobe—pink, to match the Calamine lotion dotted on the bug bites she got walking out of the swamp. Maybe she'd be snuggled in front of the TV, watching an old black-and-white movie about lost love. There'd be a pile of crumpled tissues beside her. I wanted her to be safe.

Martinez may have had a point. I like to save the day. What was the Spanish word he used? *Heroína.* Heroine.

The sun was setting, trailing a few long fingers of pink and yellow across a darkening sky. Enough light remained to see that

Emma Jean's place looked just as it had that morning, when Mama and I stopped by. Flowers still drooped; curtains were drawn. And, judging by the cat's insistent mewling, it hadn't eaten.

On the porch next to the flower pot sat a set of silver bowls, printed with cat silhouettes. One held water, but the food bowl was empty. I found a green plastic bin against the wall, with assorted cat food inside. I might feel helpless about Emma Jean, but at least I could take care of her cat. I grabbed one of the tins and popped the tab to open the lid.

At the *sssssssft* sound and the fishy smell, the cat increased its orbits around my ankles. I feared it might launch itself right off the porch. I didn't see a spoon, so I just dumped a bit of dry chow into the bowl, then scooped some wet food on top with my fingers. I wiped the salmon stink from my hand onto the front-door mat. Better there than on my slacks.

Suddenly, I heard a car engine slow on the street out front. Then came squeaks and rattles, as the vehicle jounced over Emma Jean's unpaved drive. I crouched behind the cat food bin for cover, watching between the slats of the porch railing. Headlights moved up and down, coming closer.

"Shhh," I whispered to the cat, which was ignoring me now that food filled its bowl. "None of that Siamese screeching, y'hear? As quiet as a mouse."

As the car drew near, I could see the outline of lights on the top. Then, the familiar blue-and-white markings of the Himmarshee Police Department. My breath whooshed out in relief. The cat lifted its head at me, then went right back to eating. Kind of like me, when I sit down to dinner.

The car rolled to a stop. The driver's door opened. In the glow of the dome light, I thought I recognized a military-style haircut and pumped upper body. I was just about to stand up and call out, but I hesitated. I can't really say why, except the events of the last few days had made me suspicious of everyone. I stayed put and kept watching from my little hiding spot.

Switching on his flashlight, the uniformed officer started for the backyard. I was glad I'd pulled the VW off to the side, behind the toolshed. I hadn't wanted to advertise that I was snooping around, indulging my fantasy of rescuing Emma Jean.

I crept off the porch and past the rose bushes, where Mama had pinched off dead blooms. Night was coming fast. But I still could see the old pickup as I rounded the corner of the house. The flashlight beam traveled over the truck: Across the front seat, into the space of the extended cab, then out the rear window. Like an oversized firefly, it flitted from rear to front and down to the ground. It lit on the right front tire, staying for a good while.

As I got closer, I could see him reflected in the beam. His head was bent to the tire. He ran a hand over the tread.

"Hey, Donnie." I spoke quietly, from about twenty feet away.

He jumped like the tire gave him a shock. His hand flew up, hovering just above the gun at his right hip.

I quickly called out, "It's just me, Mace Bauer. No weapon."

He dropped his hand to his side and rocked forward onto his knees. "You should know better than to sneak up on somebody who's armed, Mace. Mistakes can happen."

"I wasn't sneaking. I came here to see if I could find Emma Jean. Then I saw you down on the ground out here. I got curious about what you were up to."

"It's been all over the police radio about Emma Jean's abandoned car."

"So the Toyota is hers? I'm the one who found it, out near my house."

"It's hers, all right. I'm on overnight at the jail tonight. I thought I'd swing by here on my way in and see if anything looked unusual."

I thought I saw the slightest shift in his eyes. But I could have been mistaken. There wasn't much light.

"It seems like you'd go first to Emma Jean's door. Knock and see if she answers."

"I was gonna do that next," Donnie said. "I came around back first to see if there were any other vehicles parked out here. The more you know about who might be inside a dark house, the safer you'll be if you need to go in."

That made sense. But still. "You seem awful interested in that old pickup, Donnie."

We both looked at the truck. With a hand to the fender, Donnie boosted himself up.

"Truth be told, I've been staring extra hard at every truck I see since I got the accident investigator's report about the night you landed in the canal. I feel bad I didn't believe you. I thought maybe I could make it up by finding the truck that ran you off the road."

I wanted to rescue Emma Jean and find out who killed Jim Albert. Donnie wanted to hunt down the nutcase who forced me into the water. *Heroina* and hero.

"Do you think this truck is related?" I asked.

"I don't know. But it's worth checking out."

"Are you going inside the house?"

Donnie brushed off grass, just as I'd done to my own knees that morning. "I'm gonna have a look around." He shifted his heavy belt. "Not you, though, Mace. It's police business."

Those words had a familiar ring.

"Well, I'll wait then. I want to know what you find."

I followed Donnie to the back door. He looked into the window, then pounded on the wood frame with his heavy flashlight. "Emma Jean?" No answer. "Himmarshee Police. Anybody in there?"

The silence was broken only by the crickets, tuning up for their evening serenade.

He tried the door. Locked. There used to be a time when doors were left open. But those days are mostly over, even in a small town like Himmarshee.

Donnie bent and lifted the mat. No key. He ran a hand on the jamb over the door. Nothing but dirt. He picked up a concrete cat statue from the grass. Success.

His flashlight beam led the way inside. I stayed put, like he told me to. But I could still watch through the kitchen window. He turned on the light switch at the wall.

"Everything looks just the same as it did this morning, when Mama and I stopped by," I yelled into the house. "We were worried about Emma Jean. Those are the same dishes we saw in the sink. That's the same newspaper on the counter."

"Stay outside," Donnie yelled back. "Don't even think of coming in."

More light spilled from the windows as Donnie moved through the little house, turning on lamps. I could hear him knocking, and opening and closing doors. I didn't have long to wait. The whole search only took about five minutes. He retraced his steps, shut off the lights, and rejoined me on the back door stoop.

"No sign of a struggle," he said.

He locked the door and slid the key back under the kitty. The real cat caught up with us at the birdbath, which had a concrete fairy dipping a wand into the waterless bowl.

"I guess I better call county Animal Control about Emma Jean's cat." Donnie reached out to steady me as the cat twined around my ankles.

"Leave it be." The words out of my mouth surprised me. "I'll take care of the cat, Donnie."

He stopped and stared. "I'd have pegged you as a dog person, Mace. You don't seem like the kitty-cat type."

I bent to stroke the cat's head. It rose on its hind legs to meet my hand. "This one's kind of growing on me. I'd always heard Siamese were unfriendly. But this one's more like a dog than a cat. Maybe there was a Labrador retriever somewhere in its gene pool."

The cat had eaten. I decided to leave it, in case Emma Jean came back. If she still hadn't shown by tomorrow, I'd return to collect it with one of the animal carriers I use for possums.

"I'm going to hit the road, Donnie. I'm beat. We've had way too much excitement in our little town in these last few days."

"You said it. What do you think happened to Emma Jean?"

As we walked to my car, I filled him in on her tire iron and threats of violence.

"That's what seems weird," I said. "If anyone was to go missing or get hurt, I'd have bet on Emma Jean as the culprit, not the victim."

Donnie's brow was furrowed.

"What is it?" I asked.

214

"It seems strange Emma Jean was in a rage about being cheated on."

"Yeah, I know. But Mama told me that relationship with Jim Albert was a real whirlwind. How well can you really know anyone after just a few months?"

Donnie shone the light around the empty yard. "That's not what I mean, Mace. Word is Emma Jean herself was running around. She was cheating on Jim Albert."

My mouth dropped open. I finally shut it, afraid I'd catch a bug drawn by the flashlight.

"You know how my mom moved to the south side of the lake? She works at that fish camp restaurant in Hendry County."

"The Gigged Frog?"

"Affirmative," Donnie answered, with a nod right out of *Cops*. "Mom says she's seen Emma Jean in there. She takes a booth in the bar, way in the back. Then a dark-haired, younger guy comes in to join her. He's not just a friend, either. The two of them end up making out like high-school kids."

"Your mom doesn't know him?"

Donnie shook his head.

"Maybe it's an old boyfriend. And they quit going out once she got engaged."

"Mom says no. After Emma Jean was flashing her diamond ring last week at work, I mentioned her engagement. You know what my mom said?"

I shook my head.

"Not two nights earlier, she'd been into the Frog, cuddling up with her lover boy. Mom said she pitied the poor sap who had agreed to marry Emma Jean Valentine."

THIRTY-TWO

"Detective Martinez."

His telephone bark was more warning than greeting. I had a fleeting urge to hang up my cell without speaking. Then I remembered: I'm not in junior high.

"It's Mace Bauer."

"Again?"

My resolve to be nice wavered. "You seem busy, Detective. I'm sorry to bother you."

"I didn't mean that the way it sounded." He backed down a little, allowing a flicker of warmth into his voice. "I'm just about done out here. So, I do have a few minutes to talk. By the way, you left so fast I never had the chance to thank you for calling about Emma Jean's car."

"You're welcome." We were setting new personal records for polite discourse.

He cleared his throat. "I also appreciate that you knew enough not to disturb anything."

"Thanks."

Slapping at a mosquito, I wished I hadn't given him the bug spray before I re-armored myself. Full darkness had fallen. Squadron members of an insect air force were about to pick up the VW and take me to their private lair. Donnie was gone, running late for work at the jail. Even the cat had deserted me, slipping through a pet door into Emma Jean's house. I sat in her yard in the car, contemplating how to play Martinez. And, if I'm honest, how interesting it might be to play *with* Martinez. I banished that thought and got down to business.

"Emma Jean is the reason I called again," I said. "Do you think we could meet somewhere, maybe grab a cup of coffee? I want to run some things by you. There's a lot that doesn't make sense."

A bullfrog croaked in Taylor Slough on Martinez's end of the phone.

"Things aren't supposed to make sense to you. You're not the investigator in the case."

Trying not to be offended, I said nothing.

"I'm hot and muddy and all I want is a cool shower after I leave here," he continued. "If you know something I should know, why don't you just tell me right now over the phone?"

Because, I thought, you'll get pissed off and hang up when I try to pump you for information.

"Well, I could do that." I pretended to mull it over. "But what I really want to do is sound out some theories. Some might be useful; others might be useless. I thought it might be nice to sit somewhere cool and relax while we talk. I can hear the bugs buzzing out there through the phone. Wait ... was that a big ol' drop of sweat I just heard, splashing on the mouthpiece?"

He laughed. I had him.

"Could be," he said. "*Dios mío!* How do you stand it up here? Miami's hot; but at least we get a break when the sun goes down. We almost always have a little breeze from the sea. It's like a furnace here. And it runs on swelter, 24/7."

"I've got the perfect place," I said. "How 'bout we meet at the Dairy Queen?"

There was a long silence. A night heron squawked on Martinez's end. The bird was probably hunting for bream in Taylor Creek.

"I'd think you might be uncomfortable at the Dairy Queen," he finally said. "Since your mother was carted off in a police car from there less than a week ago."

More flies with honey, I reminded myself. "Oh, that's water under the bridge," I said generously. "Besides, I'd be no more uncomfortable than you might be, considering you falsely arrested one of their most loyal customers for murder."

"Accessory to murder." I heard a slap and what sounded like a curse in Spanish. "*Coño!*" I hoped it was directed at the mosquito, and not at me. "I thought you said that spray was strong?" Martinez said. "They're eating me alive out here." Another slap.

"The Queen is nice and cool." I was taunting him. "No bugs, either. Plus, you get ice cream. Who doesn't like ice cream?"

"I haven't had any dinner yet," Martinez grumbled.

"There's no bad time for ice cream. You can pretend it's an appetizer. I'm pretty close by. I'll head over, grab a booth, and wait for you."

"It's going to take me awhile to get there," he said.

"No problem. I'll grab a *Himmarshee Times* to read. That should kill six or seven minutes. Then maybe I'll ask around. See if anyone saw anything strange the night Mama found Jim Albert's body in her convertible."

"I wish you wouldn't do that."

"Why not? I'm good at it. How else would I have found out tonight that Emma Jean was cheating on that fiancé she cried so hard over losing?"

I interrupted his sputtering on the other end. "Wow. My phone battery's just about to die. See you at the Queen." I immediately turned off my fully charged phone. Mama always says it's best to leave men wanting more.

The sound of my voice brought Emma Jean's cat out of hiding to investigate. It jumped onto the VW's front trunk, staring at me through the windshield.

"Go on, kitty. Get off." I didn't want to scare the poor critter by starting the car. I tapped on the glass with the keys. The cat batted at the shiny silver on the other side of the windshield. Hitting nothing but glass, it looked at me accusingly—like I'd dangled fish jerky and snatched it back at the last minute. Sitting back on its haunches, it blinked luminous blue eyes.

"Don't worry. Emma Jean will be coming home soon." Did I believe the reassuring words? "We'll take good care of you, one way or another."

I wondered how Mama's Pomeranian would adjust to a feline presence. The confident way this cat acted, it wouldn't give an inch of ground to Teensy.

"Shoo." I hissed, waving my arm out the window. The cat just stared. I finally got out and lifted it from the car. "I promise, you won't go hungry." A sweat droplet rolled off the tip of my nose and plopped onto the cat's neck. "And you definitely won't go cold."

I ruffled the sweat-dampened spot on its fur. A bright red collar with rhinestones encircled the cat's neck. No surprise, considering Emma Jean's flashy fashion sense. Looking closer, I saw a name engraved on a silver charm shaped like a heart.

"*Wila*. Pretty name. Well, I may see you tomorrow."

I set her gently on the ground. "Take care of yourself. There are wild creatures in these parts." I flashed on the feeling of being stalked by who knows what near Ollie's pond. Just thinking about it raised the hair at the back of my neck. I slid back into the car. The cat still sat and stared.

If Wila could speak, what would she say? Would she echo my warning to her?

Be careful out there.

THIRTY-THREE

MORE THAN A FEW women turned their heads to follow Martinez's progress through the Dairy Queen. After a pit stop to wash up in the men's room, he was wending his way to my table. One girl even put down her plastic spoon and turned around backwards in her booth. She was drooling over the view from the rear, much to her boyfriend's displeasure.

Martinez might have been a brooding model off the pages of *GQ* magazine. His filthy loafers and muck-splattered slacks detracted a bit from the effect, though.

"I see that smirk. What's so funny?" He slid across from me onto a seat made of orange molded plastic. Not waiting for an answer, he launched in. "What did you mean about Emma Jean? And why the hell did you turn off your cell phone?"

"That phone's been giving me trouble. It died just as we were talking." I was glad the phone was in Pam's glove box, where he couldn't check the full battery indicator. "According to Donnie Bailey's mom, Emma Jean was running around on her fiancé. We don't know yet who the other man was. Ice cream now; more details after."

He waved his hand like he was dismissing the idea of ice cream.

"C'mon, my treat." I stood up. "What can I get you?"

"I don't know. I've never been to a Dairy Queen."

I grabbed hold of the top of the booth for balance, staggering in the face of the incomprehensible. "Never? Not even once?"

He shook his head, taking a small pad from his top pocket. He extracted a pen, and lined it up on the table, perfectly parallel to the pad's right side.

"Are you going to take my confession? I'll admit it: I eat too much ice cream."

There was a tiny shift in his frown. It might have been the start of a smile. Hard to tell.

I returned with two small hot fudge sundaes—no sense in spoiling dinner with large ones—and plenty of napkins. He was studying framed posters of frozen treats on the wall above our booth. Meanwhile, his real-life sundae was starting to melt.

"You need to get started on that." I spoke around a mouthful of sundae. "The hot fudge will moosh up the ice cream and make a mess."

He looked at the towering creation like he didn't know where to start. "Did you intentionally ask them to empty the whole can of whipped cream onto the top?"

"Worried about your figure?"

He ran a hand over his flat stomach. My fingers tingled as I imagined my own hand resting there. I clutched the sundae spoon tighter.

"Actually, I've lost weight since I came here," Martinez said. "I miss *Abuela's* cooking."

"Was Abuela your girlfriend?"

He laughed and settled for plucking the cherry off the top of the sundae. "It means 'Grandmother' in Spanish. She's eighty-nine and still going strong; stands at the stove for hours every day." He got a dreamy look on his face as he chewed on the cherry. "*Picadillo* to die for. *Arroz con pollo. Plátanos.*"

"Say what?"

"Some of my *abuela's* specialties: Ground-up beef; rice with chicken; plantains, which look like bananas." He put his fingers to his lips and kissed them. "You've never had Cuban food? You've really led a sheltered life, haven't you?"

"No more so than you. How could you have missed all this?" I spread my arms, encompassing the brown tiled floor, the plastic trays, and the tinny voices of customers in the drive-thru microphone as they tried to decide what they wanted.

"Right. I've been deprived," he said. "On *Calle Ocho*, there are a lot more Cuban coffee stands than Dairy Queens. That's something else I miss: Eighth Street in Little Havana and *café Cubano*, Cuban coffee."

"You mean sweet tea isn't cutting it?"

"Caffeine is meant to be consumed hot, in tiny sips of a syrupy sweet, super-concentrated concoction. Watered down in weak tea with a bunch of ice cubes? No, *gracias.*"

I used my red plastic spoon to scrape the dregs from my bowl. He'd had only a few bites.

"Cuban coffee is just as sweet and almost as thick as that hot fudge sauce you just scarfed down." Without making a big deal, he leaned over with his napkin and wiped at a dab of chocolate on my lip. He flashed a real smile this time. I returned it, hoping chocolate wasn't coating my teeth.

"Maybe I'll make you a cup sometime," he said. "I have to warn you though, *café Cubano* is addictive. We call it Cuban crack."

He was more animated than I'd ever seen him.

"It sounds like there's a lot you miss about Miami. Why'd you move here?"

Headlights from a car in the drive-thru flashed through the plate glass window, illuminating his eyes. I saw real pain, and immediately regretted putting it there.

"I didn't mean to pry," I said quickly. "I never know when to quit with the questions."

"So I've noticed." A half-smile returned to his lips. "No, it's all right. I need to be able to talk about it."

He pushed his half-eaten sundae to the side, folded his hands, and rested them at the edge of the table. And then he told me about Patricia, the pregnant wife who was murdered.

"I've heard a little about it," I said, not wanting to reveal I'd already read the details of his personal tragedy on the Internet, from the archives of the *Miami Herald*. "Something awful happened in Miami, that's about as much as people here say."

"Do they say I failed to protect my own wife?" His voice was raw.

I put my hand over his folded ones. I figured that was what my sister Marty would do. "No, they do not. And I don't think anyone would ever say such a thing. You lost your wife in a horrible crime. How could you possibly have prevented that?"

His hands felt warm beneath mine. I was new at this, comforting someone. But it felt right. When he still hadn't answered, I patted twice and then put my own hands in my lap.

Leaning in, I lowered my voice so only he could hear. "I don't think your wife would want you to keep punishing yourself. Imagine if the situation were reversed. You were at home; Patricia had to go to work. A sweet-looking old woman comes to your door, needing help. Imagine it had been you who tried to help her, only to be shot and killed for your kindness. Would you want your wife blaming herself; carrying all that guilt on top of such awful grief?"

He shook his head, staring silently at his hands on the table. I had no idea what I'd do if he lost control and started sobbing. Maybe I'd start crying, too, causing a scene at the Dairy Queen.

I needn't have worried. He covered his eyes for a moment, pinching the bridge of his nose with his thumb and forefinger. When he dropped his hand, he blinked a few times and looked up at me. Grief still clouded his eyes. But they were dry.

Just as I was feeling close enough to him to suggest we move on to dinner at the Speckled Perch, Martinez's cell phone rang. He growled out his name, which apparently is also the Spanish word for "Why the hell are you bothering me?" I was relieved to see he didn't reserve the snarling tone just for me.

He listened for a moment, then grinned. "*Hola, amigo.*" Even I understood that was the equivalent of *Howdy, pal.* "Give me just a second, will you?" he said to the caller.

He lifted his head to look at me. "Listen, I have to take this. Thanks a lot for the ice cream. I think I'm going to head on home, grab that much-needed shower."

I waved my hand at him, shooing him out of the booth. So much for dinner, and for ... whatever.

"Go on, we'll catch up later," I said. "The fact that Emma Jean had another man was the biggest news I had. I'm going to work on finding out who it was."

He waggled a no-no finger at me, but started to scoot out of the booth anyway. "Okay, I'm back," he said into the phone.

As he leaned across me to retrieve his pad and pencil off the table, I overheard a few words from the caller. Not enough to understand. But enough to tell the voice on the phone was familiar. It was a loud honk, unmistakable evidence of a boyhood spent in the Bronx.

THIRTY-FOUR

I HAD TO SQUEEZE Pam's VW past Sal Provenza's big Cadillac in Mama's driveway. So I wasn't completely surprised when he opened the door at her house at seven thirty in the morning.

We all still had our doubts about Sal. But, for some reason, Mama had warmed up to him again. Obviously, since here he was. At least he was fully dressed, in a pale pink golf shirt and burgundy polyester slacks. They were short enough to show off his ankles, resplendent in beige-and-burgundy checked socks. A braided gold chain nestled in the furry pelt of his chest. A Pomeranian snuggled in the crook of Sal's left elbow, shedding on his expandable-waist pants.

"Your mother's in the bedroom, getting ready."

I cringed to hear the words "your mudder" and "bedroom" coming out of Sal's mouth.

I know Mama had sex at least three times, since there are the three of us girls. But I didn't want to think about it, and particularly not in the context of Big Sal.

"We've got something to tell you, Mace. But I'll let Rosalee be the one to break the good news." Sal was smiling like the cat that swallowed the canary. I've seen the man eat. He might have downed both the bird and the cat before he realized what he'd shoveled into his mouth.

"I made some coffee."

I softened a bit. Sal makes great coffee, adding a dash of cinnamon to the pot.

"I got out that mug with the blue flowers that you like. It's on the kitchen counter."

He led the way into the kitchen, engulfing both of us in an aftershave fog. As he tromped across the floor, gingham knick-knacks trembled on their shelves. He filled my mug with coffee and handed it to me.

"I was just going to make myself some bacon and pancakes. Wanna join me?"

My mouth watered as I looked at the butter softening on the kitchen table next to a bottle of maple syrup. But first things first.

"I was with Detective Martinez last night when you called him on his cell phone." I added a spoonful of sugar and a splash of cream to my coffee. "What's the story between you two?"

"Why don't you ask Martinez?"

I noticed he didn't try to deny that he'd called.

"Oh, yeah. Well he did mention that thing about before." I was bluffing, trying to convince Sal I knew something—anything.

He measured pancake mix into a glass bowl. "Which thing?" he asked, watching the bowl and not me. "And what happened before?" He poured in some milk.

"You know," I said lamely.

He replaced the milk carton in the refrigerator and shut the door. Turning around, he leaned against the sink, folded his arms and plopped them where his belly met his chest. "No, I don't know, Mace. And, it's obvious, neither do you."

I studied my coffee.

"I've told you before." He patted his pompadour. Was it gel, or just naturally stiff? "Certain things I can't say, no matter how much you might want me to."

"Want you to what, Sally?" Mama came into the kitchen, tying a silk scarf around her neck. It was the same shade of boysenberry as everything else, from her earrings to her heels.

"Don't you think you're a little over-dressed for the livestock auction, Mama?"

I wanted to see what I could find out from Jeb Ennis' ranching buddies at the weekly auction. I'd convinced Mama and Marty to join me. I didn't even ask Maddie. As Martinez's new best friend, she wouldn't approve of me ignoring his warning about investigating.

Mama checked her reflection in the glass window of the microwave. "You can never be *too* well-dressed, Mace." She aimed a pointed look at my own scuffed boots, frayed jeans, and T-shirt. "Besides, I have to go to work after our mission. The girls at Hair Today would fall off their chairs if I showed up in boots and jeans."

So, instead, she'd go to the livestock market looking like Queen Elizabeth on a royal visit. Go figure.

Mama lifted the head off a dog-in-a-gingham-baseball-cap cookie jar. Teensy started cutting circles around her legs, nails scrabbling on the tile floor. The dog jumped onto a chair, leaped into midair, and snatched the bone-shaped biscuit from her out-stretched hand.

"Lookit Mama's little baby! Just like in the circus," she cooed. Still smiling at the dog, she lifted onto her tiptoes so Sal could stoop and give her a kiss. Better him than the dog, I guess.

"Your boyfriend and I were just discussing how he's cooked up something secret with Detective Martinez."

"Oh, honey, Sally's not my boyfriend."

Finally! Mama had come to her senses.

"He's my fiancé," she squealed, shoving her left hand under my nose. The sun coming through the gingham kitchen curtains glinted off the diamond weighing down her ring finger.

———

"Marty, help me out here. Mama can't marry Sal. What do we really know about him?"

The three of us were sitting in the air-conditioned interior of Marty's Saturn in the parking lot at the livestock auction, planning our investigative strategy. Of course, the topic of Mama's betrothal had been well-covered first:

How Sal had cooked her veal piccata ("I almost swallowed the ring, girls. He hid it in a lemon slice!"). How he'd gotten on one knee ("I had to help him up!"). And how he hoped to make her forget Husbands Two, Three, and Four ("He knows I could never forget your daddy!").

Now, my pleas to Marty were falling on uncharacteristically deaf ears.

"Mace, Mama's a grown woman. Your suspicions aside, Sal has been nothing but loving to her. I'm sorry to say it, but you need to butt out."

Mama shot me a triumphant look. "Close your mouth, honey. No telling what might land in there with all this livestock around."

She was unswayable with Marty on her side. But I knew my argument would win once I got Maddie involved.

Navigating the rickety wooden stairway to the Himmarshee Livestock Market can be tricky, but Mama was managing—despite the purple footwear. Marty climbed ahead of her; I stayed close behind. That way, one of us could catch her if her heel hooked on a splintery plank.

The market, the largest in Florida, dated to the 1930s. And it looked it: a ramshackle wooden building, white with barn-red trim, perched on top of a sprawling maze of livestock pens. As we made our way up, calves bawled from below. The ammonia stink of urine filled the air. Whistles and shouts came from the "alley rats," the workers who move cattle down the long, dark rows that branch off into holding pens.

Upstairs, cattle buyers were just beginning to make their way to seats that surround the sunken sales pit below. We opened the door to Miss Ruth's Restaurant, a little nook in the corner above the ring. A sign overhead said, *Cows May Come and Go, But the BULL in This Place Goes On Forever.*

Ruth Harris favored patriotic colors. Flags decorated the napkin holders. The curtains were stars-and-stripes. A cowgirl hat in cherry red topped Ruth's towering white beehive. She wore a red-and-white checked shirt, tucked snugly into a blue denim skirt. A white belt with a buckle the size of Texas cinched her still-trim waist. The only thing missing was a six-shooter on a holster around her hips.

"That's the cutest outfit you've got on, Ruth." Mama hugged the café's well-preserved namesake like a long-lost cousin. "You've sure got a theme going here."

We did greetings all around.

"You look awful pretty too, Rosalee. That shade is sure becoming to your coloring. It must be nice to dress up again after being in prison."

"Oh, honey, that was nothing but a misunderstanding." Mama waved her ring hand airily.

Ruth hadn't noticed the diamond. I figured her cataracts must be bad, as big as that stone was. Mama picked up a cow-shaped creamer from the table, turning it this way and that. She pretended to be admiring it, but really she was just trying to catch the light with her ring.

Grabbing the dappled cow from Mama, I glared at her to quit showing off. "Miss Ruth, we dropped by because we've been looking into who really might have killed Jim Albert," I said.

"Of course," Marty chimed in, "we knew all along Mama wasn't the guilty party."

Ruth nodded, still looking sideways at Mama. She didn't seem convinced. Or maybe she was thinking that a woman who'd murdered a man and stuffed his body in her trunk wouldn't think twice about stealing the cow creamer she'd picked up and was playing with again.

"Did the man who got killed ever come in here?"

"No, he sure didn't, Mace. Although . . ."

"What?" Marty and I both said at once.

"Well, I get my hair done at Hair Today. Rosalee, you know that."

Mama nodded, her chin cupped in her left hand with her ring finger splayed across her cheek.

"That sweet girl D'Vora and me were talking about how Jim Albert loaned people money. Some of the ranchers up here have been having a hard go of it. I've heard certain people were in the habit of visiting him before he got killed."

"Who, Miss Ruth? We need names," I said.

She pursed her lips. The café's owner for thirty years, her customers were her family.

"Please," Marty said. "It's important."

Still no answer.

"You know Jeb Ennis?" I asked.

She shook her head unconvincingly and moved across the restaurant to wipe down an already-spotless table. "I need to get back to work," she said over her shoulder.

Every seat in the place was empty.

"If y'all can find Old Jake, you might ask him." Head lowered, she continued swabbing the table. "He's been here longer than I have. He used to work downstairs in the pens. Now, he mostly hangs around. He knows everything about everybody. And he don't have a problem telling what he knows."

Mama touched Ruth's wrist, her fingers stretched all the way up her arm. "Thanks so much, doll."

"You're welcome." Ruth tried to pull away. Mama held tight. Ruth finally looked down. "My, oh my." Her eyes widened. "Would you look at that ring!"

"Oh, this?" Mama lifted the ring to the light. "Well, honey, my boyfriend just proposed. I'm gettin' married."

"Again?" Ruth said.

I grabbed Mama's elbow and steered her out the door.

"Congratulations," Ruth called after us as we started down the stairs.

We found Old Jake under the building, sitting on an upside-down milk crate in the shade of the pens. He looked up as we approached, his grin spreading across his white stubble beard. A few teeth were missing. Those remaining were stained brown from a chaw of tobacco, and thousands more before it, bulging in his jaw.

"Well, lookit you, Ma'am," He took off his hat and beamed. "You're as purty in that purple as a speckled pup in a red wagon."

Mama fluttered her lashes. "It's boysenberry. And thank you kindly, suh."

Had we wandered onto the set of an old cowboy movie?

"You must be Jake," Marty said.

"Old Jake, that's what they call me." He ran a hand over his head. It was mostly bald, with brown age spots and a fringe of gray. "I'm so old now, some days I'm not sure I even remember my name."

"Why, you don't look a day over ..." Mama hesitated, trying to find a number that would flatter without sounding ridiculous. "Seventy," she finished.

Jake, who'd probably passed that landmark fifteen years before, smiled so broadly we got a peek of his spit-softened chaw.

"Do you mind if we ask you a few questions?" I said.

"Depends."

He put his hat back on and spit. A brown stream hit the ground, sending up a puff of dust. Mama took a careful step sideways in her boysenberry heels.

"Do them questions have anything to do with unpaid taxes or immoral women?"

Marty blushed.

"No," I said, laughing. "Nothing like that. You remember hearing about the owner of the Booze 'n' Breeze, the man who was murdered?"

Jake knew all about it, even down to the fact that the body was discovered in the trunk of "some lady's convertible." We didn't mention the "purty" gal in front of him was that same notorious lady. He also knew about Albert's loans to strapped ranchers.

"Yep." A stream just missed my boot. "Some of these boys 'round here bit off more than they can chew. Ranching's a tough bidness. Only the strong survive."

"Who was borrowing?" I asked.

Jake opened his lips just enough to spit. Not a word escaped.

"Clarke Simmons?" I named one of Florida's best-known cattle men. Jake's thin shoulders shook with laughter. When he started wheezing, Marty patted his back until he quit.

"Simmons has got more gold than Midas," he said with a final cough. "That fellow from the drive-thru could have borrowed money from him."

"Jeb Ennis and I go way back," I said. "I know he's been having some cash-flow problems."

Jake narrowed his eyes at me. "Yep."

"It's a shame. Jeb sure did work hard to build that ranch," I said.

"Now, that might be true. But Jeb'd do better to keep his mind on his bidness. You can't serve two masters."

I waited for the wizened old man to go on. He straightened the hat on his head.

"He borrowed money from just about ever'body here, even a few bucks from me. But he always had one excuse or t'other about why he couldn't repay. Don't piss on my back and tell me it's rainin', that's what I always say."

Marty leaned down so she could look under the hat brim, directly into Jake's rheumy green eyes. "What do you mean? Was Jeb in trouble? Who were his masters?"

"The cattle, that's one. They'll keep a man up nights, always needing something. You feed, you breed, you sell for what you can, and then you start all over again. Year in, year out. Raising cattle is gamble enough for most men. But not for Jeb."

"Jake, honey, just tell us what you got to tell us," Mama said. "Who was Jeb's other master?"

"More like 'what was,' Ma'am." He spit. "Gambling got t'hold of Jeb Ennis. He's lost near all that he owned. That boy never took to heart that old advice about not betting the ranch."

THIRTY-FIVE

"I don't believe my eyes, Mace." Mama gripped my arm so tight I was afraid the skin was going to pop like an overcooked sausage. "It's that awful man."

I followed Mama's gaze through the front window of Hair Today, Dyed Tomorrow, where I'd brought her after the livestock market. Pastor Bob Dixon stood in the salon behind his wife, hands resting on Delilah's shoulders. Seated in a mauve chair, she was covered from the neck down with a drape in deep purple. She looked like a large grape with a stem of wet hair.

"I won't blame you if you don't come in, Mace." Mama turned her back to the window, just in case the minister and his wife could read lips. "You do not need to subject yourself to that man-wolf for another minute."

She clearly thought I was unpracticed at fending off unwanted advances from men.

"Don't worry about it, Mama. I'm an adult. Besides, I don't think he's going to attack with his wife sitting right there. She looks big enough to take him if he got her mad."

Mama's gaze returned with mine to the scene on the other side of the window. Pastor Bob smiled into the mirror at Delilah, the morning sun glinting off his teeth. It lit a silver cross on the lapel of his brown-checkered sport coat. His small hands looked as fragile as baby birds against his wife's sturdy shoulders. Seeing the two of them together, I realized Delilah wasn't just bigger; she was a good fifteen years older than her husband.

"He is a puny one," Mama finally agreed. "Even so, I can give D'Vora your money."

With everything I'd had on my mind, I left the shop without tipping D'Vora for cutting my hair. I'd wanted to get back to apologize ever since.

"I'm used to tusslin' with gators and snakes, Mama. How bad could one pint-sized pastor be?" I pushed open the door to a jingle of bells. "Hang onto my arm . . . a little looser, please. We'll present a united front," I whispered as we stepped inside.

"Good morning, Rosalee." The minister and Delilah spoke in unison.

"Y'all remember my middle girl, Mace." Mama's tone was cool. Not as icy as Maddie's, but heading for winter. The two of them nodded politely. I gave them a tight smile back.

Betty, the shop's owner, bustled out of the back, greeting us as she wiped her hands on a lilac-colored towel. I'd never realized purple came in so many shades.

I smelled the usual mix of shampoos, conditioners and permanent solution. Another scent fought for dominance—fruity, like overripe watermelon and bananas that have started to blacken. As we got closer, I realized it was Delilah's perfume. I backed away, putting my hand over my face as if I was scratching my nose.

Betty stopped at the counter in front of Delilah's chair and rustled through the drawer for a comb and a handful of hair rollers. She looked up at me in the mirror. "Mace, you're not blowing out that haircut like D'Vora told you to, are you? She's going to get on you when she gets back from the bank, which should be any minute now."

My hand went to my hair, made wild by the humidity and Pam's convertible. "No, Ma'am, I guess I'm not. I usually just open the windows in my Jeep and hang my head out to let it dry. It saves a lot of time."

Betty looked horrified.

"Well, guess I'd better let you ladies get to your womanly ways." Pastor Bob patted his wife's shoulders as he spoke.

He seemed oddly comfortable in the salon. I couldn't imagine Carlos Martinez or Jeb Ennis hanging around a beauty parlor. But Pastor Bob, with his bleached teeth and buffed fingernails, seemed to feel right at home.

"Every time I bring Delilah in, I think she can't get any more beautiful than she already is." He beamed a whitening-strip smile to the mirror. "But then I come back to pick her up, and darned if I'm not wrong."

He leaned toward Delilah, who offered up her plump cheek for a kiss. "I'll be back for you in a couple of hours, Mother."

"I'll be right here, Father. Betty's going to make me into a new woman, so I do hope you recognize me."

He put his hand on her face and gazed into her eyes. "Mother, I'd know you in a crowd of thousands. That's how it is with soul mates, isn't that right, ladies?"

He glanced at us for approval. Mama smiled reflexively, but I was busy choking back vomit. I hate when married couples call each other "Mother" and "Father." It's creepy.

Through the front window, I saw D'Vora hurrying along the sidewalk, breasts jiggling in her tight smock. Pastor Bob saw her, too. He dropped his hand from his wife's cheek like it was a burning coal, and rushed to open the shop's door. He stepped aside just enough so D'Vora would have to rub up against him as she brushed past. His eyes got a familiar gleam.

"It's D'Vora, isn't it?"

She raised the bank deposit bag in her hand to cover her chest, and gave him a "My, what big teeth you have" look.

"I don't believe you've taken us up on our invitation to come worship at Abundant Hope and Charity Chapel. Mother, have you seen this pretty young lady at church?" His eyes never left D'Vora's cleavage.

I glanced at Delilah. Her own eyes were full of hurt and resignation.

"No, Father, I haven't." Her lips barely moved as she studied her hands, folded on top of the drape. If she hadn't been so mean to Mama at church, I might have felt sorry for her.

"Thank you anyway, sir. Ma'am." D'vora nodded at Delilah as she sidestepped around the minister. "But I'm happy at my own church. I've been going ever since I was baptized. Thanks for thinking of me, though."

Everyone in the shop knew exactly what the minister had been thinking about D'Vora.

"Well, maybe you'd like one of my DVDs, then. Half-price, for you."

Delilah didn't give her time to answer. "Hadn't you better get to your errands, Father?"

Pastor Bob put a hand to his chin, thoughtful like. He was probably just wiping off drool. "You betcha," he finally said, as D'Vora disappeared into the back room. "I've got a long list to tackle. See you soon, Mother."

Delilah followed her husband with her eyes until he was out the door, down the sidewalk, and out of sight of the window. She continued staring until, finally, she let out a little sigh and a tiny shake of her head. What would run through your mind if you had a husband who would come on to another woman like that, right in front of you? Delilah looked like she was trying to convince herself of something. I wondered what it was.

"Okay, let the girl talk begin." Betty shook her magenta comb like a conductor's baton. It broke the shameful feeling we'd shared at seeing Delilah humiliated. "Who's got news about Emma Jean Valentine?"

We spent the next fifteen minutes dissecting Emma Jean's disappearance. I filled them in on finding the abandoned car and visiting her house. Mama revealed the fact that she might have been cheating on Jim Albert. Delilah perked up at that gossipy morsel.

"Maybe I shouldn't tell tales," she said, waiting for the go-ahead to do just that.

"Mace and her mama are trying to find out who really killed Emma Jean's boyfriend. Whoever did it may have kidnapped her, too." Betty's eyes bored into Delilah's in the mirror. "You'd only be helping Emma Jean to tell what you know."

Delilah paused just long enough to take a deep breath before beginning. "Well, I will say I couldn't believe that scene she pulled the other night at Abundant Hope. All of that about how the wicked woman who'd been cheating with her boyfriend attends our little church? And the way she tried to stare down the evildoer? Talk about a sinner casting stones!"

Mama wrinkled her brow. "What are you saying?"

"I'm saying I know for a fact Emma Jean had a secret lover. And I'm saying the man's a member of our church."

"Are you sure?" Betty asked, whipping some of Delilah's wet hair around a pink roller.

"Absolutely. Every couple of months, I collect all the hymnals and give them a good dusting."

I wasn't at all surprised Delilah was a fastidious housekeeper.

"The last time I did it, I found a love note tucked into one of the books. It wasn't addressed by name; Emma Jean had written *My Dearest Darling Man* at the top. She talked about how she could barely stand to see him in church with his wife, knowing she couldn't have him." She angled her head toward Betty, who was wedging the last roller into an even row. "And then she said things were heating up. *You know who* was going to ask her to marry him, she wrote."

She looked at each of us to make sure we were listening. We were.

"*What should I do about it?* That's what she asked her 'darling man.'"

"How do you know Emma Jean wrote it? I can't believe anyone would sign their name to a note like that," I said.

"She didn't sign her full name. The whole thing was printed, on a typewriter or a computer. There were just the initials at the end, *EJ*. Beside them, there was a red stick-on heart, like the ones little girls put on their notebooks. Get it? The initials stand for Emma Jean, and the heart for Valentine."

We were all quiet for a few moments, digesting Delilah's theory. Betty combed and rolled; rolled and combed.

"Who do you think it was, y'all?" D'Vora peeked from the back room, where she'd fled to escape Pastor Bob. "Who was doin' the dirty thang with Emma Jean?"

"That's what we need to find out, honey," Mama said. "Maybe whoever it was loved the 'dirty thang' so much he killed poor Jim Albert so he could keep doing it with Emma Jean."

THIRTY-SIX

WITH A MOUNTAIN OF meat loaf and mashed potatoes in front of him, my cousin Henry was holding court from a corner table at Gladys' Restaurant. Making a point, he waved his fork in the air like he was a judge and the fork was his gavel.

I stopped for a minute just inside the front door, feeling the sweat on my neck drying in a blast of cold air. The air conditioner felt so good, I lifted the hair from my collar and let the chill wind blow away the heat that had accumulated from outside.

Charlene, the waitress, ran an obstacle course between chairs and tables. Plates were stacked in a line along her left arm like planes waiting to take off in Atlanta. There was a blizzard of white order slips in the kitchen window, waiting for the cook.

Just about every seat was taken. The courthouse crowd was there, the men in neckties; the women in pantsuits or dresses. Three ranchers in blue jeans tipped back in their chairs, toothpicks in their mouths and pie plates scraped clean on their table. A couple of retirees from the RV park sipped coffee at the counter, their faces sunburned under bass-fishing hats with bands of breathable mesh.

I dropped my hair back onto my neck and started toward Henry's table. Marty leaned forward, smiling as she listened to whatever our cousin was saying. Maddie's arms were crossed against her chest, her face scrunched into a disapproving glare. She looked up as I approached.

"You're just in time, Mace. Henry is entertaining us—and all three adjoining tables, I'm sure—with a story about his neighbor's pot-bellied pig. Apparently, the poor creature suffers from severe flatulence."

"*Pfffbt.*" Henry forced air through his lips. "*Pfffbt, pfffbbbttt.*"

"Complete with sound effects." Maddie shook her head in disgust. "Henry, I've got middle -school students with better manners and more maturity than you."

He poked her gently in the arm with his fork. "Chill out, Maddie. If you wind yourself up any tighter, only dogs will be able to hear you fart."

Marty burst out laughing.

"Mace, please sit down and try to get your cousin under control. Marty only eggs him on."

While Maddie looked at me, Henry palmed a salt shaker from the table.

"*Byuck, buck, buck, buck.*" Clucking, he lifted his butt off the seat, reached down, and brought up the white shaker in the center of his hand. He offered it to Marty. "I believe this egg is yours, Madam Egger-on."

The harder Marty giggled; the madder Maddie got.

"All right, you two. We all know Maddie is fun to tease." I took a seat. "But get serious, now. I've got some news you're not going to believe."

I told them about the note Delilah found tucked into a hymn book.

"Maybe Emma Jean was cheating with that choir director," Henry said. "He always looks you in the eye a little too hard. I don't trust him. It's like he's trying to sell you on the notion he's a better person than you."

"That's not a hard sell in your case," Maddie sniffed. Henry stuck out his tongue in reply. "Besides, I don't think someone who only shows at church for weddings or funerals is qualified to judge others, Henry."

Maddie became a Methodist when she married Kenny. We all agreed it was a better fit for her, as the worship at Mama's church can get pretty emotional and uninhibited. Those characteristics aren't in my older sister's repertoire.

Marty spoke before Henry and Maddie had the chance to start another round. "What about Al Small, from the insurance agency? Doesn't he go to Mama's church?"

Marty dated a vegetarian in college, and both of them embraced Buddhism. The boy's long gone, but the diet and religion stuck. At first Mama believed Marty would burn in hell for worshipping a false idol. But even she eventually came around. The Buddhist philosophy of never hurting a living thing is a good match for my gentle sister.

"Al and Anna Small do belong to Abundant Hope," I told Marty. "Why do you ask?"

"Anna's in the book group I run at the library. She's been bad-mouthing her husband in between discussion questions. She says she wants a divorce. Al's been cheating."

I couldn't imagine anyone writing "dearest darling man" to portly, balding Alvin Small.

"What about Pastor Bob?" I shifted in the chair. "Y'all heard he hit on me. Then, he just about devoured poor D'Vora, even with Delilah sitting right there in the beauty shop chair."

Henry shoveled some green beans onto his fork. He stopped it midway to his mouth. "Naw. It doesn't fit, Mace." He gave his head a firm shake, as confident as a defense attorney who just caught the prosecutor's key witness in a lie. "First of all, if the pastor went after you and D'Vora, then Emma Jean's too old for him. He likes 'em younger. Second, she's not hot enough."

Maddie looked like she accidentally ate the lemon slice out of her iced tea. "Eww, Henry. I hope you're not implying you think Mace is 'hot.' First-cousin hanky panky is almost incest."

Henry swallowed the fork load of beans. "Calm down, Maddie. I'm not saying I want to jump Mace's bones. Though any red-blooded male who isn't her cousin might." He swiped a biscuit through a pool of gravy on his plate. "I'm just speaking objectively, as a man. Mace is a fine-looking woman with a beautiful build."

"Ewwww," Marty and Maddie said in chorus, as I blushed.

Henry polished off the biscuit, then eyed the final meat loaf morsel. My sisters had waited on me to order lunch. But Henry claims his blood sugar gets screwy if he doesn't stick to a strict meal schedule. Charlene was so busy she could barely breathe, let alone get back to take our order. So, as we waited with empty stomachs, we were treated to the spectacle of Henry plowing through lunch.

He speared the meat loaf sliver and pointed his fork at us. "And how do you know the note is from Emma Jean, anyway?"

He didn't wait for an answer.

"Find another woman with the initials E.J. at that church ... hell, in the whole town, or just about anywhere, really. That'd be enough for a good attorney to establish reasonable doubt. 'Ladies and gentlemen of the jury, that note could have been in that hymnal for years. Maybe a church-going woman named Elaine Johnson worked at the music-book company and slipped it in there for safekeeping. Maybe one of the teenagers at Abundant Hope did it as a prank. Anyone with a computer could have produced that note, ladies and gentlemen.'"

Henry looked at us, pleased with his performance.

"You've got a point, Henry." Maddie handed him a napkin. "But you might want to check your chin first for a glop of gravy if you ever do that bit for a real jury."

———

Charlene finally delivered the orders we gave her: A cheeseburger and extra-crispy fries for me. Chicken-fried steak for Maddie. A vegetable plate with biscuits for Marty. Henry couldn't decide between the cherry and coconut cream pie, so he got a slice of both. I pitied the unfortunate client whose Friday afternoon appointment coincided with Henry's crash from his sugar high.

He waited until I had a mouthful of burger to say, "Maddie told us you have some suspicions about Jeb Ennis, is that right, Mace?"

"Wuuuhh," I said.

"Why am I asking, or why were you suspicious?"

Maddie slapped his shoulder hard, nearly knocking a clot of coconut pie off his fork. "Hell's bells, Henry. Can't you see Mace's mouth is full of food? Just tell us what you know about that devil, Jeb." She shot a look full of meaning at me. "I can already predict, it's gonna be something bad."

Marty glanced at me with a guilty look on her face. We hadn't told Maddie about our trip to the livestock market, or about what Old Jake had said about Jeb.

"One of my clients did a little work for Jim Albert," Henry began. "Let's say his line of work is 'enforcement,' and just leave it at that." He spiked a quarter of the cherry pie slice with his fork and gobbled it down. "Anyway, this man says Jeb was into Jim Albert for quite a bit of dough."

The hamburger turned to dust in my mouth. "That's old news, Henry. Jeb himself told me he'd borrowed from Jim Albert."

I still felt protective, even as the evidence mounted against Jeb. For some stupid reason, I didn't want my family, and especially Maddie, thinking badly of him. Did I harbor some fantasy that we'd end up together, riding off into the sunset?

"So he talked about the loan, huh?" Henry said. "Did he tell you he owed more than $250,000?"

Marty's eyes went wide. Maddie let out a low whistle. I tried to conceal my shock.

"That gives Jeb two powerful reasons for whacking Jim Albert," Henry lectured. "Number one: money. He couldn't possibly pay that much back, not and keep his ranch. Number two: self-preservation. It's as strong a drive for us as it is in the animal world. Jim Albert was a dangerous man. Kill or be killed."

I stirred my coffee, which had gone cold. I still hadn't said a word.

"I know you loved the guy, Mace."

I started to protest, but Henry held up his fork. "Don't deny it. I kid around, but you're like a sister to me. It broke my heart to see how bad Jeb hurt you. You loved him, young or not."

"That's what I told her, Henry. Any man that could do Mace like that might be capable of much worse." Maddie leaned over and patted my arm. It was such a rare gesture, it almost made me cry.

"You want Jeb to be innocent." Henry's voice was soft, his eyes kind. "But you have to face the facts, Mace. This sordid romance or affair or whatever it is that might have been going on at Abundant Hope? That's just a distraction. Your ex-boyfriend takes the prize as the likeliest killer in Himmarshee, Florida."

Each of my sisters grabbed one of my hands and held on.

Henry pushed his pie plate away, even though there was almost a half a piece left. He looked into my eyes: "Let's put it this way, cousin. I'm a damned good lawyer. But I wouldn't want to walk into court right now with Jeb Ennis as my client."

THIRTY-SEVEN

"Warm you up again, hon?"

I put a hand over my ceramic coffee mug. "No thanks, Charlene. I've already had enough to be peeing like a racehorse all afternoon."

My sisters had to return to work. Henry was back at his law office, probably terrorizing his teen secretary with bad jokes and the sounds of bodily functions. I was alone with the afternoon *Himmarshee Times* on the table and a third cup of coffee sloshing around in my gut.

Mama called much earlier to ask us to hold off on dessert. But she'd been delayed. It was almost two-thirty now. I stuck around to wait for her, since my new schedule has Fridays off. Rhonda, my supervisor, decided I needed a day before the weekends to recharge my friendliness.

"You need to work on your attitude, Mace," she'd told me.

Rhonda was referring to the credo I have for park visitors: There are no stupid questions; only stupid people.

While I waited, I paged through our newspaper's slim pickings. The mayor and the bank manager of a First Florida branch squinted in a picture, their feet in dress shoes resting on shiny shovels. In construction hardhats, they looked like big-headed ants in business suits. I checked out the listings for births and deaths, making sure I didn't owe anyone a card. I read about the chances this season for the Brahmans, Himmarshee High's football team. Reflecting the town's cattle-raising roots, the team's mascot is a two-thousand-pound Brahman bull. His name's Bubba, and he's got his own e-mail address on the Internet.

And then I spotted a small item next to the police blotter, usually a repository for vandalism reports and drunken driving incidents. I scanned the story:

STORM FUNDS MISSING

Hurricane Janet took a terrible toll on Jack and Donna Warner of Basinger. Their three-year-old daughter, Ashley, died when the storm destroyed their house in June. The child was struck on the head by a roof beam torn off in the hurricane's 100-mph winds.

Now, Himmarshee police are looking into whether the Warners and other families struck by the June storm have been victimized again.

Almost $5,000 is missing from a fund designated to help hurricane victims rebuild, according to sources at First Florida Bank. Himmarshee Police Chief Ben Johnson confirmed that money is gone, but would not specify a sum.

"There are some discrepancies in the bank account," John-
son said. "We're investigating the matter. We're still hoping
there's a reasonable explanation. I hate to think anyone in
Himmarshee would steal from people who've already been
hurt so much."

The fund was begun by members of the Abundant Hope
and Charity Chapel. Phone messages left on the church's an-
swering machine were not returned. The Rev. Bob Dixon,
pastor at the church, could not be reached for comment.

Johnson declined to say whether any arrests are imminent.

I was staring at the newspaper, picking my lower jaw off the table, when Mama walked up. "Mace, you won't believe what happened at Hair Today." She pulled out a chair and collapsed with a dramatic sigh.

I slid the *Times* onto her map-of-Florida placemat, right over our red star above Lake Okeechobee. "Before you say a word, read that." I tapped the headline with my index finger.

"Well, it's about Delilah," Mama started in, ignoring me as usual.

"Not another peep." I grabbed her glasses from her purse and slapped them in her hand. "Go ahead. Read."

Mama clucked her tongue at the part about the Warners' little girl. Her eyebrows shot up when she came to the missing money. At the end, her hand flew to her throat.

"Jesus H. Christ on a crutch!"

Charlene, clearing plates off an adjacent table, shot a surprised look over her shoulder.

"Sorry, darlin'." Mama slapped a hand over her mouth. Then she leaned in and whispered through her fingers. "This is bad, Mace."

"I know it, Mama."

"It's real, real bad. I was going to tell you that Pastor Bob never did come back for poor Delilah today. That's why I'm so late. I stayed there with her. First, she was embarrassed. Then she got irritated at him for keeping her waiting. Finally, she got plain worried. The woman was in tears, Mace. She kept calling and calling him on his cell phone."

"No answer?"

"Straight to voice mail. She phoned the church office, thinking he might be there. The beep on the answering machine went on forever. Delilah said that meant there were lots of messages. She couldn't figure out why."

I tapped the paper again. "I've got a pretty good idea, after reading that."

"Finally, D'Vora offered to run her home. They dropped me off here on the way."

We both looked down at the *Times*.

"What do you think it means, Mace?"

"I'm not sure. But I aim to find out. A lot of little strands have been unraveling all around Jim Albert's murder. Money seems like a common thread. Now, here comes another string, leading straight to Pastor Bob Dixon."

———

"Delilah?" Mama pounded for the fourth time on the Dixons' front door. "Let us in, honey. We just want to help."

We called D'Vora to find out where she'd dropped Delilah. I was proud of Mama. She hadn't given away a word, just said she had something for Delilah she'd forgotten to give her.

The house was modest, a one-story white stucco on a quiet street, only a couple of miles from the church. There was no car in the driveway. A wooden welcome sign with a clump of silk flowers in yellow and white decorated a front door painted robin's-egg blue. A plaster cross hung beside the door, with a passage from the book of Joshua engraved in fancy letters: *As for me and my house, we will serve the Lord.*

I doubt the Lord would consider it in His service to rip off hurricane victims.

Mama kept pounding. Finally, heavy steps sounded behind the door. Pale blue curtains rustled at the window.

"Honey, we don't mean you a bit of harm. We figured you'd need someone to talk to. Now, open up," Mama ordered through the door.

The door cracked. A thick pair of eyeglasses and one red-rimmed eye peeked out. Delilah opened up a fraction wider and looked both ways. Her face was a mess, but her hair looked terrific. Betty had done a remarkable job.

"No reporters?"

"Not a one," Mama said.

"That man from the *Himmarshee Times* has been calling ever since I got home. I finally answered and told him I have no idea what he's talking about. Bob handled all the money for the church and the house."

"May we come in?" I asked. "The neighbors will wonder why we're talking to a door."

She stood aside to let us by, then turned and stalked away. "Suit yourselves." Her tone was hard. "I suppose you've come to gloat."

The newspaper was on Delilah's otherwise spotless carpet, open on the hurricane story.

"We're not gloating," Mama said. "We're women, just like you. We feel for what you're going through."

A sniffle came from Delilah's direction. The hard shell was beginning to crack. "Would you like a cup of coffee?" she asked in a softer voice. "I was just about to make myself a pot."

Before I could scream "No More Coffee!" Mama said, "We'd love a cup. That's very nice of you, Delilah."

As she busied herself preparing the pot, Mama and I took seats at the table. Images of butterflies were everywhere. They fluttered across the curtains. They danced on the coffee cups. They formed a butterfly bouquet in a vase on the table. The way Delilah's words stung, she was more like a wasp than a butterfly. And she was big, like a hawk. Yet, deep inside, she seemed to identify with the most fragile of winged creatures.

Or, maybe she just liked butterflies.

She poured a coffee for each of us. My bladder tightened in protest.

"I may as well get right to it, Ms. Dixon. Mama and I read the story in this afternoon's *Times*. Is it true?"

She looked into her coffee cup, avoiding our eyes. A tear plopped onto the table, and her shoulders began to shake.

"I don't know if the newspaper has it right or not." Sobbing, she took off her glasses and slipped them into a pocket on her housedress. "Like I said, Bob takes care of all the financial matters.

256

But ..." she stopped, raising her light brown eyes to ours. Hers were filled with tears.

"But what, honey?" Mama stroked Delilah's thick arm.

"He's definitely *gu ... guh ... gooonnnne.*" More sobs. "He cleaned out all his drawers and his side of the closet. He even took the envelope the cashier at the grocery gave me yesterday. It had fifty-six dollars the store collected for the hurricane fund. I left it on the hall table until Bob could get to the *ba ... buh ... baaaank*," she wailed.

Mama pulled a boysenberry-colored handkerchief from her purse. She patted and murmured. I envied her ability to let bygones go, comforting the same woman who'd razzed her about her jail stint. I hold onto a grudge tighter than Midas with his money. I'm not saying I'm proud of it.

Her sobs finally subsided into hiccups. "The whole thing is my fault."

"Why?" I asked.

"Don't be silly." Mama jumped immediately to Delilah's defense. "What could you possibly have done to make your husband do an awful thing like this?"

I said nothing, withholding judgment until I heard her answer.

"I don't think this would have happened if I hadn't pushed Bob beyond his limit. He'd already been under a lot of stress because his plans to grow his ministry weren't working. And then I come along and ..." she couldn't finish the sentence. "I'm so ashamed to admit it ..."

"Honey, there's not a one of us pure enough to cast a stone," Mama reassured her. "We've all done things we're sorry for. Go on and say what you need to say." She brushed the well-coiffed hair from Delilah's forehead.

"It's all because of me that Bob wasn't thinking straight." Delilah fiddled with her teaspoon. "You know that woman Emma Jean came into the church shouting about? The woman who was having an affair with her man?"

We nodded.

"Well, that was me. Lord forgive me, I was cheating on my husband with Jim Albert."

THIRTY-EIGHT

MAMA ACTUALLY GASPED. I kept my mouth shut, processing Delilah's confession.

She was silent, too. Staring out the window, she traced the wings of a butterfly on her coffee cup. Maybe she wished she were outside, floating peacefully from flower to flower on her trellis of Confederate jasmine.

"Why didn't you say anything the night Emma Jean came to Abundant Hope?" I asked.

Her head snapped around, and I thought for a moment she was going to slap me. She might be hurt and humiliated, but there was still a slice of mean in Delilah Dixon.

"What should I have said? 'Excuse me, everyone. I'm the wicked woman Emma Jean is yelling about.' I couldn't do that. I'm the pastor's wife. I'm supposed to be a model of propriety."

I wasn't letting her off that easy. "You just stood there, as each of those fine churchgoers looked with suspicion from woman to woman." I flashed on the pretty soprano. The way Emma Jean had stared, even I'd suspected her. "That's not right. It's not Christian."

Mama put a warning hand on my wrist. "Hush, Mace. Delilah knows she's done wrong. But she's got all sorts of trouble right now. Her husband's gone. So is the hurricane money. She doesn't need you piling on."

Delilah got up for the coffee pot. She raised her eyebrows to me. Not unless you want me to pee right here on the butterfly-covered cushion of your kitchen chair, I thought. But I just smiled and shook my head.

"No, Rosalee. Your daughter's absolutely right. I wanted to confess. I really did. But I simply couldn't get out the words that night in front of everyone. I prayed and prayed about it, asking God to help me do the right thing. I'd decided to ask Emma Jean for her forgiveness, but she vanished before I could do it."

We sat, listening to the tick of a butterfly clock over the kitchen sink. A Monarch hovered at twelve o'clock; a Swallowtail at six. As I studied the specimens for each hour, a mini lepidopterology course, Mama eyed a store-bought package of pecan cookies on the counter.

"Delilah, honey?" She licked her lips. "Would you mind if I took a couple of those cookies? I never had lunch today."

She glanced over her shoulder at the bag, but made no move to get up. She seemed completely defeated. "Of course, Rosalee. Help yourself."

Mama started struggling with the indestructible packaging. She put it between her knees and tugged. She turned it this way and that, trying to find a tab to rip. Delilah took the cookies without thinking, as if she was accustomed to being the one in the house who opens lids and unsticks drawers. The tendons in her forearms flexed like steel cables as she forced open the bag.

"You're awfully muscular, Delilah. Do you exercise a lot?" I asked.

"My heavens, no!" A tiny smile creased her mouth. "Wouldn't I be a sight in a leotard?"

Delilah spread her anvil-sized hands, staring at them as if they belonged to someone else. "No, I never needed to exercise. I've always been strong. My father was German and my mother Norwegian. They were both from hardy, peasant stock. All my brothers and sisters were big, too. But I was the biggest. My father used to call me *Schweinchen*, which means piglet in German. He meant it as an endearment."

"That's a nice memory," Mama said.

"Not really. The kids at school took my father's nickname for me and turned it into 'pig fart.'"

I pictured a heavy little girl in glasses, ridiculed and teased. Sympathy for Delilah was beginning to come easier.

But then I looked again at those big hands, dwarfing the butterfly mug as if it were a doll's teacup. What kind of damage could they do? Jim Albert was dead, tossed like a sack of garbage into Mama's trunk. First Emma Jean vanished. And now Delilah's husband had, too. Several of those unraveling strands seemed to start with the woman sitting across the table from Mama and me.

"Emma Jean called me the night she disappeared," I said, watching carefully for Delilah's reaction. "She knew who Jim was cheating with. She told me she was going to confront the other woman. So, you're saying the confrontation never happened?"

Delilah continued to stare at the table. My question hung in the air. Finally, she looked up with narrowed eyes. "That's just what I'm saying." She filed the sharp edge from her voice. "Mace, I don't know who Emma Jean believed was the other woman. Maybe there was more than one. I do know I cheated with her boyfriend. I asked God and my husband to forgive me. I was going to ask her, too, even though I was terrified after seeing her waving that tire iron."

"You've just been telling us how strong you are. Why would you be scared?" I said.

"Emma Jean's nearly as big as I am. She's ten years younger. If there was ever going to be a confrontation, I don't know that I'd come out ahead."

I looked over at Mama. She was munching on her fourth pecan cookie, looking thoughtful.

"Why'd you do it, Delilah?" she finally said.

I had no idea what she was talking about, and I'm used to deciphering Mama Code. Delilah's eyebrows were so tightly knit she looked like she was trying to do higher math.

Mama clarified. "I mean, why'd you cheat on your husband in the first place?"

Delilah sighed. Was it sadness? Or was it relief Mama was only asking about sex?

"I only did it once, you know?" She touched the tight, beauty-shop waves in her hair. They sprang back. "I'd gone to the drive-thru to pick up some sodas for the youth group's pizza night. Jim was there. He complimented me; told me how nice I looked in blue flowers. I looked like a pretty flower myself, he told me."

If Delilah had been wearing the same floral dress we'd seen her in at church, Jim Albert had been a liar as well as a weasel.

"I couldn't remember when a man last acted with me that way. I liked it. It made me feel young again." She lifted her eyes to us. I thought I saw the passage of sad and lonely years reflected there. "You may not know it by the way Bob acts in public, but I've had to put up with a lot from my husband. Bob's a serial cheater."

I shot a quick glance at Mama. Both of us remembered the creepy scenes with Pastor Bob in his office and at Hair Today.

"It's humiliating." Delilah dabbed at her eyes with Mama's handkerchief.

I was back to feeling sorry for her.

"It got so bad at our last church, the board forced Bob out. We prayed and prayed about it. He begged me to forgive him. Again. Things were good for a while, but then I saw the signs he was starting to slip. Again. And then, one night, Bob never came home at all. The next day, I met Jim Albert for the first time at the Booze 'n' Breeze."

"You'd had all you could take." Mama patted Delilah's hand, perhaps thinking of all those nights she waited to hear the key turn in the lock with Husband Number 2.

"That's right, Rosalee. And when Jim Albert started flirting, I was ripe. I still didn't know who Bob was playing around with, but I was certain he was playing around. Again. A couple of days later, I went back to the drive-thru, and there was Jim. I didn't have the first feeling for him. A man with a diamond pinky ring, can you imagine?"

She was married to a man with whitened teeth and clear-polished fingernails. Myself, I didn't see how a pinky ring was that much worse.

"He told me he had some special cartons of soda at discount prices in the back. I knew full well that was malarkey. But I didn't care. He left this girl with funny braids in charge."

I flashed on Linda-Ann, the slacker clerk.

"We went to his office and he locked the door." Delilah traced the rim of her butterfly cup. "We did it right there, on a stained couch of brown-and-white plaid that smelled like stale cigarettes. I remember looking at a bare lightbulb on the ceiling. A Dallas Cowboy Cheerleaders poster hung on the wall. The poster was crooked, and the beige paint was peeling."

Tears dropped as dark spots on the front of Delilah's pink housedress.

"I didn't feel a thing." She hid her face in the lacy handkerchief.

Mama stroked her hair. "Let it all out, honey."

Something had been niggling at me throughout Delilah's confession. I thought and thought. Her sobs slowed to whimpers. Finally, it came to me.

"Ms. Dixon, did you say you asked your husband to forgive you?"

She lifted her face from the handkerchief. "Oh, yes. I got down on my knees and begged. But Bob was furious. Angrier than I've ever seen him. I was actually frightened he'd hurt me. And I never felt that way about him or any other man."

"He must have gotten over it," Mama said. "He seemed sweeter than strawberry pie at the beauty parlor."

Delilah blew her nose. Mama's hankie wasn't up to the challenge. I tore two squares from the paper towel roll and handed them over.

She spoke from behind a wad of towel. Her voice was bitter. "Oh, Bob's a very good actor. He's had a lot of practice, pretending he isn't cheating."

"So he was angry you'd been with Jim Albert?" I asked.

She nodded, her eyes wide. "When he stormed out of the house that night, he was in an absolute rage."

"Delilah, honey?" Mama and I exchanged a look. "Did Pastor Bob own a gun?"

THIRTY-NINE

MADDIE TAPED CREPE PAPER to the wall at the VFW lodge. The garland was as straight as the center line on a flat stretch of Florida highway. Marty followed behind—unsticking the tape, draping the paper, and tying it into festive bows.

"Hmph." Maddie looked over her shoulder. "You've got it looking like a fancy birthday cake, Marty."

"That's kind of the point, Maddie." I was supervising. "It is a party, after all. It's supposed to look pretty."

"I'd hardly call a pot-luck prayer breakfast a party. What are they going to do? Put top hats on the biscuits?"

Marty made a final paper loop-de-loop. "For once in your life, could you not criticize everything, Maddie?" She tied a purple bow onto a gold streamer, keeping her eyes on her hands. "This is a big deal for Mama, even if it's not exactly your style."

I was afraid Maddie was going to toss the heavy tape dispenser at Marty's head. Ever since that promotion, our little sister had become more emboldened about speaking her mind.

"Hmph," Maddie huffed, as if she had plenty to say. But when she looked at Marty, tongue peeking sweetly from the corner of her mouth in concentration, Maddie put down her would-be weapon.

"Explain to me again why we're here while Mama's off cavorting with her obnoxious boyfriend?" Maddie said.

"Fiancé," I corrected. "They're going to be married, whether you like it or not."

With all the excitement over going to jail and getting engaged, Mama had almost forgotten about her church's annual Save a Sinner breakfast. That's not the official name. It's shorthand for my sisters and me. The members of Abundant Hope invite as many non-members as they can, plying them with a lavish, Southern-style breakfast. All the church ladies and a few of the men bring their specialties. The hope is guests will be so caught up with food and fellowship, they'll commit themselves to the Lord between the homemade biscuits and the egg-and-sausage casseroles.

Mama remembered at the last minute she was supposed to be in charge of decorations. Meanwhile, Sal had made dinner reservations at the new country club. He wanted her to meet his golfing buddies and their wives. Since it was another opportunity to show off her engagement ring, Mama hadn't hesitated. Which is how my sisters and I wound up spending our Friday night at the Veterans of Foreign Wars lodge, picking up the decorating ball that Mama had dropped.

I stood back to admire our handiwork.

A *Welcome* banner hung across the stage. Jesus held out a beckoning hand on a color poster, with *John 3:16* inscribed in big type across the bottom. The churchgoers know the Bible verse by heart. But, for the less faithful, there was a cheat sheet beside the poster:

For God so loved the world, that he gave his only begotten Son, that whosoever believeth in him should not perish, but have everlasting life.

White plastic cloths covered all the tables; a vase of silk irises and marigolds decorated each one. Purple and gold are the school colors for Himmarshee High. Supplies in those shades are always left over, so they get used for just about every party in town, except funerals.

"Well, sisters, it looks as good as it's gonna look." I said. "Let's eat."

I opened the box of pizza we'd ordered. We all took a seat at the one table we hadn't decorated. In the morning, it would be crowded with platters of grits and red-eye gravy; biscuits and fruit butter; country ham and sweet potato pancakes.

Maddie helped herself to a pizza slice from the pepperoni-and-sausage side. "What I don't understand is how they think they can still throw this big church shindig. Everyone knows the pastor vamoosed after knocking off his wife's lover and stealing from those poor hurricane victims."

"Allegedly, Maddie." Marty lifted out a piece from the cheese-only side. "Allegedly. No one has talked to the man, so we don't know Pastor Bob's side of the story." She took a tiny bite. "Haven't you ever heard of the concept 'innocent until proven guilty?' "

What were they putting in the water at the Himmarshee Library? Our mild-mannered sister was becoming a spitfire. I spoke before Maddie could come back with something mean.

"Well, he sure looks guilty. Delilah couldn't find his gun when Mama and I were at the house this afternoon. But she found the paperwork on it. It's a revolver, a Smith & Wesson."

Maddie slid the box to her side of the table. "What'd Detective Martinez say?" She rolled up her second slice like a burrito and chomped off the end.

"You know how he is," I said. "Played it close to the vest, as usual. But he perked right up when I told him Pastor Bob owned a .38."

"Is that the kind of gun that killed Jim Albert?" Marty asked.

"Martinez wouldn't say. I tried calling Henry, but he left his law office early. He's taking the kids to Disney, and you know what that means."

"A thousand rides on Space Mountain and no pesky cell phone," Maddie said.

"Anyway, Martinez was awfully interested in the Dixons' marital problems and the missing money. He planned to talk to Delilah today. Mama and I offered to be there, but she turned us down. I think it gave her something else to focus on besides worrying how everyone will react to her tomorrow at the prayer breakfast."

"Poor Delilah." Marty nibbled on a sliver of crust. She stared at us, blue eyes immense and serious in her small face. "Have y'all considered how many questions are still unanswered? For example, what happened to Emma Jean?"

Maddie chose her third slice from Marty's meatless side. "Maybe she found out Pastor Bob killed her boyfriend. He had to kill her, too, before she told the police."

I remembered how out-of-control Emma Jean had been at Abundant Hope; how distraught she'd sounded when she called me on the phone.

"Remember what Mama told us about Emma Jean's little boy going missing all those years ago?" I said. "Maybe she couldn't take losing another loved one. Maybe she walked into Taylor Creek and just kept walking until she drowned."

"Maybe a moccasin bit her." Marty shuddered.

"Then why haven't they found a body?" Maddie asked.

"She could be caught up under a fallen log," I said. "A gator could've dragged her off. You know how the swamps are, Maddie. A lot can stay hidden in there."

"You're the swamp rat, Mace. I stay out of that mess." She took a compact from her purse and swiped at a tomato sauce smear on her chin. "Anyway, there's another person whose behavior has seemed mighty suspicious. Sal Provenza. Mama's Yankee fiancé." She snapped shut her compact like an exclamation point.

Marty, studying a cartoon Italian chef on the pizza box, said nothing.

"It *is* strange how he won't reveal anything about his life in New York before he retired to Himmarshee," I said. "But all of a sudden Mama seems convinced he's on the up-and-up. Do you think he told her something to put her mind at ease; something she hasn't told us?"

"Ha!" Maddie slapped the table, causing the pizza box—and Marty—to jump. "That's a good one, Mace," she said. "Asking Mama to keep a secret is like asking a sieve to hold water."

Our little sister remained silent, eyes cast down to the napkin she was shredding.

"Well, Martinez seems to have shifted from thinking Sal is Public Enemy Number One," I said. "Sal may be okay, *if* we can trust Martinez. And I'm not saying for sure that I do."

Marty lifted her face. "Of course you can trust Carlos, Mace," she said. "He's a policeman. They protect and serve. It's an oath."

Maddie snorted. "Get real, Marty. Haven't you ever heard of police corruption? The man is from Miami, after all. Maybe he and Sal were both involved with Jim Albert in something fishy. And they murdered him to take all the profits."

We sat quietly for a few moments, digesting our pizza and our theories.

Marty finally cleared her throat, an apologetic sound. "There is one person we haven't mentioned, Mace." Her voice was a whisper, as if by speaking negatively she might unsettle the universe. I knew right away which conversational planet she was circling.

"Jeb Ennis," I said. "You can talk about him, Marty."

"That devil again." Maddie looked like she wanted to curse Jeb and spit on the floor. "I'd be the first one to march him straight to jail. But even I have to say the pastor seems to have a better motive for the murder than Jeb Ennis does."

Marty's shredded napkins were a snow bank in her lap. "He owed Jim Albert an awful lot of money, Maddie."

"Yes, but we don't know about Bob Dixon, do we? He must have been financially desperate to take that hurricane money—to *allegedly* take it," she said, with a nod at Marty. "Maybe he also borrowed from Jim Albert."

"Or, maybe the minister killed him so he could steal his money," I said.

"Either way," Maddie said, "a man as vain as Bob Dixon had to be humiliated that his dowdy old wife took up with someone else for a roll in the hay."

"A roll on a dirty plaid couch," I said. "Delilah said it reeked of cigarettes."

"Whatever." Maddie waved her hand. "The point is men do crazy things when women are involved. That leads me to the reason I don't believe Jeb did it."

Marty's eyes went round. "What do you mean?"

"No matter what else I think about Jeb, I do believe he loved Mace."

"Loved her and regretted breaking her heart," Marty said.

"So? What do Jeb's old feelings for me have to do with anything?" I asked.

"The person who killed Jim Albert ran you off the road when you started asking too many questions," Maddie said. "That wreck could have been a lot more serious, Mace. You could have been killed."

Marty gasped and grabbed at her throat, just the way Mama does.

"Yes, Maddie, but I wasn't. I'm okay." I reached over and patted my baby sister's hand.

"Thank the Lord for that." Maddie inclined her head to the poster Jesus. "Jeb Ennis wouldn't do anything to hurt the woman he loved; maybe even still loves. He wouldn't endanger you that way, Mace."

Maddie sounded so sure. I almost opened my mouth to tell her how I'd felt that afternoon in the park by Ollie's pond: Stalked. Endangered. Not to mention confused, as I watched Jeb peel out with the windows rolled tight in a truck that was supposed to be stifling.

But in the end, I didn't say a word to my sisters. I never told them how frightened I'd been that day.

FORTY

THE LIGHT FROM THE headlamps on Pam's VW bounced upward, illuminating hawk moths and the low-hanging branches of trees. At the end of the unpaved drive, Emma Jean's house was dark. Deserted-looking. As I turned left to park the car, the headlights flashed across the front porch. The cat's dishes and the rubber container of food were still there, just where I'd left them.

I killed the engine and turned off the lights. A waning moon barely broke through a thick layer of clouds in the sky. I heard night sounds: A dog barked a couple of streets away. Something small skittered through the dry leaves under the hedge lining the driveway. An owl hooted. The call sounded haunting. Lonely. I turned the car lights back on.

Talking with my sisters about all the people we knew who could have killed Jim Albert had left me feeling nervous.

"Here, Wila. Here kitty, kitty."

As I called, I lifted an animal carrier out of the car and set it on the rocky driveway. I grabbed a towel I'd put in the back seat. I'd been thinking about Emma Jean's cat. I didn't want to leave the pampered creature for too long on her own. I'd feel awful if Emma Jean did come home, only to find something had happened to her pet.

"C'mon, Wila. I've got food."

I tried not to sound too eager. I'm more accustomed to dogs than to cats. But a cat-crazy college roommate once told me that cats are just like men: Show too much interest and they turn tail and run; ignore them and they fall all over themselves for you. I arranged myself into a position of nonchalance on the bottom step of the porch. Plastering a bored expression on my face, I pretended to examine my fingernails.

"Okay, no big deal," I announced to the night and to any Siamese that might be listening. "Come if you want. Stay away if you don't. I'll just sit here for a while and enjoy the music of the mosquitoes."

I started to hum.

Within moments, the cat padded out from behind a glider with a periwinkle-blue-and-white striped cushion. She seemed to remember me from before, but who can be sure? I stroked her a few times, murmuring nonsense words to her. I had the feeling Wila wasn't going to like what was coming. But it was for her own good. Somebody had to take care of the poor critter.

I wrapped the towel around her, cocoon-like, except for her head. I lifted her into my arms, the towel protecting me from her claws. As quickly as I could, I stooped down, got her into the carrier, and shut the wire door.

Wila looked at me with betrayal in her eyes. *MEOWRRR!* She sounded like a cross between a lion and a rusty door hinge.

"You'll be out soon, I promise," I said to the cat. "It's only until we get to my house. You'll like it there, I swear."

With the cat safely secured on the passenger seat beside me, I decided to take a quick detour past the backyard on my way out. The car's lights played across the lawn as I turned. There was the bird bath. The rose bushes. The shed in the back. Then I saw a big, empty rectangle of long-dead grass. What I didn't see was the battered white pickup that had been parked at Emma Jean's house the day after she vanished.

With one hand on the steering wheel, I fished around in my purse until I found my cell phone. Detective Martinez answered with the usual welcoming snarl.

"It's Mace. I figured I'd better tell you. I swung by Emma Jean Valentine's house tonight. There's something funny…"

Martinez interrupted me, his words tumbling out the phone. "Are you all right? What's that horrible sound?"

Meeeeeooooowwwrrrr!

"That's just Emma Jean's cat," I said. "I don't think she's too fond of the carrier I've got her in."

"*Dios mío*, it sounds like someone's being tortured."

"She's a Siamese," I said knowingly. "The Internet says they're very vocal."

"Can't you make her stop?"

"The article I read didn't include anything about a volume button or an on-off switch."

Meeeeeooooowrrrrr!

I raised my voice over the racket. "Anyway, I stopped by to see about the cat. I'm on my way home with her right now." The light on Main Street turned green, and I crooked my neck to hold the phone while I shifted gears. "I noticed the white pickup truck that was at Emma Jean's last night is now gone. Did you have the police haul it off?"

Martinez answered without the usual stonewalling. "No, I didn't." He started to think out loud. "Maybe it belonged to a relative or a friend, and they came by to get it."

"Maybe," I said. "But why now? From the look of the lawn, that truck has sat there pretty regularly for a long time."

"A neighbor might have used it."

"The houses around Emma Jean's are on three-acre lots. Mama told me her two closest neighbors are snowbirds. They leave for the North in June when it starts getting hot, and they don't come back until the end of November, when hurricane season's over. She's not close to anyone else out that way, which is one reason I came to get her cat."

I passed the Speckled Perch and thought about food. Two slices of pizza two hours ago wasn't going to hold me until morning.

"We can check to see if Emma Jean's the registered owner," Martinez said. "If she is, I'll have the information I need to put out a BOLO on the truck and tag number."

"Bolo? Isn't that a Western-style string tie?"

"Be on the lookout. BOLO."

"Gotcha," I said, feeling stupid. I don't watch as much *Law and Order* as Mama does. "I'd know the truck if I saw it again. It was old and beat-up. There were beer cans in the back of the bed."

"Great. That describes half the vehicles up here," Martinez said.

"Watch it, Mr. Miami. I can hear you sneering."

I remembered the feel of the worn tread on my fingers as I ran my hands over the tires. "I didn't think about getting the tag number, but Donnie Bailey might have," I told Martinez. "We both noticed the truck had bald tires, just like the one that ran me off the road. Donnie was awfully interested in that old truck."

———

If ever five days felt like fifty, this was it. What a week. I was looking forward to a cool shower, a cold beer, and some hot salsa once I got Wila and her cat-related accessories settled into my house.

I smiled to myself as the VW jounced into my yard, illuminating the battle ring tucked off to one side. Looked like it was Mace 1; Wildlife 0 in this latest round of raccoon smack-down. The garbage cans were upright, lids still securely fastened with a collection of bungee cords. I might have feared the animals were lying in wait, prepared to punish the woman who shut down their nightly buffet. But the way Emma Jean's cat was caterwauling, any living thing within hearing distance had skedaddled.

I left the cat in the car as I got out. I wanted to prop open my front doors so I could more easily heft the carrier onto the screened porch and on inside. What I saw as I mounted the steps put the brakes on my victory-over-the-wildlife dance.

The resourceful raccoons must have busted through the screen to get onto my front porch. They'd taken their revenge for my garbage-can offensive by overturning a flower pot. Trampled geraniums and big clods of dirt littered the wooden floor. The welcome mat sparkled in the dim moonlight with shards of broken glass.

And then I looked more closely. The screen was intact. The flowerpot had been used with just enough force to break the front window, next to the door. Someone had carefully reached past the broken glass to turn the key in the deadbolt lock on the inside of the front door. The door stood open a crack. The house was a dark cave beyond.

I've seen raccoons turn a doorknob; even pull open cabinets in a kitchen. But using a flowerpot to break a window, locating a deadbolt key inside in the lock, and understanding what the key is used for? That's different. Unless the raccoons had gained a hundred IQ points and opposable thumbs since our last encounter, this burglary was beyond their skill level. The intruder had to be human.

With my heart pounding, I backed slowly off the porch and down the steps. As soon as I felt grass beneath my feet, I spun around and took off at a run.

FORTY-ONE

MARTINEZ MADE IT TO Taylor Creek in thirteen minutes. There was hardly any traffic this far from town on a Friday night. Still, he must have beaten Jeff Gordon's NASCAR time.

He was familiar with the location of the bridge on State Road 98, so when I called him from the safety of Pam's car, that's where I told him to meet me. I figured that was easier than trying to explain how to find my cottage way out in the country. And, to be honest, I hadn't wanted to stick around alone without knowing what was in my house, on the other side of that open door.

I heard his siren a long way off, and then I saw him coming. I flashed my lights. He was going so fast, he flew right past me. By the time he stopped and backed up, I stood waiting for him on the shoulder of the deserted highway. He leaned over to open the passenger-side door.

"Are you okay?"

I nodded, surprised—and a tiny bit pleased—to see how worried he looked.

But when he spotted Wila in the carrier, the concern on his face changed to annoyance.

"What do you think you're doing with that?"

"I'm not leaving her out here alone, with no top on the VW. Who knows what might try to get at her? She's already had enough trauma for one night."

He grimaced, but made room for us on the front seat. "Just try to keep her quiet."

"Yeah, right," I said, as Wila let out a long screech. "Turn left about a half-mile up, at the sign that says High Horse Ranch."

I directed him the rest of the way in. Left at the last fence post. Right at the big oak tree. In no time at all, we were pulling up in my front yard.

"You're staying in the car." His tone offered no room to argue, not that I wanted to.

"Don't worry. I'm not stupid. I'm not going up against the unknown, not when my only weapon is a noisy Siamese cat."

As Martinez got out of the driver's seat, his right hand slid across his chest, under his jacket. I knew he must have a shoulder holster there.

"Be careful, okay?" I said.

With a curt nod, he was gone.

He banged on my front wall and yelled *Police!* then edged the front door open with his foot. The longest five minutes in history elapsed after he disappeared inside. I watched as light replaced the darkened squares of my front windows. A dim glow spilled from the backyard. Martinez must have flicked the switch for the outdoor light at the kitchen door. I imagined him moving down the hallway into the bathroom and then on to my bedroom.

I suddenly flashed on all the housekeeping I hadn't had time for in the last few days. It was ridiculous under the circumstances, but I hoped he wouldn't notice the pile of dirty clothes and underwear I'd left on my bedroom floor.

Finally, I saw him walk around the house from out back. He holstered his pistol and patted its location over the outside of his jacket. I got out of the car to join him.

"All clear," Martinez said. "Whoever was here is gone now. Things look fine inside."

"Let's get poor Wila into the house." I leaned into the car and picked up the carrier.

"Let me get that." He grabbed it from me. I almost protested that I was strong enough to carry my own carrier. Then I remembered Mama's admonition: flies, honey, vinegar.

"Thanks," I said instead.

Stepping over the glass shards and through the front door, I did a quick survey.

"Aside from that broken window, everything looks okay," I told him.

"Except that key in the inside deadbolt," he said. "You know that's a dumb place to leave it, right?"

"Didn't they teach you in police school not to blame the victim?" I snapped.

"Sorry. I just wish people wouldn't invite the bad guys in."

I wondered whether he was talking about me or his murdered wife.

"Try not to disturb anything," he said. "I'm going to bag that key. Whoever broke in had to touch it. We may still want to get somebody out here to dust for fingerprints."

I led the way into my bedroom. "You can put the carrier down right there." I nodded toward the floor. I laid out Wila's things—the litter box and food from Emma Jean's, and a toy mouse I bought. Then I sprung her from her prison. She lit out, fleeing for cover under my bed.

"We won't see her for a while," I said.

"At least she's finally quiet," Martinez said.

Wila gave a short *meow*, just to prove him wrong.

"Why don't you take a good look, see if anything is missing? All I noticed out of the ordinary is that pile of clothes." He frowned at the floor. "Whoever broke in probably tossed your dresser drawers, looking for money or jewelry."

I felt my face flush. "Uhmm, that was me. It's been a bad week for laundry."

In fact, I was wearing my last pair of clean undies, the ones with the droopy elastic waist and the hole in the seam by my butt. I didn't share that detail with Martinez.

We left the scared cat in the bedroom and went into the kitchen, where I got a plastic sandwich bag from the drawer. Martinez used it to extract the key from the front lock. Then, he sealed it inside the bag.

I did a quick circuit of the rest of my house. A string of pearls from Daddy's mother, my only jewelry, still nestled in my sock drawer. Change filled a brass spittoon by the front door, including a ten-dollar bill I'd left on the top. My computer was on my desk; my share of Grandma's silver was still in the kitchen.

"Thank God they didn't get the gator," Martinez nodded toward my coffee table, a half-smile on his face.

"Yeah. I'd have to trap another one so I'd have a place to keep my car keys."

His eyebrows shot up. "Don't tell me you killed that?"

"Well, I had a little help. My cousin Dwight's the one with the license, so he had to be there," I said modestly. "Anyway, looks like nothing's missing."

With Martinez on my heels, I returned to where I'd started. Suddenly, I was aware of being alone in my bedroom with a sexy, attractive man. He was close enough that I could smell his after-shave. Spicy cloves. My bed was just inches away, the same bed that had seen no action since the down in the feather pillows was still on the ducks.

He put a hand on my arm. "Are you really okay?" His voice was husky. "It can be traumatic to have your house broken into, even if they didn't get anything." His dark eyes searched my face.

Just one step, I thought. One step. Hell, I could just tackle him and toss him onto the bed. I'm almost as tall as he is. I wondered once we got down to it, where would he put his gun?

His gun.

"Oh, my God!" I crossed my bedroom in four quick steps and yanked open the closet door. "Paw-Paw's shotgun." I quickly scanned the small, crowded space. "It's gone."

FORTY-TWO

NOTHING SPOILS A SEXY mood like the notion that some maniac might be stalking you with your own granddaddy's shotgun.

Martinez bustled around the house, re-checking everything we'd already checked to see if we missed anything. He found a piece of plywood I'd used as a shutter during the last hurricane, and nailed it over the broken pane on the porch.

I wavered between being grateful for his presence and annoyed that he thought I needed him. Even worse was the thought in my own mind that I did.

"I'm staying the night," he announced, as he hammered the final nail into the plywood.

I raised my eyebrows. "I don't recall issuing an invitation to share my bed."

"Don't flatter yourself." He smirked. "It's purely a security measure. I'll bunk on the couch."

Damn!

"Suit yourself," I said. "It's your backache."

"You shouldn't be out here all alone."

I wasn't about to admit I thought he was right. I'm not accustomed to the damsel-in-distress role. But I was tired. And it was late: one fifteen AM by the hands of the clock shaped like a large mouth bass on the living room wall. I had to meet Mama in less than five hours. I'd promised to go with her to the sunrise prayer breakfast to help lend Delilah some moral support.

I went to the linen closet and gathered up some bedding for the sleeper sofa. "Listen, I appreciate this," I told Martinez as he pulled open the couch. "There's no need. But I do appreciate it."

He grabbed an end to the sheet I held and tucked it under the mattress. "You're probably right, Mace. Still, better safe than sorry." Trapping a pillow with his chin, he started wriggling a floral case over it. I like a man who's not afraid to indulge his domestic side.

I handed him one end of a comforter from the closet. "I mean, it could have just been kids, right?" We dropped the spread over the sofa bed. "The McPherson boy's been running with a bad crowd. I wouldn't put burglary past those little juvenile delinquents. Maybe I scared them off when I pulled in with Wila, yowling in the car. Maybe they didn't get the chance to steal anything but the shotgun."

Martinez sat on the pull-out, testing the mattress with one hand. It was just as comfy as any other sleeper sofa, which is to say he'd feel like he was resting on a sack of rocks.

"Yeah," he said. "It's not like the closet is an original hiding place. Any burglar worth his rap sheet knows to check high shelves and closet corners for homeowners' weapons."

We each sounded like we were trying to convince the other there was nothing to worry about. It was becoming exhausting.

"Listen, I've gotta be up before the rooster crows. I'll try not to wake you when I leave." I yawned.

"*No te preocupes . . .* I mean, don't worry about it. I'll probably be awake anyway. I don't get much sleep as a rule."

I wondered whether those sleepless nights began in Miami, after his wife was murdered.

As I started for my bedroom, I spoke over my shoulder, "I've got an extra-large cotton T-shirt if you want something besides that dress shirt and blazer to sleep in."

"Is it in that pile of filthy clothes you dropped on the floor?"

I would have blushed, but I was too damned bushed.

"Just for that remark," I said, "I get to wash up first." I turned into the bathroom and slammed the door.

A half hour later, I was in bed, but nowhere close to sleep. Of course, I was worried about who took the shotgun—and why. But I also kept thinking about the glimpse I got of Martinez in the hallway. He'd come out of the bathroom and was standing still, looking for a wall switch to turn off the hall light. His skin was the color of graham crackers, and I wondered whether it tasted as sweet. Hard muscle rippled along his abdomen. He had a smooth chest with almost no hair. He wore nothing but boxer shorts. Light blue; intact waistband; no rip near the butt.

Would he slip out of those boxers when he climbed between the sheets?

I glanced at the alarm clock beside my bed. It was scheduled to beep me awake in about four hours. I tossed to my right side, even though I normally sleep on the left. I made a quarter turn, plopping onto my stomach to try to get comfortable. Punching the pillow didn't work. It still felt wrong. Martinez's shoulder would have felt just right. *Stop it!*

I grabbed the pillow's underside to toss it off the bed. That's when I felt something I knew wasn't supposed to be there. I shot to my feet, turned on the lamp, and stared down at the pillow. Carefully, I lifted a corner to look underneath.

"Detective?" I called into the living room. "You'd better come in here."

He was beside me in a flash, proof that he hadn't been asleep, either. I pointed at a sheet of folded notebook paper under my pillow. My name, misspelled, was printed in crude block letters between the wide blue lines: *Mase.* A love note from a demented fifth grader.

"Should I pick it up?"

Martinez's jaw was clenched. His eyes were dark, unreadable. "Do you have any tweezers?" he asked.

"In the medicine cabinet. Be right back."

He used the tweezers to open the note, and then placed it on the nightstand. In the glow of the lamp, we read it together:

You dindt stop. To many questons. See how easy I could kill you? I'm coming for you. Your mama to

The printing looked the same as on the note tossed on Mama's porch. The misspellings and bad grammar looked familiar, too.

"Get me another plastic bag, would you?" Martinez said.

"What are you going to do?"

"Not much I can do, tonight. Or I guess I should say 'this morning.' I'm going to take it in later, when I go to work. We'll compare it to the other note, and see what, if anything, we can learn from it."

He didn't sound optimistic.

"It looks a lot like the note from the mutilated toy dog," I said.

"That it does. Unfortunately, they're both written with pencil on common notebook paper. Finding out who wrote it would be easier if they'd used expensive parchment, or an unusual color of ink. Or a fountain pen. The more distinctive, the better."

"What about DNA?"

"It's possible. But you have to match it to a suspect whose DNA is known. And we don't have a suspect."

We both looked down at the piece of paper. So ordinary. So disturbing.

"This puts my burglary in a different category, doesn't it?"

Martinez's mouth was a grim line. That vein throbbed in his right temple. "Yes," he finally said.

And with that one word, I knew I wouldn't be able to get back into my bed. I knew that whoever had killed Jim Albert had been in my home, standing right here. And I knew I wouldn't get much sleep at all until we found the murderer who was now threatening Mama and me.

FORTY-THREE

"MAMA? IT'S MACE."

"Well, hello darlin'. I'm just finishing up my Cheese 'n' Ham Surprise for the church breakfast. Are you on your mobile phone?"

Mama still treats each call from a moving car as a miracle, even though cell phones have become as common as cowboy hats in Himmarshee.

I bit back a smart-aleck remark, though sleep deprivation and sheer fear might have given me a pass to make one. "I'm in Pam's car, on my way into town. I wanted to let you know I'm running a little late."

My thoughts drifted back to why I'd been delayed.

I'd finally fallen asleep, for an hour and a half, on the floor of my front porch. The idea of a killer in my house, maybe even in my bed, creeped me out. Martinez wanted to leave the sheets and pillows as they were, to preserve any evidence. Even though I'd rolled around in there, the intruder may have, too. He could have left behind skin, hair, maybe even bodily fluid. That last prospect alone was enough to make me grab a sleeping bag, plug in a fan, and hit the porch.

Martinez pulled all the bedding off the sofa and insisted on bunking on the floor next to me. His presence was solely a comfort. Feeling scared and vulnerable effectively squashed any erotic leanings I had earlier.

"I know how it feels when you don't want to be inside your own house." His voice was barely a whisper beside me. "After my wife was killed, I couldn't use the front door. For months, I entered and left from the back. Finally, I sold the house and moved here. Too many memories."

I didn't know what to say. "I'm sorry," was all I came up with. Marty would have done better.

I must have finally dozed off, because I dreamed of Patricia Martinez's murder. But everything was confused. She wasn't in the front hallway of their home in Miami. She was in the woods in Himmarshee. Throughout the dream, the faces of her attackers stayed hidden in the shadows. And then finally, just before she was shot, the two men looked up. In my dream, one of them was Sal Provenza. The other one had my granddaddy's gun. It was Jeb Ennis.

The sound of the fatal shot in my dream turned into the beep of the alarm clock I'd brought to the porch. I awoke, tangled in my sleeping bag and soaked in sweat.

My porch mate was already up and dressed. He'd folded his bedding, placing it neatly in a corner. After I showered and came out in my bathrobe, he handed me a cup of coffee he'd made.

"Sorry, no *café Cubano*," I said, sitting at the kitchen table so I could linger a bit longer.

"That's okay." He took the seat across from me and smiled. "I'll make you some when you come to my house."

I'd been parsing that sentence ever since. Was it an invitation? A promise? Or, was it like, "Let's have lunch sometime," a casual remark without real meaning? One way or another, I was oddly eager for my first taste of that Cuban coffee.

Now, I was hurrying across the bridge at Taylor Creek—just as I'd done the night Mama called from the police department to tell me there'd been a murder. I passed the site along State Road 98 where I'd spotted Emma Jean's car, pulled off into the marshy weeds.

I swerved to avoid a dead raccoon in the road. One of my garbage can bandits? I hoped not. I wanted things to be like before, when my sole worry was a gang of marauding critters.

"I'm still about twenty minutes out, Mama," I said into the phone.

"That's okay, honey," Mama said. "The VFW's only a couple of blocks away. Alice and Ronnie from next door are already here. We're gonna walk over together. I'll meet you."

No criticism about my tardiness. Not a single complaint. Mama's mood was as sunny as the September day would be. I didn't have the heart to tell her someone might be gunning for both of us with her daddy's shotgun.

"I wish you wouldn't walk, Mama. I'll be right there to pick you up."

"Don't be silly, Mace. We'll be at the hall in two shakes of a lamb's tail." She lowered her voice. I pictured her cupping her hand around the phone. "Alice begged me to walk with them. She's doing everything she can think of to get Ronnie to exercise. He's getting as fat as the only tick on a hound ever since he hurt his shoulder. The doctor says it'll be another month before he can go back to full-time work at the feed store."

Ronnie Hodges' upper arms are as big as hams. Eight-hour shifts lifting feed sacks will do that. I didn't think anyone would mess with Mama with the hulking Ronnie right beside her.

"Okay, but just be careful, would you?"

"Of course, darlin'. If this last week has taught us anything, it's that there are some crazy people in Himmarshee."

You have no idea, I thought.

"That brings up a little something I need to tell you, Mama." I downplayed. "I got another one of those notes, like the one with the stuffed dog on your porch?"

"How could I forget? That awful thing looked just like Teensy."

"This note came to my house. I'll fill you in on the details later. But Detective Martinez thinks we should be extra watchful for anyone who might mean us harm."

"I don't like the sound of that, Mace. Are you okay? What'd the note say?"

"I'm fine. And it was just like before." I dismissed the note. "'Mind your own business.' 'I'm going to come after you.'"

"Who do you think wrote it?"

"Truly, I don't know. But let's ask around at the breakfast. See what we can find out."

"Okay, honey. Ronnie's helping himself to his second biscuit, and Alice is givin' me the evil eye. I gotta go. See you in a little while."

"Remember what I said about being careful. Love you."

"Me too, Mace."

I had the urge to tell her more, but she'd already hung up. By the time I passed through a bad spot for my cell signal, then hit redial, Mama's number rang inside an empty house.

——

Guests were still arriving when I parked Pam's car in the VFW lot. It was only fifteen minutes past the time Mama had planned for us to get there. She wanted to be early so she could see how my sisters and I decorated the place. That way, she'd know what to take credit for.

Inside, I found one of the place cards holding a table for Abundant Hope members and family. I hung my purse on a chair and went off to look for Mama.

Surveying the food table, with its assortment of sweet and savory treats, I didn't see her distinctive casserole dish. She always brings the same one to every party: white, trimmed in blue asters. It's got a tiny chip on the top and her name written on masking tape on the bottom.

Mama must have gotten waylaid, talking to someone somewhere while her Cheese 'n' Ham Surprise was getting cold. I scanned the crowded room.

And didn't see her.

Maybe she'd stopped to primp. I opened the door to the women's bathroom. "Mama? It's Mace. You in there?" I called.

And didn't hear her.

My heart was starting to pound. Ronnie Hodges was across the room, moving his massive frame around the food table, eyeing the offerings.

"Ronnie?"

"Hey, Mace. It's a shame they make us wait to eat until after everybody from Abundant Hope is done praying. I'd feel more prayerful with a full stomach."

"Ronnie, where's my mama? I thought y'all walked over together."

"We did. But you know Rosalee. She saw someone she knew and ran off to say hello. She told Alice and me to come on inside. Said she'd meet us at the table."

"When was this?"

"Not five minutes ago."

"Where?"

"Outside, in the parking lot."

I left him standing there staring. Pushing my way against the faithful and the hungry, I went outside. There were at least a dozen vehicles in the parking lot: pickup trucks, battered sedans, shiny SUVs. I rushed up and down the parked rows, looking for Mama.

And didn't find her.

Taking a corner around an old Buick, I slid in something slippery. I caught my balance and looked down at fluffy eggs and cubed ham oozing on the asphalt. Shards from a casserole dish poked out from a golden layer of cheese. I stooped and picked up a shard—white, with a perfect blue aster in the center.

"Good Lord, Mace. You're as white as rice." Ronnie Hodges panted from rushing out after me. "Is everything okay?"

"Who did Mama run off to talk to, Ronnie?"

"Well, I don't know. My distance eyes ain't what they used to be. The truck was all the way over to the other side of the parking lot."

"A truck? What kind?"

"It was an old pickup. White, I think. Or something light. Why?"

"One person in the truck, or two?"

"Just one. The driver. But why, Mace? What's wrong?"

"Man or woman?"

"Well, now …" Ronnie looked heavenward, like he had to think on that for a while.

I felt a scream rising in the back of my throat. "Dammit, Ronnie, was it a man or a woman?"

"Woman," he finally said. "I'm almost sure it was a woman."

I grabbed Pam's car keys from my pants pocket. "Mama's been kidnapped, Ronnie. Call the police. Then, tell Delilah to make an announcement that anyone who saw anything should stay here to talk to the cops."

Ronnie's jaw hung open. He worked it a couple of times before some words came out. "Where are you going?"

"To find Mama," I said as I flew toward the car.

"Wait, Mace." Ronnie's heavy footsteps pounded behind me. "Delilah's not here."

I stopped and turned around.

"She called your mama this morning. She said she couldn't face the crowd after all, not after Pastor Bob took all the hurricane money. Delilah asked your mama to promise to explain to everybody how sorry she was."

FORTY-FOUR

THINK! THINK! THINK!

I pounded three times on the steering wheel in Pam's car, trying to dislodge the fog in my brain with each blow. I needed to focus, like I do when I'm tracking an animal. Get inside the kidnapper's head.

Any prey, knowing it's being hunted, will either flee or find a hiding place. I scanned the lot. There was nowhere to hide a pickup with a pint-sized captive. The driver had surely fled.

I eased the VW across the lot, to the side where Ronnie had seen the truck. In the wild, an animal leaves a trail: flattened grass, bent twigs, droppings, or tracks on the ground. I hoped to see something, anything, that would reveal the path taken by the animal in the pickup's driver seat.

There wasn't even an oil stain.

Then, just as I reached the exit, I spotted what I prayed was a clue out on the road in front of the VFW. Something small and round shone against the blacktop, about thirty feet to the right. Seeing nothing on the pavement to the left, I made the right. Slowly, slowly I drove, and then stopped. The object on the road was a honeydew-colored earring, gleaming in the rising sun.

Mama had been so excited when she found the set, which included a necklace and a bracelet, too. She had a pantsuit in that exact shade of light green, and the costume jewels were a perfect match.

I hoped she tossed the earring out of the car intentionally, like Hansel and Gretel with their breadcrumb trail. I didn't want to think of the alternative: that the clip-on was the first casualty as Mama struggled with her kidnapper.

The VFW is at the far western end of Main Street. I drove for two miles without spotting another clue. Then I came to an intersection. Right, left, or straight ahead? I parked on the shoulder and examined the site on foot. There was nothing to suggest choosing one way over another. There was only a quiet Saturday morning and empty road in all directions. Making the wrong decision might mean Mama's life.

I was about to start combing the grass alongside the intersection when I noticed an ancient fisherman. Sitting stooped in a folding chair and holding a cane pole, he was nearly hidden by the cattails that grow along the banks of Himmarshee Creek.

I came up quietly, not wanting to scare him or the fish.

He looked up, dark face nearly hidden in the shadow of a huge straw hat. "Hey."

"Hey." I returned his greeting and got right to business. "I'm trying to find a light-colored pickup truck that might have come by here about ten minutes ago."

With yellowed teeth and sunken cheeks, he looked about a hundred years old. I hoped he still had his wits. "Yes'm," he finally said. "I saw a truck. White, it was. I was just gettin' here myself to do a little fishin' when the damn fool driving nearly run me over."

"Did you see which way it went?"

He aimed the tip of his pole to the west. "Straight ahead, along the course of the creek. I remember, 'cause I was walking 'long side of the road, right there." He pointed the pole again. "They flew by me, so close I could see the look on the face of the white lady in the passenger side. Real little lady. She looked scared, like she thought they was gonna hit me."

"Did you notice anything else unusual?"

"I remember wondering why she was only wearing one of them round earbobs."

I thanked him and continued on my way. In another mile, a honeydew scarf waved from a fence alongside the road. I was on the right track.

Just before the intersection with State Road 70, a woman stood on the roadside at the back end of an old blue van. Cardboard boxes and a metal contraption that looked like a coat rack sat around her on the grassy swale. She bent into the back to pull out a folding card table and a chair. Coming alongside, I read the sign on the van's left panel: *Wendi's Whirligigs*.

By the time I stopped and backed up, she'd put up her table and started arranging her wares. She sold airplanes and birds fashioned from old beer cans.

"Are you Wendi?" I asked, shifting Pam's car into neutral.

She nodded, but didn't look at me. She hung her whirligigs from the coat rack, hoping to catch the eye of passing motorists. I asked about the truck.

"Might have seen something." Her head was down, orange spiky hair pointing to a flock of beer-can birds she was arranging on the table. "I've been busy. I have a lot of these here crafts to sell. Business is awful slow in the summer." She finally looked at me. "Awful slow."

Highway extortion. I searched for my purse on the seat and floorboards. It wasn't there. But I saw it in my mind—just where I'd left it on a chair at the VFW. My wallet was inside. Even worse, so was my phone.

"Look, I'm in trouble," I told Wendi. "My mama's been kidnapped. I need to know which way that truck was headed."

The hard line of her mouth softened, making her almost pretty. "I thought there was something off about those two gals. Love affair gone bad, right? I been there."

"Yes, that was it," I agreed, desperate for her help even if it was under false pretenses.

"Was that your mama in the passenger seat? The one with the platinum hair?"

I nodded.

"Pretty, for an older gal. They were heading west. Your mama looked right at me as they passed, about ten minutes ago. She was yelling out the window, 'Park, park, park!' It didn't make sense. I already was parked. But that's all I heard before the truck blew by."

"You notice anything else?"

"There were crushed beer cans in the back." She pulled a ciga-rette from behind her ear; lit it. "It's a shame people smash them. A good can is the foundation of my business."

"Thanks, Wendi," I shifted into gear and let out the clutch, as a cigarette-smoke cloud drifted my way. "If I get her out of this mess, we'll be back to buy a six-pack of whirligigs."

"Good luck," Wendi called out as I pulled onto the road.

What could Mama have meant? I tried to concentrate, but kept getting a picture in my mind of work boots. I'd seen mine sitting on the floorboard in the back when I was searching for my purse. I glanced over my shoulder at the heavy boots.

Suddenly, I knew exactly where Mama's captor had taken her.

FORTY-FIVE

Himmarshee Park doesn't open on Saturday morning until ten, giving the kidnapper plenty of time to … I couldn't bear to finish the thought. I didn't want to imagine what the murderer had planned in my workplace for my mama.

The slats on the wooden bridge vibrated under the VW's tires. I spotted a honeydew-colored shoe just beyond the rise of the little span. It was the mate to a heeled pump I'd seen in the middle of the street just before the turn-off to the park.

The woods were eerily still. No birds called. No animals rustled through brush. It was as if the humidity that already hung like a wet veil over the day had sucked out all the sound. Technically, we were closed. But all anyone who wanted in had to do was unhitch the steel cable that stretched across the road. The *Do Not Enter* sign would fall to the ground, and they could drive right through. Which is just what someone had done.

I turned off the car's ignition and coasted across the downed cable. When tracking an animal, the quieter the better.

The white truck was pulled off ahead, blocking a nature path. There was no one inside. It was the pickup from Emma Jean's yard. I stopped right behind it, blocking it in between a tree and the nose of Pam's VW.

Kicking off my loafers, I quickly changed into the boots, lacing them tight around my ankles. Then, I started out running for the park's office. I felt for the car keys in my pocket, glad that I'd thought to put my office key on Pam's key ring where it wouldn't be lost. The ground and foliage was still damp with morning moisture. Droplets wet my hair and splattered onto my shirt as I passed under the low, bushy fronds of Sabal palms.

It only took minutes to reach the building and unlock the door. But it felt like hours.

"9-1-1. What is your emergency?"

"This is Mace Bauer." I kept my voice low, in case anyone was lurking nearby. "I'm calling from inside the office at Himmarshee Park."

I'd made many 911 calls from the park over the years: Broken bones. Heat exhaustion. Two fatal heart attacks for senior citizen visitors. I heard my own voice, calm and steady. Only I knew the fear I was barely keeping at bay.

I continued, "Please contact Detective Carlos Martinez with the Himmarshee Police. This is an extreme emergency. A woman's life is at risk."

"Are you in danger, Ma'am?"

"No, not at this moment. But my mother is. She's been kidnapped, most likely by someone who's killed before. She's being held somewhere in the park. Please tell Detective Martinez to get here as soon as he can."

"Ma'am, you need to stay right where you are." Urgency edged into her professional tone. "Stay put until we can get an officer out there. It won't be long."

I glanced at my watch. Seven-forty on a weekend morning. The police roster would be sparse at that hour, and the park's at least fifteen miles from town.

"I can't do that," I told her. "We're talking about my mother here. Just tell Martinez to hurry."

I hung up before she could speak again. The office phone rang back immediately. The answering machine was picking up as I slipped out the door and struck out into the woods.

I returned to the trail that led to the entrance, back to where the white truck was parked. And then I took off on the path in the opposite direction, going deeper into the woods. It seemed likely that whoever had Mama would choose to stay on the marked trail instead of trying to cover rough terrain.

Here, I was on familiar ground. Some of the ferns along the path were bent back, evidence that someone had recently passed by. I saw a platinum-colored strand of hair caught in a low-hanging branch. And there was a knee-high nylon, balled up and dropped in the center of the trail.

I almost had to smile. Mama never wore shoes when she worked outside, a habit carried over from childhood. It embarrassed my sisters and me no end when we were teenagers. We'd bring home a date, and there Mama would be: standing in the yard with a garden hose, as barefoot as an Amazon tribeswoman.

"Well, I don't see what's wrong with it," she'd always say. "My feet are just as God made them."

After sixty years of unshod gardening, her soles were as hard as horse hooves. At least she'd be safe from sharp sticks in the mulch covering the path. I held on to that thought. It was the only thing I had to be optimistic about.

The woods were so still, I could hear my own breath. I strained to hear anything else—a voice, or the snap of a branch that might reveal where the killer had gone. I covered perhaps a quarter-mile before a human-sounding murmur floated toward me through the heavy air. I crept closer, following the direction of the sound. Now, the noise became a voice. It was Mama's, thank God.

"You know you can't get away with it," she said.

A low answer. I couldn't make out the words.

"If you turn yourself in now, I'll put in a good word. I'll testify and tell the jury you never once hurt me."

I stopped, staying hidden in thick trees, just short of a small clearing. Across the open space, Mama stood on top of a concrete wall. Facing her was Emma Jean Valentine, aiming my granddaddy's shotgun directly at Mama's heart. Beyond the wall was a shallow pond, home to Ollie the alligator.

Emma Jean lifted the shotgun's barrel, motioning with it for Mama to jump. "You have a choice, Rosalee. Either you go in willingly, or I shoot you and your body falls in. Either way, the gator gets his dinner."

"Emma Jean, please. Think of how my girls will feel. You know how much you loved your own little boy. I love my daughters like that." Mama wiped tears from her cheeks. "This isn't you, honey. This is someone else. You aren't a murderer."

Emma Jean lowered her own cheek to her shoulder and rubbed. Could she also be wiping away tears?

"I'm sorry, Rosalee. I didn't want to hurt anybody, I swear to God."

I moved stealthily through the oaks and hickory, trying to find an angle to approach out of Emma Jean's sight line. Every moment felt like a month. Just before I burst into the clearing, I saw Emma Jean hesitate. She hung her head and dropped the shotgun a few inches. But before I got out a sigh of relief, her shoulders squared. She lifted the weapon and aimed. I was close enough to see the fear in my mother's eyes, but not close enough to tackle Emma Jean.

"No!" Sprinting across the field, I screamed. "Don't shoot."

All in an instant, Emma Jean whipped her tear-streaked face toward me. Whirling back toward Mama, she struggled to fire. The old shotgun jammed. My mother stumbled on the wall and fell backward. Emma Jean turned and started for the woods, still hanging on to the gun.

"You do it," she yelled to the sky. "I never wanted any of this."

I had no idea what she was shouting about. But there was no time to ask. I heard splashing from Ollie's pond. Praying hard, I reached the wall and looked over. Mama was flailing, which looks to a gator just like a fat duck in distress or a drowning baby deer. In other words, dinner.

"Hold on, Mama. I'm coming in."

The pond wasn't more than six feet at its deepest, but even that was too deep for a woman of Mama's size who never learned to swim. I reached her easily. Calming her was another matter. First a fist, then a flying elbow connected with my face.

"Listen to me." I grabbed her around the neck and stared directly into her terrified eyes. "You've got to stop fighting me. It's not safe.

Now, I'm going to float you about three feet toward the side of the pond. The water's shallow there. You'll be able to stand."

She was listening, her eyes locked onto mine. I felt her relax. That was the good news.

The bad news: Ollie had noticed the commotion in the water. He slid off the bank and was swimming our way.

FORTY-SIX

MAMA HAD HER BACK to the alligator. I thought it best not to let on that Ollie was bearing down. A hysterical woman and a hungry gator make for a bad combination.

"You're almost safe, Mama." I forced a reassuring tone. "Just walk along the sand to your left until you come to the pathway out. There's a steel gate at the end. I'll be right behind you."

"It was Emma Jean all along, Mace. How could she? She was my friend."

I looked over my shoulder. Ollie had covered three-quarters of the pond's length. "Not now, Mama," I said quietly. "We need to get out of this water. Immediately."

All I could see of the gator was his snout and one eye. I knew that beneath the surface, his powerful tail was moving to and fro, propelling him closer and closer.

"Steady, now." I boosted Mama by the butt onto the steep bank. I was in calf-high water, about to follow, when I felt a hard bump at the back of my knees. Ollie. I swallowed my panic. The pond here was shallow. The slap of the gator's tail slamming on top of the water sounded like a bomb going off.

"Watch out, Mace!" I heard Mama screaming, as if in a dream. "Get out of the water!"

I didn't want to take the risk the gator would follow me onto land. He might attack Mama—a weaker, easier prey than me. I whirled around and saw acres of teeth in a mile of jaws. It was all instinct at this point: Ollie's to eat; mine to survive.

Yelling louder than a legion of warriors, I drew back my foot. The steel-toed boot struck the gator on the top of his snout. I did it again, aiming directly for his one good eye. I kicked at his closest nostril, shouting the whole time. Ollie backed off and began to turn. I sent a parting blow to the less protected skin of his underside, where the organs are close to the surface.

That last kick convinced him to move on to a more docile prey. In his thumb-sized brain, he was probably trying to puzzle out what had happened to his usual meal—the dead, whole chickens that never fight back.

Adrenaline still coursed through my body as I hauled myself onto the bank. Ollie had retreated to the far end of the pond. The damage I'd done was more irritation than lasting injury. A gator's body is like an armored battleship.

As I sat, leg muscles quivering, lungs gulping in air, I was aware of Mama blubbering beside me. She ran her hands over my arms, then my legs, as if to convince herself I was whole. "My God, Mace! Wait until I tell your sisters. You fought off an alligator!"

"Well, it was shallow water, Mama," I said. "If he'd have gotten hold of me in the deeper part, it would have been the end. He'd have grabbed me in his jaws and pulled me under in a death roll to drown me. We wouldn't be talking right now."

Mama shuddered. "I'm just glad you were here, Mace. I wouldn't have had the presence of mind to do what you did."

"Not to mention the footwear," I said.

We both looked at Mama's bare feet, covered in mud. We started laughing. It felt good.

"Before you go bragging around town, turning me into Himmarshee's Heroic Gator Gal, you should know a couple of things." I held up a finger. "First, Ollie's not nearly as big as those eleven or twelve-footers that have made the news. Those were some fearsome gators, taking three victims over a week's span in different parts of the state." I put up another finger. "Second, Ollie's used to getting regular meals. If he was hungrier, he might have fought a lot harder."

Mama took my chin in her hands. "Don't downplay what you did, Mace." She pulled my face to hers and kissed me under my bangs. "You saved my life."

Tears sprang to my eyes. I rested my head on her shoulder as we sat on the bank.

"Now," she patted my arm, signaling the moment was over. "Let's get the heck out of this death pit."

———

Pond water squished in my boots as we made our way across the clearing, back toward the park office. Mama's polyester pantsuit stuck to her like honeydew-green plastic wrap. It wasn't even eight-thirty, and already the sunlight was turning white, blinding. It was going to be a scorcher, which isn't exactly a news flash in middle Florida in September.

Birds sang. Butterflies stirred. We were about halfway across the field when a man's voice punctured the happy bubble we'd been floating in since surviving an attempted murder and an alligator encounter.

"You two aren't going anywhere." The accent was flat. Midwestern.

Mama grabbed my hand and slowly we turned.

Bob Dixon stared at us with the deadest eyes I'd ever seen. His hand was steady on his .38.

FORTY-SEVEN

"I SHOULD HAVE KNOWN better than to send a woman to do a man's job. Emma Jean is just like all of you." Pastor Bob sneered at us. "Can't be trusted."

Delilah's confession about cheating on him ran through my mind.

"Every marriage has its ups and downs," Mama said, echoing my thought. "You've committed murder and caused a lot of heartache. Have you done it all because Delilah strayed?"

The minister blotted sweat from his neck with a white handkerchief. Then he laughed out loud, showing us his teeth. "I don't care a fig about that fat sow. None of this was about my wife—or even about Emma Jean, though I was banging her."

Mama blinked in disbelief at his crude language.

"It was about money, plain and simple." He shrugged and sopped again. "Jim Albert had a lot, and I wanted some. I'm not cut out to be a poor pastor in a Podunk town."

"But you're a man of God," Mama protested.

"Yeah, that was a mistake." He picked his teeth with a pinky nail. "I'd watched some of those big-time TV evangelists get rich. Thought it could be my path, too. I tried making the DVDs; thought they'd sell a million. But they didn't. And I didn't want to wait."

"I don't understand," I said. "Who killed Jim Albert? You or Emma Jean?"

"I don't suppose it matters now. You'll both be dead soon." Sweat stains darkened his light blue dress shirt. He tented the wet fabric off his chest, trying to find a nonexistent breeze. "I told Emma Jean all she had to do was set up her boyfriend so the two of us could take his money and run off together. I knew all along we'd have to kill him, though. Jim Albert wasn't the type to forgive being robbed. I figured Emma Jean was so crazy about me, I could convince her to do it. But when it came right down to it, I had to kill him. She lost her nerve."

Mama said, "And she lost it again when it came time to kill me."

I wasn't so sure about that. If Emma Jean could have fired Paw-Paw's gun, I'd be grieving over Mama's dead body.

"There's a reason women are called the weaker sex," he said.

If he wasn't holding that revolver, I might have quibbled. I probably had five inches and twenty-five pounds of muscle on the pencil-necked reverend.

I tried to reason: "Listen, you've got Jim Albert's money and the hurricane cash. You can lock us in the supply shed and just go. By the time we're found, you'll be long gone."

"Great plan. And I did intend to go, until I saw that some idiot in a Volkswagen pulled behind the truck and blocked me in."

The sun was melting the gel in his hair. He dabbed as a glob slid down his brow.

"I thought that truck was Emma Jean's," I said.

"It is. I rode over here with her and your mother. I was in the back of the cab the whole time, crouched behind the seat under a blanket." He spoke to Mama. "It was hot and I had to listen to you yammer the whole way. You talk too much."

She pulled herself to her full stature—four foot eleven inches. "There's absolutely no call for you to be insulting."

Heaven forbid he'd insult us, I thought. Kill us, maybe—but not insult us first.

"I'll give you the keys to the Volkswagen," I said.

"Don't worry, I'll take them. Just like I took your mother's extra set from her neighbors when I needed to dump Jim's body. Too bad for you Alice and Ronnie aren't more suspicious."

He wiped at his neck again. He was unused to the Florida heat, which was taking its toll.

"I'll have to shoot you first, of course. You should have paid attention to those notes and backed off. Curiosity killed the cat, you know."

"But we had no idea," Mama said, her hand fluttering to her throat.

"It was only a matter of time until you linked me to Emma Jean, and then both of us to Jim Albert. Emma Jean was this close to confessing the whole plan to you on the phone, Mace." He held his left thumb and forefinger apart a fraction of an inch. "I cajoled and sweet-talked and convinced her to fake her own disappearance in the swamp instead."

He examined his hanky, looking for a dry spot. I took the opportunity to scan the ground for anything to get us out of this mess—a big rock, a sharp stick, even a snake sunning itself. I know how people are about snakes. Tossing him a serpent might spook him and let us get away.

When I looked up again, black rivulets ran down the pastor's forehead from his hairline. He obviously washed away his gray. He closed his eyelids, patting gently at the stinging dye.

Continuing my survey, I finally spotted something in the tall grass: Paw-Paw's gun. Emma Jean must have tossed it as she ran. It was ten feet away, on my left. I gripped Mama's hand tighter. Cocking my head ever so slightly over my left shoulder, I whispered. "Bang."

She looked and shook her head once, a nearly imperceptible *No*. I answered with a tiny nod of my own. *Yes*.

"We all have to do what we have to do, Pastor Bob." I addressed him, but the message was for Mama.

Nodding at me, she squeezed my hand and closed her eyes. Her lips moved in a silent prayer. I joined her, a little rusty, asking God for strength and guidance.

Suddenly, a distant shout shattered the park's quiet.

"Police! Get down on the ground, Emma Jean." It was Detective Carlos Martinez. "Get down!"

Bob Dixon spun toward the command coming from the far trees. Mama and I glanced at each other. Now or never. I ran, diving into the grass. Her leather-hard foot delivered a sharp kick to the reverend right where it counted. I bolted up from the ground, aiming the antique gun. Pastor Bob dropped his weapon and doubled over, cupping his crotch with both hands.

I whistled, loud enough to call a cab south from New York City. "Over here," I yelled. "I've got Emma Jean's accomplice at the business end of a shotgun."

"I was watching before." The reverend spit out the words between painful breaths. "I saw it jam. It won't fire."

"You don't want to test that," I said, lowering the barrel from his heart to his groin. "This old gun is just like a woman. You have to know how to handle it right."

Martinez came crashing from the woods, pistol raised. His face lit with relief as he took in the scene: Mama and me, still dripping, but safe. Pastor Bob, cradling his family jewels. And my granddaddy's shotgun, aimed and ready to do more damage if need be.

I heard the distant sound of police sirens. My eyes flickered to Martinez for a moment, just long enough to see the hint of a smile steal across his face.

FORTY-EIGHT

"Rosie!" A bellow like an escaped bear from the Bronx zoo thundered from the woods. "Don't worry, honey. I'm here now."

The expression on Sal's face was priceless as he lumbered into the clearing. His weapon was ready. But the bad guys were already in handcuffs, on the ground.

"Looks like your backup is a little late," I said to Martinez.

"I don't know what you're talking about, *chica*." His face was a mask.

"C'mon, it's over now. You can admit it. Sal's a cop, too, isn't he?"

"Retired," Sal said, holstering his weapon. His face was as pink as his golf shirt from jogging over to us in the heat. "Thirty years, New York City Police Department."

He leaned down to kiss my mother. "How'd you know, Mace?"

"Well, there was the way you spoke about Detective Martinez and the police. You were awfully admiring, for a mobster. Then you called the rest of us 'civilians,' like cops always do. I put it together just now, seeing the way you ran over with your revolver

316

drawn." I nodded toward Martinez. "He wasn't at all surprised, so he must have been expecting you."

"I'm sorry," Sal said. "I couldn't talk about it. When I was on the job, I was undercover. Jimmy Albrizio, a.k.a. Albert, was a link to one of my last cases." His eyes scanned the tree line, like he was searching for something there. "A good friend, my first partner on the force, died trying to protect that weasel so he could testify in court." His face got hard. Mama reached up on her tiptoes to stroke his cheek.

"When Albrizio moved south, I followed. I hoped he'd lead me to the people who killed my buddy."

Martinez said, "Sal's cover was convincing. Even I thought at first he was linked to the mob and Albrizio's murder."

"When you found out otherwise, y'all became cigar-puffing pals," I said.

"You got that right." Sal clapped Martinez on the back, man-to-man. "And now, we'd better worry about getting these two booked."

The two young officers who'd arrived after Martinez seemed uncertain about what to do next. Emma Jean was sobbing softly on the ground. Bob Dixon looked like he'd kill any one of us if given the chance.

"Emma Jean will go in with them," Martinez nodded toward the two cops. "I'll be taking the good reverend in myself, along with the murder weapon, his .38."

Pastor Bob had clammed up as soon as Martinez arrived. Mama and I filled in the blanks, telling him what the minister had revealed to us.

I stole a glance at Emma Jean. Donnie Bailey's words ran through my head: there's hardly a woman in jail who doesn't claim some man put her there. Poor, desperate Emma Jean. She'd wanted Dixon's love so badly, she went along with his murderous plans to get it. I hoped my cousin Henry could refer her to a really sharp defense lawyer.

Sal handed over a cuffed Emma Jean to the two cops. Martinez hauled Pastor Bob to his feet. As our little group walked toward the entrance, two more squad cars came screaming into the park. A caravan of other vehicles trailed them, *bump-bump-bumping* over the bridge.

Donnie Bailey was in his brother's white pickup, with Police Chief Johnson riding shotgun. The chief had apparently dressed quickly. Dabs of shaving cream dotted his face. Maddie drove her Volvo. Marty leaned forward in the front seat, clutching the dashboard so hard her knuckles were white. Mama's neighbors, Ronnie and Alice, craned their necks from the back of a custom-colored purple Chevy. The driver was Betty Taylor, Mama's beauty shop boss and fellow Abundant Hope worshipper. Betty's towering bouffant scraped the plum-colored upholstery of the roof. Behind Betty, nearly all the other cars from the church breakfast were rolling in.

The Himmarshee hotline had been busy. The 911 call I made from the park office about Mama's kidnapping had sent the country town telegraph into overdrive.

I glanced at my waterproof watch, still running after the dip in Ollie's pond. It was 9:15, forty-five minutes before opening. I hoped my boss, Rhonda, wouldn't be mad that Mama's supporters had gotten in without paying the two-dollar park fee.

Martinez stared at the convoy, shaking his head. "And I thought the crowd was bad that first night at the police station."

"Yeah, life with Mama is a circus, and I'm the reluctant ringleader." I leaned down to kiss her on the top of her patchy, platinum hairdo. "And I wouldn't have it any other way."

———

Two weeks later, Mama dragged my sisters and me to her church to hear Delilah give her first sermon. She stepped up after her husband's downfall. She was pretty good, believe it or not.

"I have an announcement," she told the congregation at the start of the service. "If it's all right with you, I'd like to change the name of our little church."

There was a low murmur from the metal chairs. I leaned around Mama to raise my eyebrows at Marty and Maddie.

"I've been doing a lot of thinking since Bob's arrest. About *all* the things that transpired, including my own behavior. I haven't always been kind. And some of you may know I strayed in my marriage. I lost respect for my vows, which are supposed to be sacred."

Several men shifted in their seats. A few women picked that moment to search their purses for one thing or another.

Delilah continued. "A cornerstone of our faith is forgiveness. I need it. Some of you may need it, too. I propose we call our church Abundant Forgiveness, because that's what I want to offer here. I intend to live my life that way. And I hope you will, too."

I felt a gentle tap on my shoulder. "What do you say, Mace?" A whisper came from behind my right ear. "Do you think there's enough forgiveness to go around?"

I turned my head to see Jeb Ennis in the seat behind me, hat in his lap, hair soaked with sweat at his forehead and temples.

"I see that AC's still broken in your truck," I said softly.

"It is." He flashed a nervous smile, looking like the shy choirboy he'd never been. "Can I talk to you outside for a few minutes?"

As I slid out of our row, Maddie whipped her head around to see what was going on. Her harrumph followed Jeb and me all the way to the door.

Outside, Jeb put on his hat and hooked his thumbs into the front pockets of a clean pair of blue jeans. They were tight as ever. They still looked pretty darned good.

"I just wanted to make sure we're okay, Mace." His eyes searched my face. "I'm leaving for a while. I didn't want to take off with hard feelings between us."

The knot in my throat surprised me. I really hoped I wouldn't cry.

"We're fine, Jeb. I already told you I've forgiven you for lying to me. And I hope you've forgiven me for suspecting you in Jim Albert's murder."

He let me stand there and squirm for a moment before he answered. "You know, Mace, you could've just called me and asked about the windows in my truck that day at the park. Maybe you can understand how I wouldn't have thought right off about rolling them down as I was pulling out, even though it was hot."

I fiddled with a loose thread on my sleeve. Truth is, I wouldn't have believed any excuse from Jeb Ennis. I'd already tried and convicted the poor man in my head. When Jeb got no response, he continued.

"Maybe I was a little upset that afternoon, seein' as how the girl I used to love—was startin' to love again—had just pointed me out as a suspect to that smart-ass detective from Miamuh."

I stared at the ground. "Yeah, I regret that, Jeb. I'm sorry."

"Anyway. I'm packing up; taking a little camper on the road. I'm going back to rodeo for a while. Cindy and I are together again. She's agreed to come along. Old as I am, she can help bandage me up and fetch my crutches after I ride."

"But what about your ranch?"

"I'm leavin' my foreman in charge. He's a good man. He's stuck with me through everything. In six months, we're gonna sit down and evaluate. I might come back; I might decide to sell to him. I just need to make things simple again."

"And the gambling?"

Now it was Jeb's turn to study the ground. He toed a crack in the sidewalk with his boot. "I'm getting some help on that," he finally said. "They've got a group just like Alcoholics Anonymous, but for people with my problem. I've got a sponsor and everything. And I found out there's a few guys I can talk to on the rodeo circuit, too."

"But you owed so much money…"

"I'm gonna pay back what I borrowed from my family and the other ranchers. But that biggest debt died with Jim Albert, so far as I can tell. That doesn't mean I don't wake up every day waiting for one of his buddies to come kicking down my door."

He took off his hat and squinted into the distance. The heat was starting to rise in waves off the street in front of the church.

"Anyway." He put a hand on my shoulder, leaned toward me, and gently brushed my lips with his. And there it was: that tiny shiver of desire. Fainter now, but still there. With a first love, does it ever disappear?

I rested my hand on his cheek and watched his long lashes close over his gold-flecked eyes. Then I dropped my arm to my side and took a step back. "Hey, we'll see each other again, won't we? I'll come and cheer you on this winter at the Seminole rodeo. You're going to ride at the Brighton reservation, aren't you?"

"Hope so." He brushed his hat against this thigh and stuck it back on his head.

"Good luck with Cindy," I said, and I think I meant it. "Any woman who will live with a guy in a travel trailer is a keeper."

"Yep. She's a good ol' gal."

Jeb sounded like he was describing a favorite horse instead of the woman of his dreams. Then again, he always was passionate about horses.

"Happy trails, Jeb. Take care of yourself, hear?"

"You, too. So, are we all forgiven, like that lady minister was preaching?"

"Abundantly," I answered.

FORTY-NINE

"WELL, I FOR ONE was impressed." Maddie lectured us over the top of her reading glasses. "That Delilah Dixon really blossomed once the police hauled her husband off to the hoosegow."

Mama, my sisters, and I had gathered at the Pork Pit after services at the newly christened Abundant Forgiveness church. I'd already filled them in on Jeb's farewell. Now, we'd moved on to Delilah's performance in the pulpit her husband had disgraced.

"I'm happy for her. She was just glowing up there," Marty said. She wet her napkin in her water glass and wiped a streak of barbecue sauce from Mama's chin. "Has anyone heard what will happen to Emma Jean?"

Maddie raised her eyebrows at me over the dessert menu, echoing Marty's question.

"Henry says the prosecutor might go easy on her," I said. "There's that whole history with her boy disappearing. Her lawyer will probably try and argue that Bob Dixon held some kind of psychological sway over her. Fact is, she didn't actually kill anyone."

Maddie tsked-tsked. "The woman ran you off the road into a ditch, Mace."

Once all the danger was over, we'd confessed to Mama that we kept that from her.

"Dixon was there, egging her on. He had Emma Jean convince Sal to meet with me at the golf course, and then call up with that fake story about Mama's heart giving out in jail. That way, I'd be out on that road all alone."

Mama decided not to wait for her own dessert. She slid Marty's half-finished bowl of banana pudding to her placemat. "We'll just have to wait and see how Emma Jean's case goes," she said, dipping in her spoon.

"Hmph!" Maddie said. "I think her case should go right to Death Row."

"Maddie, were your ears plugged during Delilah's sermon on forgiveness?" Marty's voice was as sweet as ever, but the words had some sting. "And that's my pudding, Mama." As Marty took the pudding back to her own placemat, Maddie stared at her for a long moment. She might not approve of the new Marty, but I was getting a kick out of seeing our little sister fight back for a change.

"You know, you're right, Marty. I'm sorry. I could use some forgiveness myself."

I nearly spit out a mouthful of sweet tea, hearing Maddie apologize.

"But I would like to hear why you've been so different lately. It's not just the promotion, is it?" Maddie asked.

A glance passed between Mama and Marty. Then both of them started shredding their pink Pork Pit napkins.

"Marty?" I asked. No answer.

Finally, Mama could stand it no longer. "Sal knew he was about to lose me, so he took a chance on Marty. He told her how he'd been a policeman up north. Then he asked her to convince me that he's a good man, without giving away his secret. Your little sister can be very convincing, girls."

Marty took a tiny sip of tea and gave us her sweetest smile. "He said all those years on the job had made him trust his instincts. And his instinct was that he could trust me."

I felt a tiny tug of envy. Why hadn't Sal chosen me? Maybe because I was judging people left and right, and Marty tends to accept them as they are. I guess I'll have to work on that.

Mama motioned the waitress over.

"We'll have peach cobbler all around. With ice cream. And another banana pudding for the table." When the server left, scribbling in her pig-pink order pad, Mama turned to us. "Now, let's talk about something else. Who has news?"

"I've got something. Y'all remember that New Jersey newcomer I told you about? The one who kept insisting she had a panther?"

"The one you made fun of?" Marty asked me.

"The very same." I traced the outline of a cheerful pig on the Pit's bottled sauce. "Well, damned if she wasn't right. It escaped from a pen at Pocock Ranch. The ranch owner has a license to rehabilitate injured Florida panthers."

Maddie looked over her glasses at me. "Did she say, 'I told you so?'"

"Nah. She was actually pretty gracious. I promised her a freebie on her next trapping call. She's worried now that an armadillo army is undermining her home's foundation."

The waitress returned with our desserts and a fresh round of napkins. "My news is bigger than that," Mama said, loading her fork with cobbler. "Mace went on a date with that good-looking Carlos Martinez."

Her revelation set off a seismic mood shift. Both sisters were all smiles and *Say whats*?

"It wasn't a date. We just went to dinner."

"Did you wash your hair?" Maddie asked.

"Yes."

"Then it was a date."

"Actually, Carlos is going back to Miami."

Their faces fell.

"It may not be forever. He's only taking a leave of absence from the Himmarshee Police. He says he has to face some demons down there before he can get on with his life."

The three of them looked so glum, I thought I'd toss them a bone.

"It's not like he's moving to California," I said. "Miami's only three and a half hours south, you know. In fact, I'm going down to visit him next weekend. I plan to try some *arroz con pollo* and *un cafécito Cubano*."

"Mace!" Maddie's mouth was tight with disapproval. "You may want to experiment, but I really don't think you should talk about your sexual shenanigans in front of Mama."

I laughed at their shocked expressions. "All that means is rice with chicken and a short Cuban coffee. Didn't I tell y'all? I've started studying Spanish."

THE END

Charles Trainor, Jr.

ABOUT THE AUTHOR

Like Mace Bauer's, Deborah Sharp's family roots were set in Florida long before Disney and *Miami Vice* came to define the state. She does some writing at a getaway overlooking the Kissimmee River in the wilds north of Okeechobee, and some at Starbucks in Fort Lauderdale. As a Florida native and a longtime reporter for *USA Today*, she knows every burg and back road, including some not found on maps. Here's what she has to say about Himmarshee:

> Home to cowboys and church suppers, Himmarshee is hot and swarming with mosquitoes. A throwback to the ways of long-ago southern Florida, it bears some resemblance to the present-day ranching town of Okeechobee. The best thing about Mace and Mama's hometown: it will always be threatened, but never spoiled, by suburban sprawl.